SCENT OF LAVENDER

By

Marcia P. Adams

ISBN: 0-7596-5755-6

This book is printed on acid free paper.

1stBooks – rev. 01/07/02

CHAPTER 1

Maggie Murphy sorted and snipped small squares of fabric while other women sewed and stuffed the bright cotton pieces into small pillows for the bazaar as they exchanged news in their high-pitched voices:

"Afraid...fires...carnival called off all because of the devil inspired group..."

Silently she asked herself: What are these women talking about? Devil worship? Fires? Fear? Gossip does get embroidered at times. I've got to get out of here—too many people—hard to hear.

Pushing away from the table, she stood and said, "Please excuse me, I must leave." Maggie directed the apology to the group, while ignoring the arched-brow look of disapproval from her mother.

"Margaret Ann, if you must leave, please leave a little more time for our next meeting on Wednesday. You know you're needed as a member of the bazaar committee," Mrs. Murphy said.

Maggie hesitated. Even with her impaired hearing, she had caught the undertone of her mother's veiled reprimand and watched the woman's moving lips continue:

"Oh yes, the rest of us did decide that it was not necessary to ask those outside our church to donate handmade wares for the bazaar. We'll have plenty of items with just our own church members."

Maggie merely nodded. During early-on bazaar plans, Maggie had broached the idea of opening the bazaar to all Collier residents who wished to participate with handmade articles. She wasn't surprised to learn that the six-member committee had ignored her suggestion.

1

Evelyn Murphy was the chairwoman of this year's Christmas Bazaar. Maggie knew her mother wanted this 1983 bazaar to be the best ever. For that very reason, Maggie had worked many long hours with the committee, and planned to help for the next four weeks before the bazaar on the second Saturday in December. But right now, she had to assert herself, get out, before she did something completely out of character—like scream.

"I've research to do for my book and must go to the library before the weather gets too bad." Maggie let the explanation dangle as she slipped on her heavy coat and boots, adjusted her tam, and scooped up her briefcase from the floor.

Avoiding her mother's riveting stare, she dipped her head, and with a hesitant wave of the hand to the group, she quickly left the room before more could be said. Once outside, Maggie breathed deeply of the crisp, cold Wisconsin air, feeling tension subside, and guilt surface.

She just wasn't as devoted to Community Church work as were other women in the church. A sigh escaped as she admitted that she was frustrated because church work took precious time away from her writing.

Snow had draped a glistening white coverlet over the churchyard, tempting Maggie to lie down and make a snow angel. She smiled at the image of a young woman lying on the church lawn with arms outstretched, and decided it was not a suitable activity for others to observe. Besides, the early morning's trickle of snow was now cascading in swirling sheets from the gray-veiled sky, and she had work to do before the predicted eight inches.

Head bowed—body bent to push against the whipping wind, Maggie shuffled through the crunch. Warm-breath crystals caked on the scarf wrapped over her nose and mouth. Her bright red tam, now soggy with snow, slid down over her brows so low that she had only a small opening to see the path ahead. But she was oblivious to the discomforts so intent was she on getting to the library, and finishing the research for her soon-to-be published cookbook.

Three blocks later, Maggie pushed her wet scarf and tam away from her face so that she could see the path up to the Carnegie Library. Through the grey winter haze what had been a stone building sitting on top of a small rise of land, had become a pyramid set on a snow-cushioned hill. There was no way to climb those fifteen buried steps. Trudging on to the newly installed ramp at the side of the building, she began the ascent, carefully wading through the snow, while holding on to the railing. Suddenly there was a screech of brakes—Maggie looked up—a man in a wheelchair was coming down the ramp right at her. She flattened against the rail—the wheelchair tilted on two wheels, whizzed past spraying snow to each side like a snow-blower machine. Blinking snow from her eyes, she watched the man struggle to level out, then stop the wobbling machine just inches from the street curb. Still glued to the railing, adrenaline pounding through her body, she watched the man flip his machine back toward her and say something. Sucking in a quick breath, she lifted a gloved hand from the rail and motioned as if to say she couldn't hear him.

"Excuse me." He'd removed his cap to reveal a long mop of red hair. The man's grim, unsmiling face signaled his annoyance.

"I...I'm sorry I was in the way. I was distracted by my thoughts." Eyes wide with shock, throat clogged, Maggie tried to explain.

"I'm sorry I interrupted—believe my swift descent woke you up in a hurry. Do you daydream often or on only...?" A smile crinkled bright blue eyes. He seemed to chuckle, but she couldn't hear all of what he said.

The man then tipped his cap, slapped it over his mop of red hair that billowed out around his ears, and with a spin of the chair wheeled away. Holding her breath, she watched him push the wheels at great speed toward the intersection where he safely stopped. He turned back toward her with a wave of his hand. She waved too, but the retreating figure didn't see her. He'd wheeled on across the snowy street, jumped the curb, and set the front wheels down on the sidewalk with the agility of a boy on a two-wheeler. Gathering speed, he pushed his wheelchair down the block, turned right, and faded out of sight through a curtain of snow. For Maggie it was fascinating to watch such confidence displayed in one with a deep disability.

Walking through the automatic doors of the library, the tense feeling she'd had just moments before changed to a feeling of annoyance as she recalled the beautiful old oak door of the library that had been replaced by modern technology. But a visual image of the gentleman she'd just encountered, made her realize some changes, like the ramp and door, were necessary. One thing that would never change in the venerable house of information as long as the edifice continued to exist would be the smells of old leather and glue, mingled with odors of eighty-year old wood and musty parchment.

Those smells recalled her childhood when her baby sitter Nonnie would bring her to this Carniege Library. Just as in the former days, the circular checkout desk and two brass-trimmed filing cabinets sat in the middle of the large square room. On either side of the checkout center, were rows of three-tiered wooden stacks tightly packed with books and separated by narrow aisles. Wooden tables placed at the corners of the room were piled high with periodicals and newspapers. While encyclopedias and oversized leather-bound books were stacked along the wall as if to lend support to the building.

The overall clutter of the library seemed somewhat like Maggie's own house where books, magazines, and baskets of knitting were strewn about in the living room, and spilled over into the unused dining room to cover the table and chairs. Perhaps that was why her mother made a good chairman for the Christmas craft show—she didn't mind mess.

My herb notes are a mess. With the thought, Maggie hurried past the stacks to her favorite niche in a back corner of the room to a long wooden table, and heavy straight-backed chair. Wet coat, gloves, and tam placed on the metal coils of a radiator of questionable age caused the old heater to sputter and hiss. Aromatic steam rose from its hot surface, adding a scorched wool smell to the other thick library odors—delightful, nostalgic smells. With the background clatter and bang of the coiled relic, Maggie pulled a pen and notebook from her briefcase and began to work.

Cookbook with Herbal Touches and Magic Potions would be the third of Maggie Murphy's popular cookbook series. After Maggie tested ingredients and created the recipes, her editor, a licensed dietitian, tested the recipes in Chicago. As dictated by her contract with her publishing company, her latest endeavor was to be assembled, printed and ready for sale in December. Again a touch of panic set in when she considered all that remained to be done before the due date. But past experience suggested that if she got the final research and editing done in the next few days, there would be time for printing, advertising and then ready for selling.

Maggie adjusted her reading glasses so she could read the detailed notes in her notebook:

Aromatherapy is based on the scientific studies
of the effect smell has on the memory, emotions,
and sexual arousal. Proponents of aromatherapy

claim that certain scents can ease physical maladies like headaches as well as emotional conditions such as nervousness and irritability.

She breathed in the comforting smells of the room. How true she thought as she leafed through pages on specific herbs to her notes on Lavender:

Lavender is not only effervescent. The probability of lavender having a scent, which can cure some illness, has been predicated for years. Lavender flowers brewed for tea are tasty and the mild carminative action of the blossoms could be useful for settling an upset stomach that often accompanies nervousness and irritability. The tea enhances sleep and the flowers, when chewed, give a pleasant scent to the breath.

Maggie flipped to another page, but couldn't fine the notes she needed. She was muttering to herself when Letty, the librarian, walked by and asked if Maggie had what she needed.

"Well, I need to track down a few more uses of lavender. There's a book in the stacks I may be able to use." Maggie smiled up at the tall, sober-faced woman who nodded and walked back to her work center where an elderly white-haired woman waited for help.

Maggie watched the two women. She couldn't hear the conversation, but it seemed that Letty was listening patiently to the woman's wishes with the same stoic bearing she'd shown for some fifteen years. Maggie sighed deeply, thinking how peaceful it was in the library. It was so much more conducive to getting the creative juices flowing here than at home using the computer to look up references on the Internet. It took longer for her to tap into the web page of a university library and open to information on herbs, than it did for her to get to the Carnegie Library, open a reference book, and copy material needed. Besides, she still was just a little afraid of that darn machine.

She rubbed her eyes. Why did she insist on procrastinating? A draft had to be in the mail by the following Wednesday, and it was already Friday. Tomorrow she could get the pages in order, all but the lavender section. Sunday was already filled with church functions—children's choir, fixing bread of some kind for the evening's church social. That meant only two days, Monday and Tuesday, were left to work. An anxious feeling took her breath. She had to focus and get the 'Sense of Smell' section completed today. It was like the days she remembered so well when she was a child. Concentrate had been the paramount word.

***

"She needs to concentrate so she can get out what she wants to say. That'll keep her from daydreaming so much. She's three years old, for God's sake." Stepfather Bert had little patience with the child who was often sick with colds and ear infections, and who could not speak clearly or answer when spoken to. Maggie, introverted by nature, retreated further when Bert scolded or rebuked her.

Margaret Ann Murphy did not look a thing like her mother. Evelyn had pale blue eyes. Maggie's eyes were green and almond shaped. Her mother had blond hair. Maggie's hair was jet black. And, now grown, Margaret Ann Murphy was not a beautiful woman by the Western World standards, for she was neither buxom nor leggy. She was a small, thin girl with creamy, almost translucent skin who resembled a Chinese figurine.

Maggie imagined her own coloring must be something like her real father's James Patrick Bonner. Many times, her mother had told Maggie the story of Evelyn and the tall handsome Englishman meeting while on a holiday in England. The two had married, but James could not leave his job in Dover to come to America until there was a replacement, and Evelyn had to return to the states to complete her work-exchange contract. When the new bride returned to the States, she learned that she was pregnant. James had died in England several months before Margaret Ann was born three days before Christmas day. When Maggie was six months old, her mother married Bert Murphy, a short, heavy-set man who, not understanding the cause of the child's inattentiveness, seemed always to wear a scowl—at least when he was looking at Maggie.

Maggie was three and small for her age when she started nursery school. After a few days at school, Maggie's teacher suggested to Evelyn and Bert Murphy that Maggie was partially deaf. Up until then, the parents had ignored the child's reticence, blaming it on a stubborn nature or, more likely, they simply ignored the obvious. Reluctantly, they had Maggie's hearing tested and were told that Margaret Ann had over ninety percent hearing loss.

The nurse told Evelyn, "If Maggie were educated at a deaf school for a few years, then, possibly, she could function in the public school of Collier."

Mrs. Murphy sniffed. "We've managed Maggie's difficulties very well up until now."

The school nurse countered with a nod of the head, "I'm sure, but I must advise you to have an audiologist examine Maggie. Her development would be greatly facilitated if she could be raised in a signing environment which would enable her to fully participate in any ongoing dialogue."

"I believe signing to be a crutch. Lip-reading is much less noticeable, and would not bring attention to Margaret Ann's deafness." Evelyn shot back.

Of course, Evelyn Murphy knew what was best for her child. The mother liked to tell how she had argued for Margaret Ann to stay at home. She herself would teach her. She'd get books at the library. Later, she'd thought better of that idea, and had hired an instructor of the deaf, who had recently retired from the state deaf school, to come to their home five days a week to teach Maggie to lip read.

As it turned out, Maggie's biggest help was the next door neighbor Nora Green, who was Nonnie to Maggie. The elderly neighbor had befriended Maggie before the discovery of the child's impaired hearing. Many times Maggie had gone over to Nonnie's and visited with the eighty-year-old woman on her porch, or had gone inside the house and played with Silky the cat. Maggie didn't notice that Nonnie did not hear well, and that the woman spoke to her in a loud voice. Nonnie also used the point method when she wanted Maggie to hand her a spoon, vanilla, or milk from the refrigerator when the two were cooking, for the baby-sitter was forever trying new combinations in the preparation of food. And what surprisingly delicious casseroles and desserts the woman could create from ordinary ingredients by adding a few unusual herb flavors.

As soon as the arrangements were made for a tutor, Evelyn Murphy informed her husband that she would have to work to help with the added expense of the teacher. Bert, who worked at the dairy in town when his emphysema wasn't bothering him or when his arthritis hadn't flared up, didn't bring home much of a paycheck. The money would be welcome. He'd asked what was to be done with little Biddy. That was his name for

Maggie. And that's when Maggie's mother thought of Nora Green as a baby-sitter, and the older woman said she would be delighted to have the child. The speech therapist would come to Mrs. Green's house five days a week. Since Evelyn's new job at the cheese factory required her to change from day to night shifts during the week, Maggie would stay during the week with Nonnie, and spend weekends with Evelyn and Bert. All was planned even down to what they would pay the neighbor for keeping Maggie, but Mrs. Green would take no money for keeping Maggie. She said Maggie was her soul mate sent from heaven to keep her company.

When Nonnie Green died four years later, Maggie lost her best friend. The Murphys did not know just how much of a friend the woman was until the lawyer, who came to their house after Mrs. Green's death, explained that the woman had left her entire estate to Maggie. At first Bert assumed it was for the three of them. And though his breathing had become impossible without the added use of an oxygen tank, and his doctor had said no exertion of any kind, he began to plan—a vacation to England—a new car—a cruise. But Mrs. Green's last will and testament clearly stipulated that the cash was to be put into an annuity to be used for Maggie's schooling, clothes, and health needs. The money from a large portfolio of stocks and bonds, and two pieces of real estate in Royal, Wisconsin, was to be put into a trust until Maggie was thirty years old. It was also stipulated that the trustee would have broad jurisdiction. Evelyn and the bank became joint custodians of the trust. Bert was left out.

Part of the inheritance was used to enroll the seven-year-old Maggie as a boarder in the Grennly School for the Deaf. The private school was some eighty miles northeast of Collier in a suburb of Madison, Wisconsin. When Maggie came home on special holidays, her presence seemed to make Bert uncomfortable. Maggie sensed that Bert liked Silky, the cat she'd inherited, better than he did his stepdaughter.

Although Maggie had been tutored for four years before going to the boarding school, she was still not skilled enough to go into her scheduled grade and was kept back a year at Grennly. She learned the American Sign Language method of speaking with her hands, and the joy of understanding the spoken word began to open for her. Overcoming the developmental delays associated with deaf children, Maggie began to coordinate outer speech with inner speech as she participated in signing conversations.

Maggie still remembered a beautiful spring day when nature was bursting with color on the Grennly campus. The sixteen-year-old and her mother had an appointment with a doctor concerning Maggie's latest hearing tests. A slim, sandy haired man with kind brown eyes greeted Maggie and her mother in his office:

"Maggie, Mrs. Murphy, I'm Doctor Miller, an audiologist. I'm on the clinical review staff that comes in once a year to evaluate the overall educational progress of each child in accordance with the individual child's needs. The air and bone examinations we gave Maggie show that Maggie has a mixed loss of hearing—an impediment in the middle ear plus an inner ear deficiency. Both contribute to her hearing and speech difficulties."

"But we've been told all that. What more is there to know?" Maggie recognized her mother's nervousness from the quick way the woman spoke and by the slight frown that shadowed a smile.

"For Maggie's hearing examination this year, we've used the latest technological equipment for testing hearing loss which is far superior to that used even a year ago. Maggie's hearing test results show that her hearing can be dramatically improved. Would you like for me to explain?" The doctor looked at them both.

Maggie's eyes moved swiftly from Dr. Miller to her mother. With the doctor signing, and her mother speaking slowly, Maggie caught most of what was being discussed. Her first thought had been that she'd not paid proper attention and that the doctor was speaking of some other person. But when she saw her mother asking more detailed questions, Maggie realized the man had been saying she might be able to improve her hearing.

"Do you understand what the doctor is saying?" Evelyn asked Maggie.

"I don't know." Even though Maggie had been at the deaf school for nine years and had learned to rely on herself, she reverted to the days of deep dependency when she was with her mother, which did not allow her to agree or disagree. Though she didn't ask, she did wonder how much school she would have to miss, how long the operation would take, and would it hurt.

The doctor turned to look at Maggie and signed while speaking, "Maggie, let me explain how sound is relayed to the brain, and how we hear."

Doctor Miller got up from his chair and turned to a diagram on the wall behind his desk. "These are the parts of the ear. The outer ear catches sound vibrations. The ear drum, in the air-filled chamber of the middle ear, vibrates with the sound, and the three bones, right there, pick up the sound vibrations, and send them on to the inner ear." He pointed to each section of the ear, showing Maggie locations in the middle and inner ear where hers were not conveying sound correctly.

The doctor turned back to Maggie, "In your case, Maggie, you have a 70 dB hearing loss, which is profound."

Maggie, who had been lip reading and watching the doctor sign during his explanation, remained silent. For as long as she could remember, it was easier to remain silent than to be reprimanded and be afraid. She squirmed in her seat, but settled down when her mother frowned at her.

"We were told by the first specialist who saw Maggie that there was trouble with her hearing, and hearing loss caused her speech difficulties. We were to have patience with her talking. But try telling that to a hardheaded Irishman, Maggie's stepfather. I did try to be more patient, but not him." Evelyn said.

Doctor Miller nodded, "A parent's impatience is understandable, but may have an adverse effect on the child's speaking skills. The rebukes, plus the natural tendency to be rather shy, could have had a part in Maggie's reluctance to talk."

He smiled at Maggie in an understanding way. Maggie thought he had a nice smile. Never had anyone taken so much time to explain why she was deaf.

"Was Maggie born with this?" Mrs. Murphy's voice was strident. "I was very careful when I was carrying Maggie."

"It's a birth defect, but research hasn't found its cause." The doctor added, "In the embryo stage of development, the stapes bone usually gives way to soft tissue which can move, thus vibrate. When there is a fixation of the stapes, the bone remains ridged. Maggie's is ridged. There would be a marked improvement in Maggie's hearing if we were to replace the stapes bone with prosthesis. Then with a Cochlea implant, plus hearing aids and therapy, the correction would improve Maggie's hearing to 20 dB. Or put in another way, she'd have about 75 percent of normal hearing."

With a defensive lifting of the chin, Evelyn Murphy asked, "Is Maggie doing all right in school learning to sign and speak?"

"Very well." The doctor looked at Maggie with a smile.

"Then why put her through the ordeal?" Evelyn asked with a shrug as she sat up a little straighter.

"Mrs. Murphy, research would be useless if everyone had your attitude. With the new-found knowledge available, there are ways to help Maggie lead a fuller life." His engaging smile softened the rebuke.

"Of course," Evelyn nodded, but there was a definite tightening of her mouth.

"To replace the stapes is an out-patient operation with a short recovery." Dr. Miller picked up a small plastic container on his desk from which he took a very small object, and handed it to Maggie:

"Maggie, this is the stapes bone I've been talking about. You can see it's much smaller than a baby tooth. It looks like the delicate yellow stamen inside an Easter lily doesn't it?"

Maggie examined the small bone, nodded, and handed it back to the doctor. Fascinated, she watched him continue, never for a moment letting her eyes leave his gesturing hands:

"The second operation, a Cochlea implant, is a surgical procedure that requires several days in the hospital. At that time, hearing aids are inserted, and therapy is required to help the patient adjust to her new world of hearing."

Maggie understood what he was saying and eagerly awaited her mother's approval for the operations. Mrs. Murphy and Doctor Miller discussed the cost of the corrective surgery, length of recovery in the hospital, and details of the transplant procedures.

After their discussion, the doctor smiled at Maggie and her mother, "Now why don't I leave for a while and let you two discuss all of this?" He walked out, closing the office door behind him.

"Margaret Ann, you caught most of what he said I'm sure." Maggie nodded that she had.

"Nora Green stipulated that your education, and other needs, should be considered in the dispensing of your inheritance. I believe this is a once in a lifetime opportunity. If you are willing, these operations may help you. This will be very expensive, but if we use the interest on your cash investments, even dip into the principal, it can be paid for. It's that important for your future. The bank will agree I'm sure."

The firm set of her jaw showed her mother's determination. Slumbering feelings of hope stirred. Her mother was going to let her have the operation. She might be able to hear!

Joy, subdued by fear of the unknown, filled her days as Maggie waited impatiently for the school year to end. At last, the anticipated operation was to become reality. Her mother took her to Madison for the first operation. All the while, Bert grumbled unrelenting that no one seemed to care about how he felt. His pessimistic attitude would not let him be hopeful for his stepdaughter, and Maggie needed all the prayers of hope she could get. Witnessing Bert's complaints and her mother's patience, the daughter began to understand what Evelyn Bonner Murphy had endured through the years with the man. What was love about anyway?

The first surgery was dramatic. To go from profound deafness to hearing, in the space of two hours in the doctor's office, was a frightening as well as an exhilarating experience. With time, Maggie adjusted to the dramatic change in her life, learned to make out more word sounds, and her speech improved with therapy. They put off surgery on her inner ear, because she couldn't imagine wanting to hear any better than she could after the stapes prosthesis was in place. It was also her junior year at Grennly and if her hearing improved too much she would have to leave the deaf school. She wanted to graduate with her classmates, especially her friend Linda Edwards, a tall blonde of German decent with a trusting, outgoing personality, which was the direct opposite of reticent Maggie's. Totally deaf from birth, Linda accepted her deafness realistically, and her need for communication with the hearing as a necessity. The two girls were deeply compatible, comfortable with sharing hidden desires, and always content with silence.

That Christmas, Bert Murphy was seriously ill with pneumonia. Evelyn had to take a leave of absence from her work to take care of him, which left no time for Maggie. The eighteen-year-old was asked to spend the holidays and her birthday with Linda's family on the Edwards' farm some eighty miles north of Collier.

The visit was a dream come true for quiet Maggie. Linda and her two older brothers included Maggie in their activities—ice-skating, going on horse-drawn sleigh rides and playing card games with the whole family in the evenings. Everyday was a teasing, laughing, and carefree time, which was magical for the lonely child. Linda's brother Tim, became the boy-prince in Maggie's dream world. Linda's boyfriend, a young man she'd known since kindergarten, was Linda's prince. Late at night, snuggled under the eiderdown comforter, the girls exchanged wishes and wove fantasies of love.

Bert died in the spring. Maggie graduated and, not yet sure of a career, she decided to have the inner ear surgery that the doctor had recommended. Recovering in the hospital, Maggie could make out the footsteps of her nurse when the woman walked into her hospital room. The occasional scream of a siren, and the squeal of tires turning a corner were frightening at first, then became exciting symbols of life outside her room. She could even hear the faint peel of the phone on her bedside table. But when several people were in her room talking, her ears picked up jabs and starts of sound waves, and the message

Maggie received was rumbling, not words. The doctor had suggested that separating words from incoherent chatter might be possible if she were standing close to the person who was talking to her, and listened with determined concentration. There it was—the childhood word concentrate, a part of her adjustment to hearing. But now, it did not signal pressure to do the impossible. The surgeon also assured Maggie that the slight buzzing she could hear would lessen as she got used to sounds she'd never before been able to distinguish. Another dramatic dimension was added to Maggie's world.

Sidney Smith, Grennly's headmaster, had encouraged Maggie to go on to college to be a teacher for the deaf. But insecure, and not yet ready to leave the shelter of Grennly, Maggie stayed on at the school to work as head of the cooking staff in the school's kitchen. She rented an apartment and moved all of her belongings but Silky. The cat remained with Evelyn in Nonnie Green's house that had become Maggie's and Evelyn's home after Bert's death.

Remembering how she and her friend Linda had agreed that the cafeteria food was too bland and fattening, Maggie switched from plain meat, potatoes, and gravy dishes to chicken, pasta, and fish dishes marinated with oils and dried herbs. Vegetables were enhanced by a subtle use of spices. She experimented with egg whites, less sugar and other low-cal ingredients to make low-fat desserts. The changes were accepted and enjoyed by faculty and students, and encouraged Maggie to take some evening courses in nutrition at the University of Wisconsin in Madison. She easily passed the required courses in nutrition, food science and food systems management for becoming a Registered Dietitian. But when required to take an oral exam before an examining board, she became physically ill and had to drop the study. Content to work without the RD degree, but with nutritional certification, she became known for effectively planning menus and creating innovative dishes that were deliciously edible and healthful. The challenge of her work inspired her to create a cookbook entitled, A Fresh Approach to Cooking for Large Groups. This book led to another on the preparation of soups and sauces. A new career began to grow for Maggie from the seeds that were planted long before in Nonnie Green's kitchen.

After nine rewarding years of creating nutritious foods in the Grennly school's kitchen, and having established a name for herself in the cooking world, Maggie decided she wanted to come back to Collier and concentrate on food preparation and writing cookbooks. With the approval and help of her mother, Maggie changed their 1930's kitchen into a modern, state-of-the-art workstation in which she created nutritional, as well as flavorful foods. Only tested recipes were used in her cookbooks, which were successfully selling to the health-minded public.

She wrote regularly to Linda:

"No doubt, my life seems quite boring, what with it revolving around my writing, my mother, our church, and Richard Stevenson, the bachelor minister of our small Community Church."

Linda also wrote about her life and asked questions:

"What is this Richard person like? Has he made any passes yet?"

Maggie laughed at the questions but it did make her consider what her life was like. She was honest with Linda:

"No, there have been no exciting passes made by Richard. I like his company (most of the time), he's kind and helps me make decisions (like mother), but he's only a friend. Besides, my work keeps me too busy to become involved."

Linda had written:

"Richard sounds boring! I've found my man, and want you to find yours. Listen, you're untouched by real living in that town of yours. Go out and find yourself a man!"

Linda's remarks were not offensive. Maggie agreed. She was a twenty-nine-year old girl-woman untouched by real living, whatever that was.

***

It was stone cold in the small-town library. All of the radiators throughout the room clanged and wheezed trying to stay hot and keep the bitterly cold weather at bay. Maggie shivered and pulled her coat over her legs, as she tried to concentrate on the quote she wanted to use:

> In the Middle Ages, lavender, Lavandula, was known as the herb of love. In our modern age, Lavender's fragrant flowers continue to inspire devotion.

Chewing on the stub of her pencil, she looked up from the book and over to the library entrance. Her thoughts drifted to the man with the penetrating gray-blue eyes and bushy red hair, who pushed his wheelchair so forcefully down the ramp and on to the street corner in an apparent attempt to escape. He'd seemed so powerful, even though he was crippled in some way. Power with a disability. It was something she'd never been able to achieve.

CHAPTER 2

It was four o'clock and Maggie had been in the library for over three hours. She'd wasted time dreaming, but had taken some richly informative notes on the properties and possible edible parts of certain herbs, which would complete the research for her new book. All that was left was to gather a few more edible uses of lavender.

The natural light of the recently installed skylights had been blocked by a heavy layer of snow, and the library flouorescent lights were just not bright enough for her to read the fine print. With an audible sigh, Maggie decided to call it a day. Bundling up in her pleasantly warm coat, tam, and scarf, she lugged heavy resource books to the librarian at the checkout desk.

"Thanks Letty. I'll need these for overnight. Tomorrow, I'll return for that reserve book, The Book of Lavender, by Jackie French. I'd appreciate it if you could put it on hold for me." She said, noticing the librarian's hesitation before she stamped the take-out books.

"Somebody took the book out." Never raising her eyes from the out-moded procedure, the librarian spoke quite loudly for Maggie's benefit it seemed.

"But it's a reserve book, Letty. It's only to be used here in the library. Besides, who would be interested in lavender but me?" A note of exasperation was evident in Maggie's voice.

"Mr. Thomlinson, that's who. He's just returned to live in Collier and continue his writing. He needs to research the uses of some herbs, including lavender, for one of his mystery novels. He'll have it back on Wednesday. I couldn't refuse him. He needs a friend around here." Letty said this as she stamped the last book with a thump of finality.

Resigned to the fact that someone had gotten Letty to waive the rules of the library, Maggie reluctantly asked that the book be saved on Wednesday, and proceeded outside. Spirals of wet snow driven by strong gusts of wind greeted her with a vengeance. Quickly pulling up her scarf to buffer the stinging wetness that greedily attacked her cheeks and eyes, she walked down the snow-hidden ramp and recalled the near-mishap with the man in a wheelchair. Could that wheelchair person be Mr. Thomlinson, the mystery writer?

Just last week, she'd heard that someone had seen lights in the Thomlinson estate. It was thought that the owner Mr. Collier Thomlinson, who wrote mystery novels, was back. Curious, she'd driven by the Thomlinson property with its ornately scrolled wrought iron entrance, through which she could see a long winding drive and a distant lake. She couldn't recall ever seeing the reclusive novelist, but she'd been gone from Collier most of her life. He needs a friend? Letty's remark intrigued her.

Using her briefcase as a shield from the bitterly cold wind, Maggie trudged her way through deep-layered snow the five blocks to their home, still pondering Letty's remark. Why would a mystery writer need a book on lavender for research? There were some weeds in the herb books that would be excellent for committing murder. The henbane plant with its innocent clusters of yellow, purple-veined flowers could be used for painkillers, as well as to induce sleep. It was also a deadly poison that could be used to kill. Or, take the digitalis-filled leaves of the foxglove, which could be used to increase blood pressure and slow down the heartbeat. It certainly had deadly properties. But why lavender?

Maggie's cheeks were stiff, her hands and feet numb with cold by the time she entered the warmth of the mini-warehouse dwelling. Maude Green's two-bedroom house had been adequately furnished when Maggie and Evelyn had moved in accompanied by all of the Murphy furnishings.

As she entered the house stomping off snow, Maggie's Persian friend swished down the hall. But before the usual rub-against-the-leg greeting, the cat stopped to lick a paw that had come in contact with a patch of melted snow. Maggie leaned down to tickle behind soft ears, but Silky danced away, and with a swish of long tail, regally ambled into the living room.

"Hello to you, kitty." A smiling Maggie followed the independent feline, into the warm room. "Hello to you too." Maggie greeted her mother who sat by the flickering fireplace, diligently working on a needlepoint piece.

"How was your afternoon at the library?" Evelyn asked, never looking up from her needlework. Maggie had caught the question that required no answer. Her mother hated the library with its musty smell and dreary appearance.

The living room reflected Evelyn Murphy's preference for uplifting, bright surroundings. From blue linen-covered occasional chairs grouped in corners of the room with Tiffany table lamps, to the multi-floral chintz couch with its large down-filled pillows, and sunlight-yellow fireside chairs placed close to the blazing fire, the room looked like a flower garden growing on a field of grass-green carpeting.

Maggie picked up needlepoint books, magazines and other periodicals strewn in her path as she went to the fireside chair opposite her mother. Removing a basket of yarn from the chair, she sat down facing the woman who looked up, smiled, and looked down again at her handwork without missing a needle stroke. Silky jumped up on Maggie's lap, and curled her body into a ball that quivered with pleasure as Maggie gently smoothed hands over long fur.

The vibration of Silky's purr, the scratch of Evelyn's moving needles, the wind whistles seeping around a window sash, the sizzle of gas-fed logs were sounds as soothing as the hum of a Jacuzzi tub—the bath luxury that was first on Maggie's after-published wish list.

Her mother's hands skillfully moved over the needlepoint canvas stitching ivy swirls in variegated shades of emerald, cream, and gold, interlaced with petite point flower petals of pink, yellow, and lipstick red. The original canvas would become a large pillow to be auctioned off at the Christmas bazaar. With not a little pride involved, all knew, including Evelyn, that Mrs. Murphy's pillow would be the highlight of the church affair.

Evelyn Murphy was a bundle of energy who enjoyed juggling the care of their home, sewing, and doing volunteer work at the church. Evelyn often gave credit to God for directing her life, and easing the painful migraine headaches she'd had to endure when Bert was alive. She also gave thanks that she no longer had to work those grueling hours at the cheese factory. She tapped Maggie's knee with a knitting needle.

"Richard called to say we're to go to the Methodist Church in Etin tomorrow afternoon to see the set-up for their bazaar. We're fortunate that there's to be a break in the weather. You know it wasn't very thoughtful of them to have chosen a Thanksgiving bazaar when our Christmas bazaar will be held in four weeks. Why is it when one gets a good idea, others like to copy it? Of course, Etin is several miles away, but still in this age of driving everywhere, we may lose some customers to their earlier bazaar. Ginny said…"

While Evelyn went through the complaints-of-the day, Maggie's mind looped to daydreams. She didn't go anywhere except to church functions and an occasional trip to Chicago to confer with her publisher. Sometimes she and Evelyn would go to a stage play or a movie while in the city, but Maggie couldn't follow the dialogue, and her mother found most stage productions and movies to be scandalous—so why attend?

She'd like to get in the car and go to someplace far away— maybe Arizona, or Florida, or a trip to California to see the vineyards and learn more about the wines she could use in recipes. But her driver's license was limited. She could only drive in and around Collier. Maybe a cruise by ship or sailboat would be nice. There were so many wonderful places to see, yet here she sat at home, cat on lap, letting her mother drone on about things Maggie had already heard, or would be hearing again.

She tuned in to her mother's run-on conversation. Evelyn had switched from complaints with people and food to again discuss the bazaar. "Well, we may get a few ideas from their bazaar for ours. Oh, after we go to Etin, Richard wants us to have dinner with him at the Fairchild House. Isn't that nice?"

It was difficult for Maggie to express an opinion with Evelyn. Perhaps it was a holdover from the days when her mother had felt the need to talk for the two of them. Maggie gently nudged Silky off her lap, and leaned over to pick up the weekly newspaper from the pile at the side of her chair. Absently looking through the paper, Maggie noticed an article dealing with witchcraft. Fires had started in woods, and a journalist had written an article on the possibility of devil worshipers practicing in the vicinity. Not into sensationalism any more than gossip, Maggie lay down the paper. And though sure of what her mother would say, belatedly answered in a faint voice:

"I believe I'll stay home from the trip to Etin."

"But dear, you must go." Evelyn said as she laid aside her needlework. "The ladies will need your ideas on the arrangement of booths in our church basement. It's so cramped. And Richard has so thoughtfully planned the trip.

He'll be disappointed if you don't go. Now let's see, we'll pick up Ginny and Blanche, motor over to the church in Etin, see the booths, then return to drop off the two ladies. After that, you and I will have dinner with Richard at the Fairchild Hotel. I understand they have a new chef who is more than adequate, and you know how Richard likes good food."

Maggie regarded her mother. With her plump body and tiny feet that barely touched the footstool, she looked like a cute little doll propped up in the over-sized wing-backed chair. Evelyn Murphy was small and round, but she was definitely not a limp baby doll. She was a sober-minded, no nonsense type of person. The old adage of idle hands mean mischief could be the woman's slogan.

When Evelyn Murphy, born in a suburb of London, England, wanted to make a point emphatically clear, she slipped into a noticeable English accent. Catching the accent, and the do-not-argue tone of voice, made Maggie wonder if there might be more involved than going to check booths. Perhaps Richard was getting ready to tap Maggie for a large donation for the church building program so the cramped basement could be enlarged. Under the trust, Maggie would be in charge of gifts after her birthday this December. She intended to give a sizable amount for the church expansion, but didn't like to be manipulated.

Maggie mumbled, "I'd planned to finish writing up my notes for my new book while the information is still fresh in my mind." As soon as she said it, she knew it wouldn't be a good enough reason.

"Oh my, that shouldn't take you too long if you go and do it instead of sitting there like a stick. We'll have a nice afternoon and see the layout for the bazaar. Some say it's the best charity affair Etin has ever had. They probably have quantity, whereas we'll have quality like this piece." Mrs. Murphy ran her hand lovingly over her needlework.

"We'll not leave until one." Evelyn said with an air of dismissal, as she returned to her project.

Heat flushed Maggie's cheeks. She loved her mother, trusted her judgment, and admired her accomplishments. But at times, she felt as if she were in a sterile bubble observing life through her mother. What was the use of arguing?

"Yes, Mother." She sighed, and walked out of the room to the den where she began to write up her notes about the downy hawthorn tree. A tea made from hawthorn flowers could be used to lower blood pressure. She presumed she would be a good subject to test the brew's effect right now.

CHAPTER 3

After the excursion to see the Etin bazaar, Richard drove the other committee members to their homes. Maggie, Evelyn and Richard drove on to the Fairchild House. The restaurant was formerly the home of the well-to-do Fairchild family who had made their money in the cheese and dairy business. The home had been stylishly converted into several intimate dining rooms. The hostess led the three to the Walnut Room, the former library in the home. Antique silver, crystal, and sprigs of bittersweet graced four round tables. To the side of their table, an antique brass screen fronted a fireplace modernized with steadily flickering gas logs. They were served the menu of the day—lamb chops with mint jelly, tiny new potatoes garnished with parsley, buttered asparagus, and crisp spinach salad with red raspberry vinaigrette dressing. After which, the waitress left them to enjoy their dessert and coffee.

Throughout the dinner, the conversation had been mostly between Richard and Evelyn. Maggie had been content to enjoy the romantic setting—a flickering fire, soft piano music in the background. She observed Richard and tried to imagine such an evening with him. He'd removed his glasses, and his eyes looked sunken and hollow. The attempt to be better looking, if that's what he was trying to do, made him look older than his thirty-seven years. But she supposed the aging could be caused by the weight of responsibility he had with his parishioners.

He'd been discussing the subject of cults, which he'd chosen for tomorrow's sermon. Now, he was apparently on another subject. She'd lost the first part of a comment Richard had just made: "...a perfect hall for their bazaar."

He apparently was referring to the Methodist Church Fellowship Hall they'd just seen. The church basement had been spacious enough to have wide aisles, and fifteen large booths filled with handmade aprons, towels, table linens, hand embroidered children's clothing, needlepoint items, and various kinds of baked goods.

"They have loads of space," Richard remarked.

"My, how glorious to be able to have that much room," Evelyn Murphy exclaimed. Apparently the minister and her mother were into a discussion about improvements needed in their own church.

Several times Maggie inserted a comment, but she knew they weren't listening to her. Smiling a little wanly, she thought of the difference between the hearing impaired and hearing individuals. Certainly she listened more carefully than they did, even though there were inflections she still didn't catch.

Wonder what would happen? She firmly said, "No."

"What did you say?" Her mother asked.

"That's my line, mother." Maggie raised her shoulders with a smile. "I'm sorry. I must have missed your question."

Dreaming dreams is a child's and an invisible woman's delight. Maggie tuned out the voices of her dinner companions, and concentrated on the rich textured flavor of her favorite dessert, Crème Brulle.

When it was time to go, Maggie watched her mother pay the bill. It was the usual finale to an evening with their minister. The pastor suggested a nice place to dine, to the tune of thirty or forty dollars apiece, and Maggie and her mother paid for it.

"Thank you, Richard. We had a fine afternoon and evening, didn't we Margaret Anne?" Evelyn Murphy prompted Maggie.

Maggie smiled and waited for Richard's thank you. Instead, Richard got out of the car and came around to help each woman out. He walked between them up to the door where he deposited each with a flourish of smiles, then drove away, leaving them to enter the house by themselves.

For just a moment, she wondered what it would be like to have Richard kiss her. She remembered one kiss after the Grennly School senior ball. Linda's brother Tim had been her escort. How thrilled she'd been when he'd given her a brotherly kiss that night. She'd believed she was in love, but he'd left for law school, met and married a girl, and set up a law practice in Royal near the family farm.

She again felt the insecure reticence born of years of being left out of much of life. So cloistered, she barely knew the rudiments of sex—what it would feel like to be in love.

The evening had been nice, if not exciting, Maggie admitted as she and her mother silently went about turning off lights and checking door locks. Evelyn retired to the only bathroom to do her usual preparations for the night.

Maggie went to her bedroom at the end of the hall where she was immediately greeted by Silky, the huge Persian cat, rubbing against her leg.

"You love me, don't you, Silky?" She stooped down to give the cat a pat, but Silky scooted by her and out the door. "So much for my allure; even my cat rejects me."

Maggie slipped into her pajamas and housecoat. Returning to the living room, she turned up the gas jet and watched the flames lick around the ceramic logs. Suddenly, the face of the man on the library ramp with his cap and fringe of red hair floated above the flickering fire. She felt the heat on her body and with it restlessness.

"It's strange I've never seen him before in our town," she muttered, walking out of the room and into the den, where she absently began pulling papers from her briefcase, while thinking about the gentleman with red hair.

29

Of course, she'd heard of him. He was a legend both because of his family and his own accomplishments. She'd never paid much attention. She wondered how old he was. Apparently he was not social, for she'd heard nothing about him, just listened to remarks about his questionable books. Not much into local news, she spent her time in her recipe-creating kitchen, and going to the library and church.

Her hermit-style life agreed with Maggie. Sunday service was her meditative time to commune with God since Richard's sermons were too difficult to hear other than a phrase or a word now and then. If they moved up to the front of the church, it might be better, but her mother didn't want anyone to see the back of her head if her hair was not just right.

The tinkle of a bell, a habit carried over from the days when Maggie could not hear, signaled that her mother was out of the bathroom. Catching the scent of her mother's fragrant lavender powder that drifted through the hall and into the den, reminded Maggie of the author who was supposedly returning the book on lavender to the library Wednesday morning. He had his nerve! She wondered if he was able to use any of the research on the lavender plant. It would be nice to have a talk with him about the reason he wanted the book. But that was out of the question. Her mother might not approve. And yet, why not? Her mother didn't own the life of a twenty-nine-soon-to-be-thirty year old woman. The enormity of the thought was strangely challenging.

With flutters of anxiety induced by thought-provoking guilt, she quickly hurried to her mother's bedroom to extend the usual goodnight kiss. "I've a few more pages to do on the new book before I go to bed. If I'm not too sleepy, I may whip up a new bread."

Maggie spent over an hour organizing her library notes on the history of flora, and the uses of the various herbs, trees and plants. At last, satisfied that she'd done all she could do until she got the facts on medicinal uses of lavender, she decided to experiment with the lavender herb as a flavor for bread. Going to the kitchen, she greased and flour-dusted baking pans, turned on the oven and, using her commercial mixer, whipped up a basic quick bread batter to which she added sugar, spices and dried florets of lavender. The smell of baking lavender bread was as soothing as a tranquilizer. Maggie wrote down another use of lavender.

***

"Good morning, dear," Evelyn sang out. She wore a bright pink dressing gown, a pink ribbon in her silver-flecked hair, and a smiling countenance, which made her look younger than her fifty-six years. She hummed as she busily arranged china and silverware, poured their coffee, and placed a plate of the fresh bread in the center of the table. "I couldn't resist the fresh bread you made. It's delicious. Is it lavender flavored? Did you make it for the church pitch-in? I thought you were going to prepare some sort of casserole. Perhaps we could use one or two loaves of this bread for the bazaar bake-goods booth."

"I can't share the recipe yet. It's going to be a special in my new cook-with-herbs book. However, I will bake cheddar with herb biscuits for the bazaar, and share the Pansy salad dressing recipe." Maggie pacified the request.

Her mother sniffed. Ignoring the hint of dissatisfaction, Maggie pinched off a slice of the bread, and was concentrating on the taste and texture of the sweet bread when she felt a tap on her shoulder:

"I really don't know how we can possibly have Mrs. Woods in charge of the bake booth. She's never tidy enough, always just a little soiled looking and with half of her teeth out. She's just too unkempt to be in a food booth for heaven's sake. We should have someone at the door to greet people, and make the shoppers feel welcome. Ginny told me about Judith Sauter— you remember her, don't you?"

Without waiting for her daughter to reply, Evelyn continued, "She's having an affair with John Aims. I don't know how she can show her face in church."

Maggie noticed her mother's cheeks had taken on a tinge more color, and presumed that the last remark had embarrassed Evelyn. Intimacy between two people was never discussed in their home.

The grievances continued like the chirp of a tiny English sparrow scolding away strangers from her nest. It was hard to defend or agree with any of it, because the woman didn't listen to anyone during her outpouring of negatives.

Evelyn slowly buttered a slice of lavender bread. "Sometimes, I believe Richard is just too nice, letting those Conners come to church in coveralls like a bunch of mountain people. Perhaps it shouldn't, but it makes me uncomfortable to see them so out of place. They don't give a thing to the church. Someone mentioned yesterday that they even attend some of that Irishman's meetings."

Evelyn stopped and looked at Maggie as if waiting for a reply, but, in truth, she might have stopped only to catch her breath.

There can be contributing factors other than dress, looks, or habits that make people seem different. Perhaps some people talk about me—"Poor child...deaf you know...can you imagine? Evelyn Murphy is a saint." Maggie sighed audibly.

After her unloading, when Evelyn had revealed her low opinion of some people, the woman would at last admit what was really bothering her. It could be that Mrs. Aldrich did not speak to her, or Ginny Philips, her best friend, had discussed the bazaar with somebody other than Evelyn. Or possibly a barb of complaint concerning her mother's bazaar leadership had hit, and Evelyn felt compelled to deflect it by criticism of others. Maggie silently waited for the habitual apology.

"Of course, I did overhear the minister say something about people changing by example when we were discussing the Conner family."

Maggie took a deep breath—end of tirade.

Evelyn took a quick sip of coffee, put it down, and looked over at Maggie who winced at the determined gleam in her mother's eye. Not wishing to discuss any more grievances, Maggie quickly looked away to add sugar to her already sweetened coffee.

"Margaret Ann, look at me."

Maggie picked up her cup, breathed in the fresh-brewed smell, and took a sip of coffee before looking over the rim of the cup at her mother.

"I think it's time we had a talk about marriage and the obligations of two people in such circumstances. You know about sexual things don't you?" Evelyn asked.

Maggie choked on a sip of coffee and discreetly covered a smile with her napkin, before acknowledging that she'd taken a sex course at the Grennly School, and that she and her friend Linda had discussed sex.

"Well," her mother continued, "I believe Richard is going to ask for your hand in marriage. Now, mind you, he only hinted at it, but I believe it'll not be long before he wishes to speak to you." The mother smiled in satisfaction, touching each corner of her up-turned lips with a white linen napkin.

"Mother, that's ridiculous! He hasn't said a word to me. Anyway, I'm not in love with Richard." Maggie lowered her voice. "There should be some sort of private communication between two people before they can know if they're in love. Don't you agree?"

"What do you mean? He just now asked you out to see the bazaar in Etin. He's always at your side to help in difficult situations. He never fails to remember your birthday, even if it is just three days before Christmas and one of his busiest times as pastor of our church."

"I know. It's dear of him to remember me—to take care of me if he feels he must. I believe we two are more like a habit than two people in love." Maggie said.

Flashbacks of Evelyn and stepfather Bert arguing made Maggie uncomfortable with the conversation. She switched the subject. "Mother, do you know Collier Thomlinson?"

Evelyn Murphy slowly poured more coffee into her cup, added two teaspoons of sugar, stirred, and took a long drink of the hot liquid. With the palm of her other hand, she kept smoothing over one small wrinkle in the otherwise crisp, white tablecloth. Maggie started to repeat her question when her mother answered in such a faint voice that Maggie had to read her lips.

"Yes, I know the family. I've heard stories about him, his writing." Eyes still averted the woman rubbed her forehead causing Maggie to wonder if a migraine was coming on.

"Why have we never met him?" Maggie asked.

Evelyn slowly wiped both corners of her mouth with her napkin. With her gaze fixed on the tabletop, the woman finally answered Maggie's question. "The Thomlinson home is on Lake Thomlinson. The father died about twenty years ago. The son's been gone ever since he was a child. He's just recently returned to live in the old mansion. And a group of people meet on his property to worship trees, or something heathenish I imagine." Like a wind-up toy, Evelyn gave the bare facts about the author, then added:

"Ginny told me, and she heard it from another woman who's a friend of the housekeeper, that he's now writing detective stories that are quite racy. I've heard that Mrs. Tuttle, the housekeeper, you know, that nice black lady we see in the grocery store, is quite fond of the man, even though it's said he's a snobbish oddball."

In just a few hasty minutes, Maggie had learned a lot about the gentleman, but nothing had been said about his wheelchair. Maggie wondered if he had been injured recently and asked as much.

"No, he's been a paraplegic for some time." Evelyn abruptly got up and gathered dirty dishes from the table, proceeded to the sink, and hastily rinsed them for the dishwasher.

After a lengthy silence, with her back still to Maggie, Evelyn Murphy added, "I believe it best we not discuss that man. I've heard he puts pornographic material in his novels. And in your condition you shouldn't think about him."

With that, the tiny woman marched out of the kitchen leaving Maggie to look after her, wondering what the condition was to which her mother referred.

CHAPTER 4

"Mr. Thomlinson, I'm going now."

"Yes, Mrs. Tuttle. I plan to go to the library and will return about five."

"I'll be back at four." The housekeeper's words carried behind her as she left the room.

With a nod of thanks, which the housekeeper could not see, he acknowledged her leaving. As so many times before, he considered how much he needed Mrs. Tuttle, and the fact that being needed was all the thanks she needed from him. She was indeed a fine woman and a prototype for the real martyrs of the world. Never expecting reward for her good deeds, Bessie Tuttle was first in Collier's book of saints. Saint Teresa of Avila was a close second.

During the mile journey in his wheelchair to the town library, Collier ignored familiar surroundings as he reflected on his life with Mrs. Tuttle and his valet, Robert. He knew he had tunnel vision when he was working, and tended to ignore his household help when he was in the process of creating. He'd try to be more thoughtful in the future. They both were as close as he would come to having a family.

Safely arriving at his destination, Collier rolled up to the library reception desk where Miss Lavitia Levert stood. The figure of dignity in her long, gray princess-style dress had been the librarian in Collier for over fifteen years. She seemed intelligent and was genuinely solicitous. Though shy to the point she could not look at a person directly, something happened when a person asked about a book. A light switched on, and a bashful smile communicated her eagerness to please.

As always, he tried to analyze the "first look" response of a person confronting a man with a disability. As she greeted

36

him, her dark eyes with their short thick lashes were twitching and fluttering like twin butterflies caught on an overhanging branch. Were her eyes darting around the room to find something to look at besides his covered legs? Or, could the keen gleam in those flashing black eyes be for him? Ridiculous! Pessimism, a part of his life, once again forced down optimism.

"Good morning, Miss Levert. I've again come with a request. Seems I need more information on the olfactory properties of flora." His request, though somewhat stilted, was lightened with a smile and lift of the brows.

"Yes, there are several flower and herb books, besides the one you took out yesterday. I'll look." With a spin of the heel, she turned her back on Collier and walked to the other end of the large room.

"Thank you," he mumbled, observing her retreating figure with its generous rear. Swiveling around, he examined his reflection in the glass door of the library's entrance. I'm a fairly good-looking man, he thought as he studied himself. The bright red hair, which defied a brush, and his lean, chiseled features were genetic gifts from his father. Vivid blue eyes with slashes of character lines stared back at him somewhat disdainfully. There might be just a trace of grimness to the set of the mouth that could indicate willfulness. A knowing tilt of the lips gave credence to the observation.

He was proud of his manly pectoris and muscled torso. The exercise program, paralyzed legs massaged to maintain what muscle tone he had, and upper torso strengthened by lifting weights executed by his valet Robert's badgering, was programmed into his daily routine and was faithfully adhered to regardless of other pressing commitments his writing demanded. Today, his upper body, was clothed in a white open-collar shirt and navy V-neck sweater. He could feel the swell of his chest against the starched fabric as he breathed in and out. The lower torso hidden by a tartan-plaid, woolen coverlet was clad in gray flannel slacks. He wore black wing-tipped oxfords. Thank God for Mrs. Tuttle's husband, Edward, who'd helped with the necessities of dress today since Robert was on vacation in England. The library door opened, bringing swishes of cold, snow-filled air in with another patron. The sting from the bitter wind of the November day caused chills to tickle his chest, and his narcissistic observance to cease.

The librarian returned with three rather small books. After he'd leafed through them, he praised her on her excellent selections and said he'd take all three. Wordlessly, she took the books, removed the identification cards, and stamped the due-date. He watched with wry amusement and something like a feeling of nostalgia. A computerized sign-out machine hadn't been introduced to this old Carnegie.

"Mr. Thomlinson." With lowered eyes, Miss Levert hesitantly addressed Collier. "Please don't forget to bring the book on lavender back this Wednesday. Another person has asked for it."

"I will bring it back as promised. I do thank you again. It was a most needed favor." With a slight nod, Collier put on his black wool cap, adjusted his fleece-lined car coat, and placed the books under his heavy lap robe. Steering his wheelchair through the automatic doors to the outside, he pressed the brake to slow his dissent down the icy, snow patched ramp.

"Oh, whoops!" He chuckled out loud at the memory of yesterday's swift ride down the ramp, when he'd barely missed a woman. Fortunately, he'd seen her coming up the ramp in time to tilt left on two wheels to keep from barreling into her. When he'd gotten the infernal machine stopped, he'd call out to her. He'd gestured with his cap and it was almost whipped from his hand when a buffer of wind slapped at the brim.

How could such a tiny person withstand the onslaught of snow-driven wind that flattened her long green coat against her ankles, and snapped thick, black hair from under a disheveled-looking red tam? A scarf was pulled down from her face and almost, but not quite, covered her full lips. When she'd spoken, he'd picked up a distinctive accent with a lilt that slightly slurred at the end. Was it Irish? Her flashing green eyes could have been. He hoped her laugh had been friendly, and that she was not laughing at his appearance, as he rushed away looking like a stiff-feathered peacock with plumage of cart and wheels—an analogy he'd often thought appropriate.

He pushed swiftly toward the stoplight, mimicking himself aloud with puckered lips and a lift of the head in exaggerated disdain. "Do you daydream often or on only rare occasions?"

That's what he'd called to the girl. The idiotic question had been accusingly harsh. He hated trivial pursuits, avoided them, and was most uncomfortable bandying words in useless conversation. Especially when he knew damn well that the underlying problem at the time had been his feeling of embarrassment and more than a little shock.

Hunched low in his chair, with a scowl as black as his cap, he stopped at the street corner for a red light. Slushy snow slapped at his face and tried to curl inside his ears, forcing him to pull his coat collar tighter under his chin. With the green light, he pushed across the street and jumped the curb.

Curb jumping was a sport for him. To roll up and over the low barrier of cement was a maneuver that called for strategy and skill. He had to hold up the front wheels of his wheelchair, with tense muscles of wrists and forearms long enough to propel the back wheels up and over the curb, then slap the front wheels down quickly to stabilize the machine. The mental image of a gymnast's lift-off from the ground, onto the balancing bar, and finishing with an upright landing on the gym pad, did help him master the art of curb jumping without a mishap.

Today, the challenge, enhanced by the uncertainties of snow, had been met again. Especially sweet was the certainty that the young woman on the library steps had observed his curb feat yesterday. Bragging was not his nature, but he'd have liked to see the girl's face when she saw that trick.

He wondered who she was; then ego-deflating thoughts of normalcy in social situations sobered him. Nothing was quite normal for him. She might have given her name had he asked, but how could he ask when she'd give it only out of sympathy? He didn't require sympathy. He knew his limitations. What he had was better than living with hope for what he could never have. Yet, there had been times when he'd thought there might be a chance for more. He remembered a thirty-year-old therapist. She was a pretty young woman named Brenda, who had been hired to come in each morning to help him exercise his upper body and massage the lower half. He'd been sixteen, two years after the accident.

Collier stopped before the closed wrought iron gate of his home for a moment to recall the professional zeal with which she'd massaged his legs and flaccid genitals. One day, her administerings got a slight response from his penis. The unexpected phenomenon must have given her a sexual charge, for she pressed her heavy bosom against him, and gave him a moist kiss. He kissed her in response, and they hungrily explored each other's mouths, tongues, and upper bodies. He pondered the memory.

He recalled being embarrassed, and somewhat chagrined, when she'd nullified his further advances by saying the physical pleasure he displayed was indeed gratifying to her as a therapist. Collier chuckled at the memory, and her feeble attempt to keep the experience on a therapeutic level. But she didn't stop.   The physical exercises with his sweet little therapist continued until the day his mother saw them. At that time, Brenda was asked to leave.

He tried to remember what fondling the woman's huge globes had been like and imagine that he could still get a slight pulse to quiver in his unused parts.

Collier clamped his mouth tightly shut, and touched the gate opener on the arm of his wheelchair. The heavy, intricately scrolled barrier slowly slid open to a snow-covered road that curved behind a glen of cedars. Collier drove through the cocoon of trees, where no snow could penetrate, to be greeted at the end of the grove by pelting snow as he passed the side lawn to the house.

The large structure in front of him seemed to rise out of the veil of frozen air. Collier chuckled aloud remembering how in his three-year-old imagination, perhaps having been programmed by the Grimm brothers' fairy tales, the mansion was a huge stone-faced monster with three horns protruding from its massive head. Dormers and a deep overhang that, to a child, could resemble thick, black eyebrows over slatted eyes pierced the black mansard roof of slate. The mansion, with its two wings that curved back to a lake, sat sprawled over the land with arms outstretched as if to guard the people inside the home from the frightening witches and goblins that lived in the dense woods at the far side of the property.

His mature observation saw a two-story, flat-faced structure of gray stone with rows of red brick-trimmed windows. The entrance was graced with a fourteen-foot mahogany door with fittings of brass and an embossed Thomlinson crest of hammered copper. Stone steps with ramps at each side and a wide driveway girdled the front of the mansion. The French Chateau design had been somewhat modified with the two wings to the lakeside shortened and rounded to allow a more open view of the surrounding Thomlinson property and Lake Thomlinson.

Great-granddaddy Thomlinson must have designed the massive structure to impress others, rather than to adequately accommodate the inhabitants of the house. At the present time it seemed so, for the staff consisted only of Mrs. Tuttle, the cook and housekeeper; Robert, the valet, chauffeur, and butler; Mrs. Tuttle's husband, Edward, the gardener and handyman; and an occasional cleaning girl who always got flustered when she saw Collier ride by. Years before, there had been a full staff of maids and butlers to serve the extended family of aunts, uncles, and guests who flowed in and out of the grand manor. At the present time, most relatives were gone, and the rest never visited.

Suddenly, the five-foot carriage lights on either side of the entrance blinked on. Collier warmed with love for the old place as he eagerly pushed up the flagstone ramp and into the wide, marble vestibule. Shaking off snow from his fleece-lined coat, he paused to gaze down the length of the long hall in front of him. Doors were closed to the seldom-used formal reception room, billiard room, and dining room. Tiny candle-shaped bulbs in electrified sconces illuminated rows of ancestral portraits. Collier began a slow roll down the highly polished parquet floor, and stopped to study the five by seven-foot portrait of his portly great-grandfather, George Collier Thomlinson, an immigrant from Germany.

The soft light showed a gentleman whose pink-flushed cheeks were partially covered by a white bushy beard. Collier imagined the beard was greatly appreciated by the man when he went about on snowy days in his horse-drawn milk delivery truck. The frugal relative had learned the dairy business working on a dairy farm near Milwaukee and had saved his money to acquire five milk cows, one horse and a truck. Later, he added three trucks and a herd of Holsteins that were the envy of other milk supply houses.

The portrait hanging beside the one of the founding father was of great-grandmother Bessie. She presented a stern, unsmiling face to the viewer as she sat on a dark green velvet chair with hands clasped on her lap below an ample bosom. Collier could see a resemblance to Brenda the therapist.

The thought brought a smile as Collier shifted his gaze from the first inhabitants of the Thomlinson mansion to the two portraits on the opposite wall between the garden room and the library. The first was of an impressive looking man, Collier's grandfather, George Collier Thomlinson II, who had no beard but sported long sideburns and a sagging mustache. George II had added to the budding wealth of the clan when he married Julia, the heiress to the Fairchild Cheese Company fortune. He'd been forty, she twenty. Her portrait showed a drably dressed woman with red hair pulled back in such a way as to show off her prominent ears.

"You must have had hidden talents, old girl," Collier told her as he passed by, and felt a momentary stab of sadness. His father had never known this woman, his own mother, for Grandmother Julia had died giving birth to George Collier Thomlinson III. Collier pushed on past the closed library doors to gaze up at the portrait of his father. With no mother, and a father who was dedicated to the German work ethic, George Collier III was sent to England to be educated at the early age of ten. At the age of twenty-five, having had enough knowledge crammed into his head to last a lifetime, as George Collier III had often told Collier, the young gentleman had come back to help in the family business where he was neither needed nor wanted. What his father's life must have been in the days of his youth, sent to school in another country for years with very few Wisconsin visits, Collier could only imagine.

Collier whispered aloud, "Dad, you once eluded to the fact that you weren't a good businessman. But what chance did you have? You lived with a father consumed with business, no bonding with father, no mother."

The man, standing tall in the portrait, was an even-featured, handsome man, with red hair and keen gray-blue eyes. Collier wondered what it must have been like to have been in the prime of life when he returned from England and been so rejected. There had been nothing for the young scholar to do for the Thomlinson dairy business.

Two managers who oversaw contracts with the various dairy farmers adequately ran the two Thomlinson Dairies located in Collier and Etin, towns of less than fifteen thousand each. The twenty-some drivers of Thomlinson milk trucks and the staff of bookkeepers and secretaries were from Collier, and Etin, as well as surrounding areas. All facets of the operation were well supervised by Grandfather George until he died at the age of seventy-five. By that time, his son, Collier's father had found other occupations—raising thoroughbreds and driving them in sulky race tournaments.

Collier recalled that the day his therapist Brenda left, she'd told him that his father, George Collier III, was a womanizer. She'd said that a man like George Thomlinson, who cut a dashing figure driving his low-slung, expensive automobiles in and about the town, and riding his thoroughbred horses over the rolling hills of the area, was hard for women to resist. At the time, Collier was reminded of servants laughingly saying that the Thomlinson men were handsome and lusty.

He now studied the painting of his father. The rendering of the artist did show a somewhat sensual expression in the eyes and smile. Yet Collier remembered his father as a dignified gentleman. He chose to believe his buxom therapist Brenda had told him that bit of gossip about his father to get even for being fired from her job.

Just beyond his father's portrait, Collier smiled up at the portrait of his mother Valerie. Her soft blue eyes continued to look directly at him as he moved closer. He imagined he could smell the scent of her favorite English cologne. In the lift of the head and delicate lines of the face, the artist had captured her pride and beauty. She would brag about the fact that she was a Brumsley of the Pittsburgh, Pennsylvania Brumsleys who were in the steel business. He could still hear her teasingly call his dad, "Sportsman George."

How she loved to describe the evening when she, only eighteen, had met the forty-year-old bachelor, who had attended the party that her uncle and aunt held in their Madison home. George Collier had not left her side that night. And after a brief courtship of four months, they were married. Collier was born only six months later. He pointed a finger at the woman in the painting, "Yes mother, I learned that family secret from a playmate when I was ten. I also heard that the marriage was called by some citizens of Collier another prudent acquisition of the Thomlinson clan." Did he imagine it, or did the smile tilt a bit?

He rode on thinking that whatever the circumstances, he'd surely been blessed with two loving parents. "I've been blessed with intelligence too, thank God." He chuckled at his admitted boastfulness. Perhaps his intelligence came from the ancestral gene pool. Another likely factor could be the diligent hours of study that had replaced most forms of play in which his peers indulged.

Taking one last look back down the hall at the Thomlinson portraits, he said aloud, "Sorry, but I'm not yet ready for the six foot framed portrait of George Collier Thomlinson IV to join you all." With a dip of his head, he gave a short salute, and moved through wide, double doors into the stately drawing room of the home.

The all-purpose room for family and friends was dark but for the brightness of blazing fireplace logs, and a thin line of light from terrace lanterns that crept between closed drapes of large French windows at the side of the impressively large room. Shadows danced in and out of the dark edges of the room, seeming to give the room a life of its own now that it was so little used as a gathering place for humans.

French antiques made the room look stiff and formal. It was a museum exhibit of long-dead values placed in a nineteen-eighties world. But he loved the ambiance, because it reminded him of his mother who'd designed it as she wished to live. Valerie Brumsley Thomlinson loved silk brocades and velvet cushions. Her chosen colors of rich reds, forest greens, and cobalt blues, now somewhat dimmed with age, gave him a feeling of peace and timelessness.

Collier wheeled himself over to the wide French doors, now tightly closed against the winter gale, and pulled back a heavy silk brocade drape to gaze out at his favorite scene in all seasons. A veil of steadily falling snow laced with golden arrows of lantern light hid the view. But he could imagine the lake, whipped to froth, lapping up over the rocky ridge of shore. By morning, winter would have left its calling card, with a scum of ice on the surface of the lake. Hedgerows of bushes and clusters of trees would be laden with thick mats of snow. And children would be sledding down the high, snow-covered hill on the other side of the lake. Wanting to keep alive the vivid memory of his own exhilarating snow days careening down Devil's Backbone, the name given to the steep rise of land, Collier had invited the children of the village to use the hill anytime they wished.

He moved nearer the fire to warm his hands before the wood-burning fireplace, and gazed up at the portrait above the mantle. It was of a small boy standing on the shore of a lake. The youngster with the flaming red hair in a round-collared white shirt, blue velvet knickers, long white socks, and black patent leather shoes, dressed much like the Blue Boy painting, smilingly gazed up at a kite which sailed high above him in a cloudless blue sky. Collier's glance traced the child's sturdy legs with their dimpled knees and thickset ankles. It was a portrait of him, George Collier Thomlinson IV at the age of eight, six years before the accident. He had strong legs, had feeling in his limbs, could feel excitement in his lower regions. This canvas was proof that at one time he'd been ordained by God to be a normal boy. He'd enjoyed writing short stories even then, but also enjoyed the heady feeling of winning a swim meet. Later, at age thirteen, he enjoyed the unbidden sensual feelings of girl-discovery. A different spin was put on his life when the fast-moving truck hit him on his bicycle. Dreams of tennis or baseball fame had to be replaced by survival tactics and home schooling until he was sixteen, when he left to go to his father's college in England.

With a rueful smile, he ran fingers through his thick hair, considering those high school and college days abroad where he became a scholar of some repute. Even Collier had considered that some of his philosophical utterances were gems in those rarefied academic surroundings. He muttered to the silent room:

"That illusory belief that all I wrote was created for posterity was shattered by advanced philosophical research and study. The more I learned the less I knew. The only thing I learned for sure was that nothing nor anybody is deserving of adulation but the Divine Being."

He picked up a pen and pad that lay beside the Good Book on a stand by the couch and quickly wrote, "There are guidelines for life's destiny, which are dictated by God. But sometimes we take detours of our own choosing."

His thoughts went to the ebony haired woman of the day before as he rolled back to the glowing fire, and there on the flickering fire before him, danced a lovely Wedgwood figurine in a billowing coat. She'd been a real person, but too an illusion of someone he'd dreamed of knowing. His chest felt light for a moment. Then he growled:

"Hell! Get real! You're a wheelchair person for God's sakes. A forty-four year old man, paralyzed beyond repair for normalcy, should not lust after healthy, sweet-faced young women." Cursing with frustration, he pushed himself over to the fireplace, grabbed the poker, and started jabbing at a log, muttering an aphorism which he had repeated to himself many times:

"Stick to writing mystery novels about the adventures of Detective Bertram Strand. Let him get involved with sweet young things, and give the readers added earthiness of plot as demanded by the publisher. I don't have to live it; I write about it."

The sound of Mrs. Tuttle's banging, whistling, and slamming of pans and drawers echoed from the kitchen through several rooms to the living room. The noise was the housekeeper's usual theatrics to let him know she was in the kitchen with her gourmet quality meal almost completed and would soon be leaving. He rolled around the room, turning on lights wondering why the lights had been gleaming brightly in the entrance, but not in the hallway or here in the central room of the house.

"I'm not blind, just crippled," he grumbled.

"It's beginning to snow," the housekeeper called from another room. "Did you get wet?"

Her remark annoyed him for it was obvious that he'd been out in the snowstorm and had indeed gotten wet. His sheepskin jacket was soaked and hard to shrug out of, which he finally succeeded in doing. In his frustration, he tossed it on the stone hearth to dry. Still, he shouldn't take his black mood out on the generous woman. His discomfort was not her fault. A foolish fancy about a young woman with emerald eyes and black satin hair was what frustrated him. Collier turned his chair to view the verandah and lake now covered with snow. Clumps of the white stuff stuck to tree boughs and mounded on the curved steps leading down to the lower lawn. He cradled his chin with a hand, and closed his eyes letting the warmth of the fire surround and lull him.

After a while, his mouth began to moisten with the distant tangy smells of tomatoes simmering with onion, garlic and a subtle essence of oregano and thyme. Moving over to the hunt table, he uncorked a crystal decanter containing a cabernet sauvignon and poured a generous amount into a stemmed goblet. He sniffed, sipped, then rolled the fruity liquid around on his tongue. His taste buds absorbed the musky grape; mouth juices pleasurably exploded, tightening his throat with a surge of pleasure. He recognized the blissful contentment he felt. It had taken years to acquire. There had been feelings of rejection through the teens, futility in the twenties, and resigned acceptance in the thirties. How much more could he expect than what he was experiencing at this moment? He was humbled by his existence.

"Cheers and down the hatch," he murmured aloud, and took a hearty gulp of the vintage wine.

The russet-colored liquid gently swirled in the crystal glass. A tiny piece of cork floated in rhythm with the motion of the wine—like a bee caught in amber. Seen from afar, was there shyness in the eyes of the woman? Was she comfortable within herself? He wondered about the library beauty as he sipped the robust wine. He'd acquired a Pavlovian denial response to the female population, and zapped the young woman's image from his fertile brain. Booze and drugs were also relegated to his denial list. But he believed that the two small drinks a day he allowed himself were good for his autoimmune system and the indulgence good for his soul. He was reminded of a lecture he had once given to a religious group:

> "The purpose of human experience in a man has nothing whatsoever to do with reassurance or conflict adjustment. Man is to see the world of reality for himself and is challenged to find this reality even though it is forever elusive and ahead of him. No one is ever fixed. He may gain insight into his interpretation of himself in a certain period of time, but there will always be different insights with changing experiences."

Like the chance meeting of the woman on the library steps? Perhaps he should have suggested it might be possible for experience to bring wisdom so that one does not have to repeat mistakes. He wondered, and held the thought as another swallow of the smooth liquid slid down his throat. Heavy footsteps, announcing the approach of his housekeeper, kindled the anticipation of veal scaloppini, undoubtedly to be served with a crisp salad and hot buttered rolls.

She began to talk as soon as she entered the door. "We're supposed to have more snow. Robert won't be back for another week. Is there anything extra you want Eddie to do?"

Eddie was her seventeen-year-old son who helped with extra chores. For the past three weeks, Edward and Eddie had taken care of most of Collier's physical needs, but he missed

Robert, and felt relieved that his valet-companion would be back soon. Every year at Thanksgiving, Robert went to visit his relatives in England. The English holiday was good for Robert, but Collier's routine was sadly neglected in his absence. Perhaps he would go to England with Robert next spring, if his new book got good reviews and became a stage production. His agent had suggested such a possibility.

"I'm sure I'll think of something by the time Edward comes to help me prepare for bed." Collier had made a half circle to face the impressive black woman who had come into the living room from the pantry. Such a classic bearing with head held high, back straight, hands lightly folded over her stomach. He recalled his father's remark: "Carries her weight well."

She'd come to work for the family when she was only sixteen and Collier an infant. He thought of what good friends Grace Tuttle and her husband Edward had been through the years. She was the one who'd kept the house, made his bed, and cooked when he'd come home for short stays during his years abroad. Since England, Robert had traveled with him, looked after his personal needs, but she'd been the one he'd relied upon to keep his home. And in all the years he'd known her, he couldn't recall a time when she'd ever been in a hurry, out of sorts, or unprepared for any emergency that might arise. Collier smiled at the woman who was busily rearranging a long-stemmed mixture of flowers in a flute-shaped vase that stood on the high table by the door.

"Perhaps Eddy could bring in a supply of firewood. Looks as if we're in for some heavy snow this time," he suggested.

How much he appreciated her. It struck Collier that he seldom thanked her for her many thoughtful acts of kindness. "Thank you," he said.

Collier could have said more, but he knew it would make her uncomfortable. She was not used to anything approaching affection from him.

"Mr. Thomlinson, you mentioned that your publisher is rushing you to finish that new book. Now, don't get yourself all sideways trying to hurry it. It won't do you nor your writing any good."

Collier's lips twitched with a suppressed smile. "Mrs. Tuttle, I thank you for your concern, but I believe you have slanted your information in my favor. I'm the one rushing, and my editor is telling me to take my time. He prefers crossed T's and no misspelled words, which I'm perfectly capable of designing if I rush."

"Well, food's ready when you are. I'll finish up and go."

"I'll enjoy your excellent meal a little later. Like the Spanish diners, I want to anticipate for a while."

"Seems one has to taste to enjoy," she said, and quickly left the room with the gentle reprimand dangling between them.

The woman didn't like to have her good cooking left to get cold, but she would never strongly confront Mr. Thomlinson with her opinion. No, she confronted only if it referred to his publisher. He chuckled at the thought as he listened to the thumps and bangs of slamming linen cupboard drawers. It sounded as if she were stacking lumber. Undoubtedly, she was only choosing a freshly laundered table spread and napkin for the lonely diner, or rummaging through velvet bags for flatware. The dinner routine would then take her to remote corners of deep cupboards where dishes and other bric-a-brac used for his evening meal were hidden.

Strange how smells make one recall past incidents, he thought. The smell of the burning cherry wood recalled cherry wood burning in the fireplace the day of the near-fatal accident he'd experienced. It had been cold that day, when his mother had sat on the couch by the warm fire. He'd told her he was going to football practice and let her tie a scarf around his neck. Then he'd put on the required boots, wool cap and coat and ran out of the house, calling to his golden retriever, Ace. A running leap onto his bike, and he had headed for the school with Ace following close behind. He'd been on a straight stretch of pavement when a hit-and-run driver slammed into him, so he'd been told. He could remember nothing.

Later, in the hospital, he'd awakened to pain in his head that lit up brain sensors like fireworks on the Fourth of July.

A tight ache in his chest clamped down hard now as it had then when he'd learned that his dog Ace was dead. There was no pain anywhere else—just the chest. And the choking fear that clogged his throat with unshed tears when he'd first looked at his paralyzed body could still be experienced at times. His mother and father had held, touched, and lived with his helpless despair while they hid their own.

"It's not good to look back," Collier mumbled aloud.

He rode over to savor the cloyingly sweet scent of lavender that floated above the perfumed essence of other flowers in the vase by the entrance. And again, childhood memories floated through the barrier of reality. He'd known where his mother was or where she'd been by the scent of her lavender cologne. The acrid smell of burning wood and tobacco smoke brought back fond memories of his father. His eyes misted with longing and pride as he thought about those two, who had given him the courage to endure and use the self that was left to him.

He breathed in the kitchen smells of Mrs. Tuttle's cooking, and grinned at the memory of another time when he was about three and company was expected. He'd been allowed to sit on a stool and watch Mrs. Tuttle whip eggs, add sugar, almonds and other interesting ingredients together. Then she'd poured dollops of the white sticky sweet on brown, paper-lined baking sheets and slipped them into the hot oven. Later, he'd watched her pull the cookie sheets from the oven and, like a miracle, the creamy liquid placed in the oven would come out flaky macaroons ready for strawberries and whipped cream. Thoughts of that sugary smell made his mouth water, and caused his heart to quicken in proof that smells can evoke feelings. He would have to make use of that idea in his writing.

In the far kitchen a heavy door closed. Soon the hum of an engine sounded and gradually dimmed as Mrs. Tuttle's car drove off.

CHAPTER 5

"I'm so glad you could come with me this evening." Richard smiled over at Maggie.

"I felt almost forced to come," Maggie said with a grin. "Mother and you insisted. And you know when you two gang up on me, I usually do your bidding." It was meant to be a teasing remark, but Richard's clenched jaw showed he didn't think it was funny.

He eased the car from the curb. "I asked you, because I believed it would be an interesting experience for you. The program is to be a discussion led by three well-known authors. I thought if I were there to help you listen, you might enjoy it. Etin isn't far to drive for an evening of intellectual pursuit. It's to be held at the new auditorium of the Presbyterian Church." Richard explained.

And Richard wanted her to see the new auditorium, for he planned to start the drive for the church building fund, and she was to be the designated donor to match funds with the rest of the congregation. Maggie's sudden flash of insight was disturbing. Why didn't he just come out and say what he wanted from her? Oh, for some honesty! Aloud she asked, "Do you know who these authors are? What do they write?"

"I believe they write fiction. I know that's not your interest, but Mrs. Hughes gave me the tickets."

"I like fiction, Richard." And she did appreciate the invitation, even if the tickets were free. It would be exciting to listen to some who plied the craft she so diligently pursued. She closed her eyes as if to sleep and thought about her manuscript. She'd yet to finish her research because she needed the lavender herb book. The weekend had come and gone. Now, Tuesday, heading for Etin with Richard, seemed the most unlikely adventure she should be having. She should be home trying to at least get the chapters in order for the manuscript. Tomorrow, she'd go to the library and hopefully the book on lavender would have been returned.

Thirty minutes later, they drove up to the church, parked and walked into the lower level of the building. Only a few seats remained in the large auditorium as they and a few others drifted in.

After they were seated in the next to last row, Richard leaned toward Maggie. "I see Reverend Hanes. Excuse me while I go say hello." He rose and smiled down at her. "You look very nice tonight, Maggie. I like that suit."

Silently, she questioned his motive. Her red wool suit was adequate for the occasion, but was not praise-worthy. Could this excursion, which certainly was not a date, have anything to do with her and her mother's discussion about marriage? Maggie studied Richard who now stood over to the side of their row of seats, talking to the other minister. She'd heard others say they thought he looked like a young Abraham Lincoln with his tall frame and sloping shoulders. His Roman nose did add to the resemblance. She recalled Linda's note, in which her friend had suggested Maggie should find a man. She would not become paranoid about Richard or his intentions. Her mother and her friend Linda might worry about her, but Maggie knew that a man was the least of her concerns.

On Saturday Maggie had received an invitation to Linda's wedding that was to be at the end of February. Linda could not talk on the phone, so had enclosed a note asking Maggie to be her only attendant. Maggie gazed over the crowd, fondly recalling the remembered letter, and the little details Linda had written about her love, John Jenson, who had a hearing deficiency. She'd asked if Maggie could come early so they could catch up on news.

Maggie could remember former girl-talk, and the outrageous description of the male anatomy as observed by Linda, who had three brothers. Maggie straightened in her seat and smoothed her hands over her skirt. A smile pulled at the corner of her mouth as she demurely folded her hands tightly together, thinking she was glad that no one could read her thoughts.

Perhaps she would go a day or two before the wedding, so that she and Linda would have time to catch up on their lives. There would have to be arrangements made to get there for it was a seventy-five mile drive, and her driver's license was only valid for short distances. Since her mother wasn't too fond of Linda, something to do with wanting Maggie to have only hearing friends, her mother wouldn't go to the wedding. That was one reason she had put off as long as possible telling Evelyn about Linda's wedding. It was childish to keep secrets, as well as foolish to have to clear everything with her mother, but it saved trouble.

Richard hurriedly sat down beside her just as the lights dimmed. Voices hushed as a man stepped out in front of the curtain, and the stage lights came up. Even though the master of ceremonies used a microphone, Maggie had difficulty hearing what he said. She caught the words "fiction writers." Since they were seated too far back for her to lip read, she eased into her relaxed mode and prepared to have another evening of introspection.

Richard tapped Maggie on the arm and leaned over to whisper in her ear, "Can you hear?" She shook her head no. Again, he whispered, "Reverend Hanes suggested we come up front to the left of the stage. In a minute, after the MC's introductory remarks and the audience begins to applaud, we'll go there." He motioned to a spot to the left where two chairs were placed.

The curtain had opened, and the master of ceremonies moved to the podium. Three people sat on the stage. With a start, Maggie recognized the mysterious Mr. Thomlinson. Of course, a well-known fiction writer, living in Collier, would be asked to speak.

She couldn't help but notice that the man with the mop of long, unruly red-halo of hair seemed very much at ease in his navy blue jacket, white dress shirt and striped tie. His slacks were gray, and his shoes placed on the metal step of the wheelchair were black tasseled loafers. The anxiety that had clogged her throat at the thought of moving to the other seats in front of all the people was quickly snuffed out as she studied Collier Thomlinson. If he could be up there on stage with his disability, she could walk closer to the stage so she could hear. Giving Richard a nod when the applause began, the two excused themselves to others in their row, and quickly made their way to the chairs set up for them.

They were seated just as the applause ended, and the MC began to introduce the first speaker. "Miss Monroe has been on the best seller list..."

Maggie's eyes skipped away from the speaker to again observe the man with the flaming red hair. He sat as if somewhat aloof. No, that wasn't it, he really didn't seem bored, or indifferent, but just uncomfortable being in front of an audience, on stage, in his wheelchair. She watched, as now and then he'd brush back the hair that kept falling down over his eyes. She was close enough to observe how his eyes would crinkle at the outer edges when he smiled at some of the woman's remarks, as if he were genuinely interested in what the speaker had to say—not self-absorbed. Maggie imagined she could feel his gentleness.

Janet Monroe, who wrote children's books, had the audience laughing as she told parts of her newest children's book, <u>Christmas in an Anthill</u>. It would surely be a best seller for Christmas gift giving.

The remarks of the second speaker, a soft-spoken gentleman whose name she didn't catch, were lost on Maggie. Thoughts drifted to the ramp encounter of last Friday, then switched to consider what she'd like to write other than cookbooks— maybe something to do with deafness or other disabilities.

Thirty minutes later her daydreaming was interrupted by applause. The second speaker had finished, was seated, and the MC was introducing Collier Thomlinson. Maggie sat up straighter and listened intently as the Master of Ceremonies said:

"Doctor George Collier Thomlinson the Fourth, is better known as Collier to his friends. Collier has had a diverse life; educated at Eton and Oxford outside London England, back to the states for his doctorate in English literature and philosophy at Yale University, back to Oxford with a fellowship in philosophy, and on to teach philosophy at the prestigious Bern University in Bern, Switzerland. After eight years in Bern, he returned to the states to be head of the philosophy department at the University of Wisconsin. Now, he's retired from teaching, and is devoting himself full-time to writing. And what tales he can spin as a writer. I hesitate to be so bold as to ask my old friend if his novels come from his past experiences."

There was a rumble of laughter from the audience. Maggie smiled at the subtlety of the MC's last remark. She turned a smiling glance to Richard, but he was not laughing. Instead, his arms were crossed, and the firm set of his mouth made a muscle twitch in his jaw.

After the Thomlinson discussion she'd had with her mother when the woman had referred to pornographic material, Maggie had gotten the author's books from the Carnegie

Library and found them fascinating, and not at all objectionable.

She eagerly listened as the MC ended the introduction:

"I give you, George Collier Thomlinson the Fourth." The prolonged applause indicated that he was by far the most popular author of the three.

Maggie watched Thomlinson, fascinated with the movement of his heavy head, the half smile, and the small gestures with his hands. She could not catch all that he said, but watched fascinated throughout his thirty-minute talk on writing style and subject matter. There were remarks that brought laughter, but mostly his subject was seriously informative. Close to the end of his presentation, when he seemed to be summing up, he was talking about art and looked over her way. She could see plainly what he was saying for he faced her:

"I've never forgotten a remark Robert McKenna, author of The Sandpebbles, made to the faculty of the University of North Carolina: 'Each of us is living our own personal work of art.'

"I was struck with the beauty of his thought, and decided it was time I pursued my work of art. Be it notable or only gratifying to me, I would try to convey art through the written word. But in the years I've tried to capture such beauty, I have found that, as Mr. McKenna suggested, true beauty is within each individual, the essence of which is hard to capture in words. You don't have to write novels to be a person of substance. We all have dreams and achievements. We all are works of art."

His words brought a rush of tears to Maggie's eyes. Aches for her own unfulfilled dreams filled her chest as he again spoke.

"I've been asked by the literati," Collier turned his wheelchair to acknowledge the other two speakers, "with whom I'm privileged to be associated, to thank you for your interest in us."

He again faced the audience. "Thank you for listening to us this evening."

The audience was pleased with the charismatic author and showed it with their clapping ovation that lasted until the MC held up his hands for silence. After questions from the floor, the MC announced that there would be a reception following. Richard suggested they leave.

"Since we're here, I really would enjoy meeting the speakers." Maggie had to meet the mystery writer. She was ready to beg, but before that was necessary, Richard suggested that they leave in about fifteen minutes after they had some punch. Maggie declined his offer of punch, and watched him walk away.

She couldn't believe she'd had the nerve to ask Richard to stay. It gave her the courage to walk up to Mr. Thomlinson, who had just come down the ramp by the stage. "Hello." Her voice sounded rather breathless to her own ears.

"Hello," he answered with a raised-brow expression as if he might be trying to recognize her. He sat there intently studying her, while moments of silence continued.

He certainly wasn't making it easy for her to talk to him she thought as she nervously glanced around for Richard. He was talking to the Presbyterian minister. Maggie gave up hope of rescue and blurted out, "I find your writing stimulating—I mean, very interesting—at least, from the writing point of view."

"I found you stimulating to say the least when we had our near collision on the library steps." His mouth turned up in a one-sided grin. "Did you find it so?" He moved a little closer to her.

She backed away. "Yes, I—it took my breath. And when you jumped the curbs going across the street—how did you learn to do that?" The words whooshed out. There was no way to retrieve them.

He chuckled. "The sport of jumping curbs was learned with a lot of practice and one wheelchair destroyed beyond repair."

They laughed at the same time, stopped, studied each other, then spoke at the same time. "I…"

He waited. Maggie continued. "I enjoy your style."

Then she quickly added, "I mean, I enjoy the mystery and intrigue in your books. I am especially interested in the research you do." And feel like I'm being researched when you look at me like that, Maggie thought, feeling her cheeks flush.

"My research is very boring to discuss. I'd rather discuss how I live vicariously through the lives of others." Briefly, he looked down at his legs, "You might call me a Peeping Tom, but I would object to the title." His penetrating blue eyes held hers. "Do you write?" He asked.

Maggie hesitated. "I'm a writer of sorts."

"What kind of sorts?"

She laughed. With a tilt of her head and shrug of her shoulders she explained, "I write cookbooks."

"Fat free? You seem to be a nice example of what a lower calorie diet can do for one." A smile sealed the compliment, before he glanced behind her to acknowledge someone.

Richard had come up to stand by Maggie, and apparently had overheard Collier's last remark. Unsmiling, he gave a short nod to Thomlinson and looked firmly at Maggie.

"We'd better go, Maggie." And in his authoritative way, Richard took Maggie's arm and prepared to move on.

Maggie pulled away from Richard. Turning to Collier, she said, "This is Reverend Richard Stevenson. Thank you for this evening, Mr. Thomlinson. I enjoyed your presentation."

Collier merely nodded in answer to her compliment, then added, "Don't get caught on any ramps." He cocked an eyebrow and smiled a one-sided grin that implied more.

Richard took Maggie's arm and marched her away from the author, while Maggie looked back over her shoulder to smile at Collier.

The minister was quiet on the way home. Maggie was equally silent, furious that Richard had been rude to Collier Thomlinson. Endeavoring to calm herself, she thought about some of Thomlinson's remarks. At one point in his talk, he'd said his publisher wanted racy details to make the books sell, and Collier had countered that he didn't feel obligated to describe what went on behind closed doors. She'd liked that, and felt Richard must have thought it a commendable reply for the author to make. But right now, it was probably best that she not attempt to discuss Mr. Thomlinson with Richard.

She knew she'd missed several remarks he'd made when the audience interrupted with laughter. Perhaps there'd been a witty remark about sex that had disgusted the minister. And Mr. Thomlinson's reference to ramps, though innocuous, might have seemed suggestive to Richard. How, she wasn't quite sure.

They got to her house, and Richard came around the car to open her door. He helped her out of the car, then, holding on to her arm, he stopped her from going ahead of him, "Maggie, I..."

"Richard, I'd invite you in, but it's late and you said earlier that you have a busy schedule tomorrow. I've enjoyed the evening. Thank you."

He smiled as if relieved. She wanted him to say what was on his mind, and yet didn't, as if what he might say would change what they had. Linda would probably ask if he wanted to talk about money for the church or sex.

The thought of her funny, uninhibited friend lightened Maggie's mood, and she took Richard's hand as they walked to the house. At the front door she looked up with a smile and paused, "Thank you again, Richard. It's been a wonderful evening."

He smiled. "I'll see you tomorrow at the noon meeting?"

"Yes." She lightly kissed his cheek, surprising herself as much as him, and went into the house.

Evelyn greeted Maggie while looking over her daughter's shoulder with a questioning look, "Where's Richard? Why didn't you invite him in? It's only ten o'clock. I've made some hot chocolate." Evelyn had come out of the kitchen and stood in the hall.

"I didn't ask him to come in. He was tired and so am I. Thank you for thinking about us." Maggie's smile was forced.

Walking on into the living room, Maggie had to stop for a moment to adjust her eyes to see in the shadowed room. The Tiffany lamp on the drum table by the window was not turned on. Matching crystal lamps on another table at the far side of the room gave off a soft flicker. The only bright light came from the gas-fed flames casting a soft glow over two fireside chairs that had been drawn up in front of the fireplace as if inviting an intimate conversation. Her mother had gone to a lot of trouble to create the perfect romantic setting for Maggie and Richard.

Maggie felt sick at heart and disgusted too at the measures her mother had taken to orchestrate the two of them. She panicked, felt walled-in, and flew out of the room past her mother, to her own room. She closed the door and leaned back on it until her heart stopped pounding. She would not let her mother control her feelings.

Undressing and putting on a flannel gown and slippers, Maggie sat down in the old rocking chair. It was the first time she'd not told Evelyn about an evening spent away from home. She would have liked to talk about Collier Thomlinson, but knew a conversation about the questionable author was unthinkable.

Maggie was surprised that she'd had the nerve to actually have a conversation with the author. She was inhibited—he seemed so confident. No doubt he could laugh, say silly things, be wrong without the feeling of shame or guilt with which she lived. Maggie felt that she didn't know how to converse on a personal level with anybody. Her mother and she only shared opinions that were pre-decided. Her mother might ask:

"Maggie, what color do you think we should paint the house next year?" But it would be the same as five years before— white.

There ought to be some interest between a mother and daughter that might lead to a deeper level of conversation, even if it was about finances or the trust. Maggie didn't have a clue about managing her trust from Nonnie Green, and her 30th birthday was coming up the twenty-second of December.

Once she'd suggested that she and her mother go to Dover, England, to see her father's grave, but that idea didn't go any place, for Evelyn had said she couldn't stand the trip by air, and a ship would take too long.

Many times Maggie wanted to suggest that she and her mother sit closer to the front of the church so Maggie could hear Richard's sermons. She never did ask.

She used to make decisions for herself when she was at Grennly. Was it because it's just too much trouble to confront when the conversations would be diverted to talk about the day's schedule, appointments, meetings, what was needed at the grocery store, and what was going on in the church? Birthdays and other immediate happenings were discussed, but they never ever talked about personal things like hopes, wishes and fears.

Even if she'd gone to her mother's room to say good night, the discussion would have gotten around to Richard, and she didn't want to talk about him. She'd decided long ago that Richard's interest in her was because he felt it his Christian duty to fulfill the role of protector for an afflicted woman, who couldn't meet life as a complete person. Either that was the role she played in his life, or he saw her as the moneyed church member, who could lead the drive for a new church auditorium. Perhaps all kindness was patronizing. She felt disgust with herself, and was disillusioned with her attitude.

No, it would be best to stay away from her mother tonight. She'd face the inquisition tomorrow morning. Pulling off slippers and robe, she climbed into bed, and lay wide-eyed, thinking about the romantic setting her mother had arranged. She wondered what Richard would have thought. He'd have probably taken one look at the intimate setting, and run for his bachelor-style-life. She stuffed the sheet in her mouth, and shook with laughter until she was gasping for air and wiping away tears.

"Mother, it would be nice if you could weave a lovely tapestry of love between Richard and me, but people can't be designed like needlepoint patterns," she whispered. Besides, she'd rather think about Collier Thomlinson than Richard.

***

"I've no time for breakfast, Mother." The next morning, thrusting arms in her long green coat, Maggie clomped into the kitchen in heavy snowboots. She gave her mother a peck on the cheek before adding:

"I have to get this rough draft to my editor. I promised it for Friday, and it takes two days to get to Chicago."

Evelyn followed Maggie out into the hall. "I'm to pick up Ginny. You'll get to the church meeting at noon, or do you need a ride?" Evelyn asked.

Although Maggie could drive with her limited driver's license, her mother usually drove. The early insecurities about hearing horns toot, ambulance sirens, and road noise in general, plus her accepted low self-confidence, had left Maggie a hesitant driver.

"Yes to the meeting. No, I'll walk. It'll be cold, but it's too pretty a day to ride. I'll be at the cleaners, then the library if you need to reach me," she called over her shoulder, as she scooped up her briefcase and dry cleaning, patted the cat, and quickly walked out into the cold, crisp day that Nature had dressed in fresh snow. Added to such beauty were the occasional sunbeams that would blink from behind fast moving clouds and shimmer down diamonds.

Her breath came out in misty puffs as she trudged down the street sidestepping drifts. At the corner of Cherry and Main, she had to dodge snow that sprayed out from runners of sleds being pulled by school-free children. In the distance she saw others sledding down the steep hill on the Thomlinson property. It would be as good as any roller coaster ride on a thick-snow day like today. Apparently that's why the hill got the name Devil's Backbone because the ride down was as scary as the devil.

Ben Jackson was shoveling snow off the entrance to his dry cleaners shop, when Maggie walked up. For fifty years, the man had never missed a day cleaning off his walk at the stroke of eight be the weather rain, shine, sleet, or snow.

"Beautiful day, Mr. Jackson." Maggie greeted the man, who nodded and followed her inside the shop. A town meeting bulletin lay on the counter top—something about the Devil's Backbone Winter carnival being canceled.

Each year, there was a Devil's Backbone Winter Carnival held at the base of the steep hill in the wooded area of the Thomlinson property. The women working on the bazaar had suggested that there might not be carnival this year. Last Sunday Richard's sermon had been about the sin of devil worship. And the newspaper story she'd glanced at had an article about some sort of cult. Devil, sin, cult—what was going on in town?

She left the cleaners and approached the still-snow-covered Carnegie Library, noting that the building gave a look of stability to the center of town—pride too, as did the Thomlinson property beyond the sledding hill. She cautiously walked up the ramp. It was too early to bump into people, like important authors who undoubtedly didn't get out this early in the morning.

"Good morning, Letty." She called to the librarian who acknowledged the greeting with a nod, but apparently was too busy to look up from a book on her desk.

Maggie wondered what Letty's life outside the library was like. The quiet woman was single like Maggie, and in Collier there was little opportunity to meet an interesting man. Moving a stepping-stool to the spot where Jackie French's book on lavender was kept on file, Maggie looked on the shelf—it wasn't there! She had to have the information on lavender to include in the manuscript to be mailed today. Frustration and panic propelled her to the checkout desk to confront Letty.

"Letty, has Mr. Thomlinson brought the herb book back? It isn't on the shelf." Maggie's voice quivered with suppressed anger.

Letty muffled a sneeze behind a tissue. With noticeable hesitancy and, avoiding eye contact with Maggie, the librarian spoke barely loud enough to be heard. "Excuse me, I have a cold."

Maggie tapped her foot, trying to stay calm. She did have sympathy for the obviously sick woman, but was exasperated with Letty's avoidance of the question. "Letty, I'm sorry you don't feel well, but please..."

Letty interrupted, "The book on lavender is still out. I imagine it will come in today, because Mr. Thomlinson is very punctual." The red-nosed woman grabbed another tissue before a sneeze.

Maggie had to struggle to keep her voice steady. "But I need it right now, before the mail goes out." A slow intake of breath stifled a stronger comment.

"I told Mr. Thomlinson it was most unusual to allow the book to leave the premises, but he assured me that it was not a book anyone other than himself would wish to read. I let him take it, after he promised to bring it back first thing Wednesday morning. I told you that the other day, Maggie."

Avoiding eye contact, Letty busied some papers on her desk. "Today is Wednesday, it's still early, and he has important work..."

And my work isn't? Mr. Thomlinson had apparently charmed Letty. Something he did very well as Maggie knew from the night before. Uncontrollable indignation spilled out.

"The nerve of him presupposing no one else has an interest in a certain book he apparently wanted to take home. I suppose he's copying whole sections down on his computer. I've heard of people like him who plagiarize!" Aware for a few seconds of cold air that had been sweeping into the vaulted room from an open door, Maggie clamped her mouth shut.

"I'm truly sorry, Maggie." Letty's apology was accompanied by the closing thump of the entrance door.

A voice rose from nearby, "All over the little tantrum are we?" She looked over her shoulder, and saw Collier Thomlinson in his wheelchair by the main entrance.

He shoved over to the two women. "I believe, before I turn over such an important document, I should defend myself." His voice was ringingly loud as he enunciated each word with slow deliberation, while holding Maggie's eyes with his piercing blue ones.

Maggie's insides shook. He'd heard everything she'd said and appeared just as indifferent as many accused him of being. Well, she'd said what she thought, and she did think he'd been wrong to intimidate Letty with his charismatic charm.

Letty started to get up from her chair. Maggie moved to put a hand on the woman's shoulder, indicating that Letty was to stay seated and out of this. Then with raised brows, and a tilt of the head, Maggie addressed the man. "Mr. Thomlinson?"

"You know damn well who I am. And I might ask why you're following me around? Let me get somewhat paranoid, and suggest that you have been trying to glean information about my latest book from me."

Her head shot up. "I have a book deadline to meet before the mail goes out today. I need to refer to some material in that book of lavender, which you took out of the library." She pointedly added, "Even though it was a reserve book."

"Ah, maybe you are going to copy it on your computer?" There was a slight loosening of the tight jaw; a sparkle appeared in his eyes.

"I don't own a computer." Maggie's lips tilted with the beginning of a smile.

"Too bad, either a copy machine or a computer is necessary when one wants to plagiarize sections of a book," he countered.

"I'm sorry for the accusation. I had no right to say—well, whatever I said." Warmth tinged Maggie's cheeks. An all-too-familiar feeling of awkwardness diffused her anger. She stood silent, subdued by the tilted grin that could indicate understanding. Yet somehow she doubted that he was being kind or tolerant.

"I feel responsible because I let you take a book which wasn't to leave the library. Please, Mr. Thomlinson, is that the book?" Voice husky with cold, Letty had stood to ask about the book on the man's lap.

"I'm sorry if I've caused you unnecessary worry, Miss Levert. And you, Miss...?" Smiling at Maggie, with arched brow, Collier Thomlinson asked and waited.

"Murphy—Maggie Murphy." Maggie clutched her briefcase in front of her as if to ward off his piercing gaze.

"Miss Murphy is it? You failed to introduce yourself last evening." Letty blotted her nose, looking from one to the other with a questioning frown as Collier continued:

"I'm sorry, but the book is back at my home. If you would care to go with me, I'll be glad to give it to you."

He swung around with a charming smile for Letty. "Miss Levert, one of us will return the delinquent book. Is that agreeable with you?"

The librarian's eyes went huge. She silently nodded, and plopped back down in her chair.

"Well?" The man gestured to the door, apparently waiting for Maggie to go out of the library with him.

She did need the book and it would be best to go with him and make sure she got it. Flustered and somewhat reluctant, Maggie dipped her head to Letty, shoved on her coat, tam and gloves, and walked out of the library, leaving him to follow. She hesitated at the top of the ramp to indicate that he should go first.

He nodded with a knowing smile. Slowing the wheelchair before he descended the ramp, he said, "We'll have to walk," and rolled down.

His comment that they'd have to walk was obvious for there was no car that she could see. He was a thoughtless, self-centered egotist who presumed every woman would do his bidding. Letty had done what he wanted, and now she was doing the same. Aware that she was more annoyed with herself than with him for having agreed to go to his home, she bit back a snappish reply.

"I walked from home. It's a nice day to walk." Maggie clamped her mouth shut. She would not prattle in useless conversation, especially since he seemed determined to move at full speed. She briskly followed, remembering the other day when he'd stopped at the corner, and looked back at her with a wave of the hand. The gesture was almost as if they were old friends just saying good-bye. Perhaps he could be charming, but right now she had her doubts.

Maggie was tempted at times to reach out and help him through a mound of snow or up a curb. But remembering how well he maneuvered the wheelchair up curbs and through snow with astonishing ease, she decided it best not to help. He'd probably make some brutish remark if she tried. How had she ever thought him to be kind?

She hurried along, holding herself erect, concentrating on keeping up with his fast pace. He did mumble something as they went through the ornate arch of the Thomlinson estate, but she was too busy admiring the view to listen. A distant lake appeared far off through the mist of snow that lazily floated from the sky. What a wonderful wonderland! The beauty of the landscaping dazed her—the avenue of trees through which they passed, the wide circular drive that led to the mansion.

"Please come in." They'd reached the entrance without Maggie's realizing it. As she ascended the front steps, he rolled up the side ramp, and proceeded to open the massive wooden door with a press of a button on the arm of his wheelchair.

"I'll get Mrs. Tuttle to bring some hot tea into the drawing room. There's a fire going in there." He'd ushered Maggie in, and quickly led her down a seemingly endless central hall.

She wanted to stop and study the life-sized portraits of stern looking men and black-velvet-gowned women, but dared not linger. Instead, she followed him past the ancestral display to the arched entrance of a large room. The warmth of a roaring fire in a gigantic fireplace greeted them, dissolving Maggie's shivers of cold.

She slipped off her coat at Collier's suggestion, and stood holding it, not sure what to do with the damp wrap.

Collier rode up to her. "Here, I'll take that. Are you too cold? Do you need to take off those boots?"

"Oh, I'm sorry." She looked down at the puddle her boots had made, and glanced back to see if she'd left a trail of melted snow behind her on the beautiful rug. "I tried to stamp them when we came in, but..."

He grinned. "Think nothing of it. My wheels do more damage than your small boots. Take those wet boots off, and I'll get you a pair of socks to put on." Having delivered the command, Collier took Maggie's coat and laid it over the back of a chair close to the fireplace.

"Ah, Mrs. Tuttle! We're in need of some nourishment and hot tea if you please." Collier had turned toward a woman who had just entered the drawing room.

Maggie acknowledged the introduction to the housekeeper, and sat down to pull off her wet boots. Holding the boot, Maggie watched Mrs. Tuttle leave to get the tea Thomlinson had ordered—another person who obeys without question. Well, I won't this time!

While hurriedly telling Collier that she couldn't stay, Maggie struggled to pull on the boot, and stood up. "I thank you but I really must go. I'm quite warm, very comfortable.

"May I have the book?" She asked as she walked over to pick up her coat.

"Well, I'm afraid my study is rather a mess. I'll have to look for the book. I've got a tour coming up, and I'm doing a lot of research. If you'll excuse me for a minute, I'm sure Mrs. Tuttle will return shortly with our tea. You can wait that long." He smiled and wheeled out of the room, leaving an outmaneuvered Maggie.

With a sigh of resignation, Maggie dropped her coat back on the couch, and walked over to look out the French doors. Like the snap of a camera lens, a flicker of sunlight flashed into her eyes, then vanished behind storm-swollen clouds. Squinting sunspots from her eyes, Maggie turned back to the spacious room. She gasped at the sight of the beautiful rug that all but covered the hardwood floors of the huge room. Its intricate design, faded with age, was woven in shades of beige, gray, amber, warm reds, and deep cobalt blue.

Maggie's gaze roamed over small dove-grey velvet and gold brocade couches grouped in conversational clusters, and punctuated by small tables with bead-capped shades. A brown leather-topped table with cane-backed chairs was in the far right corner of the room. While in the far left, shadowed corner was an intricately carved antique Grand piano with a silk throw draped over the closed crescent-shaped bow. A nine-by-twelve inch, gilt-framed painting of a woman graced the top of the instrument. On either side of the stone fireplace, where flames circled and spit at a huge Yule log, pearl-gray silk drapes with tasseled edges covered floor-to-ceiling French doors, and puddled at the sides of wide, long windows. It was a wondrous room gowned in opulence like nothing Maggie had ever seen.

A flutter of panic made her heart skip. What was she doing in such a setting—a room that displayed such an ornate lifestyle? Something caught her eye in the gold-baroque mirror, which hung above a high, marble-topped table by the entrance. The reflection was of a tall crystal vase overflowing with a colorful mix of freshly cut alstroemeria lilies, lavender, baby's breath, and tall sprays of feathered fern. Human hands had arranged those flowers. There was a note of comfort in the thought, and in the vaguely heard tick of a grandfather clock close by. The surrounding grandeur wasn't intimidating; it was inviting.

More at ease, she walked closer to the portrait of a red-haired child that hung above the mantle. The little boy's happily smiling face was lifted to watch a kite, floating in a cloudless blue sky. This lovely child had to be Mr. Thomlinson before his accident. Sadness for that innocent being welled up inside and caused tears to press behind Maggie's eyes.

Feeling a presence, she turned. No one was there, but the housekeeper had been there, and had silently left a tea service on the table that sat between two damask love seats. Walking closer, her eyes skimmed over a heavily scrolled silver tray holding dainty slices of pound cake, and tartlets covered with white mousse and dollops of raspberry jam. Lemon slices, sugar, creamer, spoons, and the most delicate of Dresden teacups and saucers sprinkled with dainty swirls of roses, awaited the ritual of afternoon tea. The lovely rose design reminded Maggie of her mother's petite point pieces.

Mother! With a gasp, she glanced at her watch. It was ten-forty and she had to finish her writing, go to the post office, and be at the church by noon. Hurriedly, she went to get her coat off the chair, and was putting it on, when Collier came into the room.

He had a broad smile on his face as he wheeled over to her. "I have these for you." He triumphantly held up the book in one hand, and a pair of white tank socks in the other.

His grin turned to a frown. "What are you doing?"

"I must go. I must finish that small section on lavender, and mail my manuscript before going to the Community Church for the noon meeting. She rushed to explain as she poked arms into her heavy coat and fumbled with buttons, trying to ignore the set mouth and solemn eyes of her host. "Thank you for your time, Mr. Thomlinson."

"Call me Cole for God's sake. I feel much too old when you address me as Mr. Thomlinson and Collier is a bit too formal."

He rolled closer. "Here, give me that coat." He smiled most charmingly, though his eyes held a glint of determination as he continued. "We have over an hour. You can go to the library, and use my typewriter to type up the bit on lavender you need. That way, I'll be able to keep the book here for my research, which I haven't quite completed. After you're done, I'll send you off to the church in my car in time for your meeting. My driver will take explicit directions about the mailing and relieve you of the trip to the post office. That will also give you time for some of Mrs. Tuttle's tea and pastries." He held out his hand for her coat. Raised eyebrows and a one-sided grin suggested that he was pleased with the arrangements.

Maggie hesitated, then handed Collier her coat. Exchanging boots for socks, she told herself that agreeing to stay was no big deal. She did need to get her research completed.

Again, he laid her coat on one of the fireside couches, rolled to the tea set, tilted the teapot, and proceeded to pour two cups of steaming tea. "Do you want sugar, lemon, milk? No? Well, come select a treat and we'll proceed to my study."

He held out the herb book. "Here, you take this. I'll carry the tea and sweets on the tray. See my lap is good for that." He grinned at his attempt to be humorous at his own expense.

With a weak smile, Maggie obediently walked over, took the book, and silently followed the quickly rolling wheelchair. It carried a man who wore the most endearing little boy smile, while balancing on his lap a silver tray with two cups of tea and desserts. She had to admit there was something very special about the man.

Pungent smells of parchment and leather, the astringent wood scent of furniture polish and Murphy oil soap greeted her as they entered a large open room with floor to ceiling bookcases. It was not as spacious as the grand-scaled drawing room, but with an equally charming statement of affluent comfort as conveyed by the accordion-carved walnut wainscoting, open-beamed ceilings, parquet floors, and scattered oriental rugs. The view from the floor-to-ceiling French windows was the same as from the living room—frozen lake, woods, and Devil's Backbone hill.

A highly polished six-foot mahogany desk dominated the left side of the study and angled toward the lake. On the desk, two phones, stacks of periodicals, files and papers sat on top of a large leather-trimmed blotter. On the wide credenza behind the desk was a large-screen computer with the printer and fax machine sitting to the side. Nearby, was a table holding a typewriter, which had blank paper on the spool. He set her cup of tea on a small round table beside the typewriter, and looked at her as if pleased with his own efficiency.

This man was full of surprises. When he'd gone to get the socks, he'd apparently set up the typewriter in hopes she would do her final pages for her editing there in his study. She smiled at his tenacity, pleased that he'd won. Seating herself on the swivel chair he offered, she took a bite of the tart, a sip of hot tea, and started flipping through the herb book to the pages she needed.

"Well..." He hesitated by her side as if he might stay and watch her work, then apparently deciding against it, wheeled away to his desk, where he began to open some ledgers.

She had an intuitive feeling that he was watching her. It was hard for her to concentrate, but she did, and after thirty minutes or so, she had finished her work. She glanced at her wristwatch, and was relieved to see that it was only eleven-fifty.

"I believe if I hurry to the post office, and mail this, I can still get to my meeting without being too late. May I have that ride?" Maggie asked Collier.

"A ride and the mailing of your manuscript are the least I can do. I did cause all of your worry. If I'd brought the book back yesterday—or not taken it at all..." He smiled with a shrug.

"I really must go." Her smile forgave him.

Collier nodded toward the tray table. "You must at least have one more bite of the sweet. I can't tell Mrs. Tuttle that you didn't eat her delicate pastries. Undoubtedly the tea is cold. I'll ring..."

Maggie held up a hand. "No, please, don't bother about the tea." She started to add that she didn't have time for the pastry either, but he spoke first.

"Then I'll ring for the chauffeur." He wheeled over to a tapestry rope that hung on the wall and pulled. The peel of a bell sounded.

He rolled around to face Maggie, who had decided to take a last bite of a cream-filled tart. Pleased with the taste of the smooth vanilla custard that melted in her mouth, she gladly finished the pastry while he watched.

Licking her lips, she said with a satisfied nod, "There, it's truly delicious. You can tell Mrs. Tuttle I said so, and now I must rush. My publisher will be very happy when she receives this final draft."

With a warm smile, Maggie slipped on her coat that Mrs. Tuttle had silently brought from the drawing room. Boots were substituted for the tank socks, and Maggie quickly walked to the front door where Robert's substitute waited. Collier followed, and introduced the driver.

"This is Edward Tuttle. He's helping me during the absence of my chauffeur and will take you where you want to go. Please explain to Edward about your manuscript getting safely to the post office. I would suggest a Return Mail receipt."

What a masterful male! She thought as she hurried down to the car where Edward Tuttle held the door.

With a smile and a wave, Maggie leaned back to enjoy the ride to the church. It came as no surprise to her that she had heard every word that Collier had said. It was partially because of his commanding voice, unfortunately a tone she was used to.

CHAPTER 6

There was a flurry of activity in the Murphy house. Maggie had changed clothes three times before she settled on a black knit suit. She was finally dressed with boots on and hurried out to the entrance hall to get her winter coat before going into the kitchen.

In the kitchen, the large woodblock worktable was cluttered with open jars, bread crust scraps, and empty plastic storage bags. Evelyn was hurriedly spreading mayonnaise and mustard on slices of bread. Lettuce, ham, turkey and cheese were ready to assemble the sandwiches that she was making for the committee lunch.

"We'll see you at noon." Evelyn 's statement was more a command than a question.

Maggie's heart sank at the mess and the reminder. "Mother, I told you I was going to Royal this morning to meet Linda about plans for the wedding. You know she can't talk on the phone."

Maggie hated to use Linda's lack of hearing as her excuse for going to the neighboring city, but she didn't dare add that the main reason she planned to go to Royal this Thursday was to see Collier Thomlinson. She'd not seen him since the lavender book incident two weeks ago, but had read on the library bulletin board that he was to be in Royal on Thursday, December 12 to autograph his new book, <u>Forbidden City</u>. She'd bought a bus ticket as soon as she'd read the article, and planned to go to the Mark Twain Bookstore in Royal to see him after her lunch with Linda.

Exasperated and just a little upset with her inability to speak up to her mother, Maggie uttered a weak reminder. "Linda's counting on me. I told you about our luncheon date."

Evelyn's eyebrows shot up. "Why is it so important that you see her? You could have corresponded by E-mail, your favorite pastime. Besides, how will you get there? I need the car too."

The look said it all—the final preparations for the bazaar must be priority one. Maggie had been at every committee meeting. She'd designed the layout for the booths, helped take out unneeded tables from the meeting hall, and engaged a music student to play background music during the bazaar. She'd even volunteered to be the treasurer this Saturday since her mother was going to be busy in the needlework booth, but it had been decided that Ginny Phillips would be the cashier and treasurer. What more could she do for the important event? Nothing was going to keep her from going to see Linda and attending the book signing.

"Mother, you use the car to get to the church. I have a bus ticket." Maggie absently began to put lettuce, ham or turkey between the slices of the bread that her mother had prepared.

Her mother stopped stirring the soup on the stove. "But you must come. I want to thank all of you committee members for your work on the bazaar by preparing this lunch. I've made vegetable soup, have sandwiches, molded salad, the angel food cake I persuaded Mrs. Reed to bake."

Her mother had worked so hard on the bazaar, and was now treating her committee to thank them for their fine work. Maggie knew she had to go to the luncheon. It was important that she be there for her mother's sake. There was a later bus. She could take it, see Linda for awhile, and still get to the bookstore before six. It would shorten her visit with Linda, but they'd already corresponded about most of the wedding plans.

"Maggie..." The set-mouth look on her mother's face had not changed.

Maggie pulled off the jacket of her suit. "OK. I'll go and take a later bus. Where's the cheese for the ham sandwiches?"

***

The Mark Twain Bookstore was still full of people even though it was 5:40. Collier stretched his fingers. His jaw hurt from the thank-you smile on his face as he waited for the next person in line to have him sign. How many had he signed—fifty or more?

It had been quite a day. Since ten that morning, Collier had sat at a desk and signed books. He'd had a brief intermission at noon for a cup of tea and a sandwich, but two men, who'd asked him to sign their copies, had shortened the break. He was pleased that his fictitious hero, Bertram Strand, who did feats of varying degrees to solve crimes, was becoming a household word in mystery-buff circles.

In one of his books, Bertram catches a quarterback rigging plays for a bookie racketeer. In another, he becomes a member of an Argentinean polo team so that he can catch a clever group of thieves selling stolen Irish thoroughbreds. Bertram also is the undercover agent who helps United States Immigrations officials find a thief with some rare documents. And when a very wealthy man is found dead with no apparent cause of death, Bertram Strand is the clever fellow who discovers that a hatpin thrust into the victim's ear killed him. Veracity laced with a bit of whimsy flavors all the stories. And at times, much like James bond, the protagonist falls victim to a fille de joie. But always Bertram remains a brave man of good character who defends law and order.

Whenever he delved into the fictional world of Bertram Strand, Collier felt like a complete person. True, there were moments of reality when he surfaced from the pages he wrote, and asked himself if it was wrong to live the existence of a hermit dreaming dreams on paper. But if his books brought enjoyment to readers, who were given another dimension to their lives by reading his novels, he'd accomplished something. "Live each day trying to accomplish something, not merely to exist," was a motto he'd chosen long ago.

Now, minutes away from closing time at the Royal bookstore, tired and over-exposed to people, Collier was feeling the need of a stiff scotch and a quiet niche where he could relax before he had to make the snowy ride back to Collier. He flexed his hands to get out the cramps before he wrote in the few remaining customers' books.

As Collier acknowledged the woman who waited patiently for his brief note and signature, a flash of red caught his eye. Collier pushed up from the seat of his chair to look beyond the woman and three others waiting in line behind her. Miss Murphy? Here?

The waiting woman was honored with a seldom shared, dazzling smile from the author as he handed her the signed book. Hurriedly, he scrawled his name on the next two books, wrote notes, and had no idea what he had written. She was here, standing in line to get his signature.

Collier attempted to improve the shakiness of his writing as he signed for a man just ahead of Maggie. Not ready to acknowledge the girl in the dark coat and red tam, he kept his head down, noticed her boots, and wondered what her legs looked like. Back to the present moment, he read the message he'd just written: Let's keep sailors' interest on the legs. Hastily, he changed the inscription to read: Let's keep sailors' interest on the lakes. The book was about sailors on the high seas, not the lakes. He frowned. He'd just written an inane inscription, which completely refuted his sense of credibility.

The man read what Collier had written, frowned, then grumbled, "Enigmatic authors," as he hurried away.

When Collier dared look up, Maggie was across the table from him. He caught the sparkle in her eyes, the slight tilt of her lips that formed a smile, and for the first time, Collier knew the power of a look. Shakespeare wrote about it, love songs tried to capture the magic of it, but until experienced, a person couldn't really know what artists were trying to convey. He felt a weakness, a loss of breath as if he couldn't breathe deeply enough. He fought the feeling her smile stirred within him. Frowning, he did not look at her, rather held out a hand for the book. She hesitated.

"Don't you want me to sign that thing?" he inquired stiffly.

"It isn't necessary for you to put a note in my copy," Maggie said, clutching the book to her chest.

"Well, give it to me." Collier knew his voice had sounded gruff. He was sorry as soon as he'd spoken, but having had no experience in saying that he was sorry, merely pulled the book from her hands, and wrote: To the lovely Lavender Lady. He then signed his name with a flourish: George Collier Thomlinson IV.

She read the inscription, smiled warmly and turned to leave.

"Where do you think you're going? Wait over there on the couch. I'll be through in another fifteen minutes," he growled.

Maggie gave him an inscrutable look, pushed through the short line of people waiting behind her and started toward the door. She hesitated, then, with head held high, she walked over to the couch Collier had indicated and sat down.

He'd watched her actions, and was strangely affected by her apparent indecision. Perhaps she was afraid, yet wanted to stay—much like his wanting to know her, yet questioning the wisdom of it. A normal woman, who had no encumbrance in her life, how could she possibly become interested in someone like him?

He hurried to finish signing for the remaining people, and rode over to the corner of the large room where she sat, and leaned toward her with a look of intent concern in his blue eyes.

"Hello. Are you all right?" He wondered how such green eyes could get so black.

"I'm just fine, thank you." Her voice shook.

She was upset. Why shouldn't she be? He'd almost commanded her to wait for him. Damn this style he'd cultivated, yet Collier decided commanding might still be the best approach.

"Good, let's leave this place and have a bite to eat. You're hungry, aren't you? I haven't had a thing to eat or drink for five hours, and not much before that," he said as he swung the wheelchair around.

Maggie stood, and the book fell off her lap to the floor. She grabbed it up and her coat slipped to the floor. Struggling to put on her coat, she started the first button in the wrong hole and had to start again. Finally in exasperation, she yanked on her gloves, slapped on her tam, and gave the patiently waiting Collier a piercing look.

"I'll get your purse on the couch." Before she could protest, he'd scooped up her purse, wheeled over to the manager to say good bye, and left amid a flurry of "thanks". A dazed Maggie followed Collier and her purse out the door.

Wordlessly, the two proceeded along the treacherously slick sidewalk. Maggie uttered a few breathless protests, grabbing the back of Collier's wheelchair for balance when she stumbled over occasional hidden clumps of ice that his machine easily bumped over. Reaching the restaurant, Collier motioned for the doorman to help Maggie.

"I'll meet you inside." Without waiting for a reply, Collier rode to the ramp at the side of the entrance.

By the time Collier met Maggie at the coatroom, he'd learned what the soup of the day was, what specialties were exceptional and announced:

"At our table, there will be a bottle of Veuve Clicquot La Grande Dame for our full concentration," Collier said, as he handed Maggie's coat, scarf, and tam to the hatcheck attendant.

He was rather pleased that it had taken only six minutes to drag Miss Murphy to this excellent restaurant. He intended to enchant her while enjoying the best of cuisine, and the finest of champagne which he'd reserved earlier for his own enjoyment—so much better to share it with this sprite of a woman.

He sneaked a peak at her while he waited for the coat tag. Her full lips were tightly closed, her green eyes flashed, as a foot tapped a displeased message. She was still angry at his "style." He noticed the way her silken hair draped her face with blue-black shimmers, how the fitted black wool pantsuit molded to her slender body. Perhaps honesty would be the best course of action to take.

"You're beautiful," he said. It surprised him as much as it had apparently surprised her. And stirred some embarrassment, so the becoming flush of her cheeks would indicate.

He extended a hand. "Shall we dine?" She turned and followed the waiter who led them to a table in a quiet corner of the restaurant.

Collier knew the evening had not started out well. He'd been rude about signing her book, because he'd felt vulnerable and didn't want to show it. He'd been domineering about coming to the restaurant, but she might have bolted if he'd not forced her to come with him. He'd sincerely wanted to compliment her, and had botched it in his usual bungling way.

They were seated. The waiter opened and poured the bubbling wine into stemmed glasses, and left their table after handing each a menu. Collier looked over his menu at Maggie who was intently studying hers.

"For two weeks I've wanted to call and tell you how much I enjoyed having you in my home. Did your manuscript get to your publisher on time?" he asked.

"It did, thank you. And I arrived at the church in time for the luncheon. But after Mrs. Tuttles'delicious treats, I wasn't too hungry." She laughed lightly and smoothed a finger down the flute of champagne.

"I propose a toast to the lavender lady for the kindness shown to me in coming to the book signing, and for accepting my rather forceful dinner invitation," Collier said. They clicked glasses and sipped the wine.

"May I, Sir, propose a toast to the successful book signing." They touched flutes and sipped again. Maggie's lifted brows, and slight tilt of her lips seemed to indicate that she was enjoying the evening as much as he was.

The waiter brought them a selection of appetizers. Before the man left, Collier ordered parchment wrapped salmon, a medley of vegetables, and a fresh green salad for two, while Maggie chose a canapé with a tiny sprig of lavender on top.

"I use lavender as an edible herb in my writing. How do you use it in yours?" Maggie held up a sprig of the herb as she asked.

Collier grinned with a shrug. "I use lavender in my writing as an intriguing scent to lure young women to my hero's den. I know nothing about eating it." But I'd like to devour you. A deep drink of champagne prolonged his thought.

"I imagine your hero does more than that to entice his women." Maggie's cheeks flushed.

He lifted his glass. "To lavender." Their glasses lightly touched. In a more serious tone, he added, "Lavender will forever be my favorite of the herb family whatever the use," and extended his glass again.

"I must admit that I was upset with you at the bookstore. You told me to sit down in a very commanding manner." Maggie said, tipping her glass for the last drop of wine.

"I was rather abrupt wasn't I?" Collier leaned forward to pour them more wine and tried to explain how sudden surprises always made him perform badly. It was as near an apology as he could muster. They both relaxed after that bit of honesty, and continued a run-on, non-stop conversation until the end of the meal. The waiter came back. Maggie ordered a mint liqueur instead of dessert. Collier decided on a brandy.

With a sip of his Cognac, Collier asked, "Did you drive? I hope not on a night like tonight. The roads are treacherous."

Maggie finished the sweet after-dinner drink, between giggles, asking if he wrote like he talked. He answered with a smile as he absently smoothed the sides of his glass. "At times, the characters I'm drawing in the plot take over."

"Good. I'm glad they can assurr…t, themselves." Maggie struggled with the word. She leaned forward and whispered. "It's very important to assert oneself." She sat back with a nod of satisfaction, blinking her eyes as if she were having trouble holding them open.

Collier leaned toward her. "Maggie, did you drive?"

She shook her head. "I didn't have to drive. I came on the bus." Her head tilted. She asked with a frown, "How did you get here?"

"My driver brought me. And how are you to get home?"

With lifted brows and an impish smile, she placed one finger to her lips and unsteadily leaned toward Collier until their faces were inches apart. "You see, I had read one of your books at the library. Letty Leffert, the librarrr...ian, told me about the book signing, and I came."

Collier wiped a smile with his napkin. "You're avoiding the question. How are you to get home? On the bus? If so, we're going to abandon the bus idea. You'll come with me instead." He signaled for the waiter.

Squinting at her wristwatch, Maggie shook her head with a little sigh. "The last bus left at ten o'clock. It's eleven-fifteen. I suppose I'll have to, won't I?" She sat up straight, and looked at Collier with a serious expression. "I didn't plan it you know."

"You don't sound too enthusiastic, but, yes, you will have to come with me." He reached over and gave her hand a squeeze. "I'll be very glad for the company. Now, if you'll excuse me for a minute, I'll go fetch Robert." He pushed away from the table.

"Who's Robert?" Collier missed her question, for he was already headed for the vestibule to summon his chauffeur. He then turned to the hatcheck girl to whom he gave a ten-dollar bill with the request that she look in on the young woman who was carefully steering a course to the ladies room at the far end of the vestibule. The girl followed Maggie into the ladies lounge just as Robert arrived. Collier explained the situation, and Robert went out to get the limo.

A short while later, Maggie, looking somewhat refreshed, joined Collier. He extended a hand to steady her, and they went outside where they were met by a very tall, handsome man. Although he wore no white plume, with his stiff bearing and mask-like face, the man looked more like a Grenadier ready for the Changing of the Guard than a chauffeur.

"This is Robert, Maggie. He's my driver, companion, handyman and nurse—when I'll let him help me."

Eyes lowered, with no show of emotion, Robert acknowledged the introduction in his perfect English. Hesitantly, Maggie acknowledged the introduction as if embarrassed, leaving Collier to wonder if Maggie might take the man's austerity as disapproval for her slight intoxication. Hadn't she had champagne before? He knew so little about her. And yet, it was as if he'd known her forever.

Collier quickly offered the serious-faced woman a hand and held it tightly as the three went down the ramp with Robert guiding the wheelchair, and Collier giving a shortened biography of his friend and chauffeur:

"Robert Charles Winfield is English and has been to the classic school of therapeutic science in Greenwich, England. Which is the city where the zero longitude has always been marked as the base for the International Time Zone. Or was, until 1954 when it was moved to Sussex County. Both my time and physical systems are regulated by Robert's excellent care. He has the strength, discipline, and concentration of a mountain climber on a vertical slope."

The on-going, one-sided conversation continued until, once down the incline, Collier pushed forward and waited for Robert to help Maggie into the van. The large, powerfully built man then joined Collier on the other side, and maneuvered him onto the car-lift and into the van. Collier slipped into the leather seat, and the silent man closed the sliding door. Maggie leaned back against the soft leather seat and closed her eyes. Collier continued his commentary.

"Robert comes from a long line of Royal Naval officers. In World War Two, Robert was blown off a carrier into the water, and came home to Greenwich to heal. We two met at the Greenwich Rehabilitation Center, where I faithfully went for therapy on weekends during my school years. Those weekends, I stayed at the cottage my father had invested in located between Greenwich and London. I've thanked father over the years for many things, including his visits to see me." He looked over to see that he'd lost his audience to sleep.

He studied Maggie's delicate face in repose. Long black lashes brushed her cheeks, full red lips were ever so slightly open, skeins of ebony hair spilled over her shoulder as her head tilted toward him. He'd called her beautiful in the restaurant. The comment had been sudden, unrehearsed, just saying it had stunned him with the truth. Now, having spent the evening in her company, he found her even more beautiful. What was it about her that so intrigued him? She could be serious, yet teasing—interested in listening, yet had her own opinion. She was enchantingly innocent, which was rare in a modern woman. She appeared to be young, perhaps in her late twenties?

He'd felt an attraction in the library, because of her audacity—he plagiarize? He silently chuckled. She had been shy, rather hesitant in his home, yet somewhat defiant too when he'd forced her to stay. And again tonight, there was that pull, as if he'd known her for a long time. Collier placed an arm close to pillow her head and closed his eyes, savoring the delicate scent of her perfume.

"Could you direct me to Miss Murphy's home, sir?" They were stopped at an intersection at the edge of Collier when, three hours later, Robert's voice floated back to them. Maggie awakened and sat up.

"Can you come to my house for a nightcap?" he asked, noticing her move to distance them, and again wondered at her shyness.

"No thank you. I've overstayed, and over indulged. I don't know how I'm going to explain." Maggie sighed heavily.

"Why should you explain anything? You look like a grown woman to me." He leaned toward her.

As if pulled by a magnet, Maggie leaned toward Collier. The scent of mint on his breath mingled with her perfume. Their lips touched and held for a brief moment before he pulled away. He looked intently at her, then abruptly turned to look out of the window.

"Where do you live?" He asked in a flat tone.

Maggie quickly leaned forward to direct Robert to her street. The chauffeur turned the car onto Main Street. Stores were dressed with sparkling Christmas lights while holly wreaths adorned street lamps and draped across the street. The only sound was the crunch of the heavy car's wheels moving over the dry snow.

Collier was thinking about the sweetness of the kiss while wishing he'd not kissed her. After all, how was a carefree young woman to manage a relationship with a man in a wheelchair? She was problemless, clueless. Normal people simply didn't understand. And what would be demanded of him if she should want such a relationship? It was too unimaginable to consider.

"Cherry, Elm, Locust, sounds like a nature lover of trees named the streets." Collier's loud voice filled the silence.

Maggie continued to look out the window. Collier cast a side-glance to watch the streetlights touch her face, and highlight the curve of her chin. She seemed to be watching the passing scene, but he guessed she was scolding herself for going to dinner with him. They'd shared a little wine, and had a small after-dinner drink. Perhaps the kiss was not a good idea, but she hadn't resisted. Asking her to his home at this late hour was a mistake. After all, it was after two. Hardly the time of night a lady would be going to a man's house with a man she barely knew. That had to be the reason she'd withdrawn to the other side of the seat and was staring out the window so intently. He wondered to whom she had to explain her evening? Odd for a girl in this modern age to worry about what another person might think, but perhaps mores were different in a small community.

The limo slowly curved onto Elm Street where the glow of street lamps had turned snow-covered yards, sidewalks and trees into delicious looking creations. At Maggie's direction, Richard stopped at the last house on the right side of the street. Collier watched lazy chimney smoke curl gray then dissolve into the cloud-scudded sky. He glanced over at Maggie's shadowed face in the dim glow of the street lamps. His throat tightened. Would she too vanish like the smoke? Would he ever see her again? And did he really want to?

With a raised eyebrow and one-sided grin, he said derisively, "I won't get out." Then quickly added, "Thank you for honoring me with you company."

"Thank you, Cole." A slight smile formed on her lips as she said his name. "It was an evening I won't forget." Maggie's smile wavered. Hesitantly, she touched his cheek with her gloved hand, then quickly slipped out of the car.

"Thank you, Robert. You don't have to take me to the door." She waved to Collier and quickly went up the walk with Robert escorting her.

When she'd said his name he'd felt a hitch in his throat that seemed to ache with the sweetness of the word. Not many called him by the nickname his father had used. Collier was pleased that Robert followed her up to the door, and waited until she'd gone inside. As they drove away, Collier turned to look out the rear window, and watched the lights in Maggie's home grow smaller until the limousine curved around a corner.

CHAPTER 7

"You and Linda," Evelyn emphasized, "must have had a nice evening." Evelyn Murphy was sitting at the table when Maggie walked into the kitchen for breakfast. Maggie's place had not been set, nor was coffee ready for her. The evidence was enough to show her mother's displeasure. Maggie was in for a lecture concerning late hours, the bus ride with all kinds of terrible people, and what could she be thinking?

Without a word, Maggie got her own cup of coffee, spooned in sugar from the canister, and poured milk from the carton, which stood on the counter. No china creamer or sugar bowl this morning. Apparently Maggie was in for a triple-decked censure. But after all, she'd known her mother for a long time, hadn't she? Fortunately, she could tune her out if necessary.

Maggie pushed aside her rather heartless thought as she stood sipping her coffee at the kitchen window. She noted the blue sky tinted with sunshine, and how the gusting wind pushed snow away from the flagstone walkway. The scene stirred something deeper than resentment within Maggie. It was joy. It was so seldom that she felt such ease that she found herself laughing aloud at a bright red cardinal with fluffed feathers, skittering to a stop on a drift of snow to peck at seeds beneath the feeder.

"What a beautiful morning, mother. The sun is shining, and birds are congregating to eat right outside our kitchen window. See?"

"Margaret Ann, look at me." Evelyn's voice was loud.

The voice of disapproval interrupted Maggie's praise of nature and somewhat dimmed her happy feeling. She sat down in the chair across from Evelyn and ignored the grim-faced woman by pouring herself more coffee, and disturbing the silence with the stirring of the mixture.

"Did you, or did you not stand Richard up last night?"

"Did he tell you that?" Maggie's cup, half way to her mouth, was slowly lowered, and carefully placed on the saucer. She traced a finger over the edge of the cup.

"Yes, and more. He said that you took the bus to Royal, and he believed it was to go to the bookstore to see that awful Mr. Thomlinson. I've forbidden you to see that man. What could you be thinking? People do not approve of him or his books."

Maggie felt heat flood her cheeks. "How could Richard have possibly known all that? Where did he get his information?" Then, with a sigh, "Of course, Letty told Richard."

One look at her mother's vividly red cheeks warned Maggie to say nothing more. She closed her mouth, and, with shaking hands, attempted to again lift the cup of hot liquid to her lips. The hot coffee splashed, and spilled over into the saucer, and out onto the table.

"Oh dear," Evelyn exclaimed, as she jumped up from the table avoiding the trail of hot liquid that slithered across the table toward her.

"I'll get it, Mother." Maggie leaned over and slowly, pressed down hard with her napkin to wipe up the mess. She wanted to share the evening she'd had with Cole, but to tell Evelyn that the intelligent man intrigued her, and that she'd drunk champagne, and kissed him was too staggering a confession to make. Anyway, it was her special memory and she didn't want it tarnished.

"That's a good linen napkin, Maggie. Here, use this toweling." Evelyn hurriedly grabbed some paper towels, threw some over the table to Maggie, then pressed some of the towels over the spills that had started down the table leg by her own chair. "What a mess. What has gotten into you?"

"I didn't have a date with Richard last night." She skirted the other two accusations as she took the coffee soaked paper towels to the wastebasket.

"I don't like your tone of voice, young lady." Evelyn pointed her spoon at Maggie, then lowered it and her voice. "It's not like you to do something and not share it with me."

"Mother, you love me, I love you, let's not hurt each other with words. Please remember I'm almost thirty." Maggie said.

There was no satisfaction in being accused, just as there was truly no gratification in doing something that Evelyn was not in on. Maggie poured them both some more coffee, and the two sat and discussed tomorrow's bazaar. Maggie promised to go to the church to help with flowers, and that led to Maggie's visit with Linda the day before, and the plans for her friend's wedding at the end of February.

"Ask Richard to go to the wedding. It would be nice to have someone with you, and I won't be able to go because that's the weekend that Ginny and I are in the canasta tournament." Evelyn repeated information already shared.

"I'll plan to go on the bus on the Wednesday before the wedding for the parties and rehearsal dinner. I did ask Linda to invite Richard to the wedding so I can come home with him, unless he's too involved with church duties."

She was tempted to remind Evelyn that rumors were starting to link Richard Stevenson with Letty Levert, but she decided it best not to share that bit of gossip. It would open up another discussion about love and marriage, and she didn't have the time. Other projects were too pressing, and anyway, years of her own defensive wall building seemed almost insurmountable at the moment. Evelyn's crisp voice interrupted Maggie's thoughts:

"Your plans sound as if you've thought them through quite nicely. I'm sure Richard will want to come to the wedding. If nothing else, he'll want to be with you. Now, I must go. This day will fly, and we're not entirely ready for the bazaar tomorrow. Will you be coming?"

"I'll be at the church by ten." Maggie had mixed emotions as she watched her mother walk out of the room. Undercover plans were not Maggie's usual style. She wanted to be more assertive, but didn't quite approve of her own method of accomplishing it. She dimly recalled having shared something about being assertive to Cole last evening.

A fuzzy memory and aching head were evidence that she'd had too much to drink the night before. A guilt trip skimmed along well-worn nerves, but she quickly zapped the feeling with the thought that she was a grown woman. Cole's remark of last night was recalled with a smile.

She absently began to clean up the remains of breakfast, while she considered that the anxious feeling she had just now was the same as she'd had years ago. She'd been a very young sixteen when she'd sneaked out, after curfew, to the gazebo of the private school with Linda. They'd talked about sex and at one point Maggie remembered what she'd signed to Linda: "Maybe the sexual act between a man and a woman would be something like giving away something only you possess and in return receive something that makes you feel good about yourself. In the Bible Jesus says it's better to give than to receive."

Linda had a flashlight hidden under the blanket they were sharing while they'd been reading Lady Chatterly's Lover. Linda signed to Maggie: "You've certainly put a new twist on sex. Chatterly says something about sharing sex with too many can make it lose that special feeling."

Maggie had signed: "Do you ever feel guilty about thinking about sex?"

Linda signed quickly: "Heavens no.   Sex can be wonderful...at least my mom in her kind of shy way suggested as much to me when I asked. The way she explained it to me, two people who are devoted, share, and become one with each other. That doesn't seem sinful to me."

Signing rapidly, Linda had lightened the subject: "Being who we are, hearing-impaired, lets us hear things other people don't know about and some of it's pretty funny. Remember that time at school when we were trying to get the janitor to open the gym in the evening? He said, 'How about six?' And lip-reading, we thought he'd said sex."

Maggie signed: "And the way some people whisper, thinking we don't know what they are saying. Like the time you and I were in the drugstore, and we read that woman's lips telling the pharmacist she'd like to go to bed with him? She didn't know we had lip-reading hearing and knew what she'd said?"

Linda added: "We have super powers! And they'd slapped hands and formed the word: 'Yes'!"

That evening so long ago had been special for Maggie. She'd done something daring, slipped out to the Grennly garden after hours, talked about unmentionables. And though not as confident as Linda, Maggie experienced for the first time in her life what it was like to be independent. Something like last night with Cole had been.

Later in the week of the Chatterly adventure, Maggie had shared the news with Linda about the surgery that would restore Maggie's hearing: "You've been my dearest, my very good friend for nine years. I don't want that to change. I don't want to lose you. I'd rather not have the operations than have you not like me anymore."

Linda's answer had been quick and decisive: "You'll have something I'll never be able to experience, but you won't be shutting me out. You'll just be opening up to let others in. Our friendship is deep enough to survive sharing. We'll always have deaf secrets."

And now, her dear friend was getting married to a hearing-impaired man. Linda would have a relationship much closer than friendship could ever be.

CHAPTER 8

On the last Wednesday in February, Maggie went on the bus to the Edwards' home. For the three days before the wedding, she'd shared pre-wedding festivities with Linda and the family. There had been time to have long conversations with Linda. Highways were clear enough for wedding guests, but there was enough snow the day before the wedding to take a bobsled ride on a country road behind the matched pair of Mr. Edwards' favorite Clydesdales. The rehearsal dinner at the Racket Club banquet center thirty miles away in Madison was gay with toasts, teasing, and fun, and appropriately poignant.

Now, the wedding day had dawned gloriously bright and sunny. After frantic, last minute preparations, the bridal party rode to the small Catholic Church where the organist was playing an interlude of soft music as guests were being seated. As Bach's "Jesu, Joy of Man's Desiring" began, the mothers walked down the aisle and were seated and Maggie followed. Then the traditional wedding march with all its golden flurries announced the bride's arrival and accompanied Linda down the aisle. She joined John who waited with his best man, Tim Edwards, and Father Lewis and the service began.

It had been hard for Maggie to hold back tears during the part of the ceremony when John and Linda had knelt as the vocalist had sung, "Oh Promise Me." But she concentrated on the joy she felt for her two friends who looked at each other with such love. An hour later, nuptial prayers having been given, spoken vowels and communion shared, John kissed his bride. The formal Catholic wedding ceremony ended with thunderous organ chords of Bach's glorious Brandenburg Concerto No.3 filling the church as the newly wedded couple and their attendants walked down the aisle and out of the church. After the photographer took pictures, Maggie rode with Tim and his wife June to the reception at the Royal Cumberland Country Club.

When they got to the club, Richard was waiting. Before Maggie could get out of the car, Richard had opened the door.

"Hello Tim, June—sorry Maggie and I are going to have to leave early." Richard turned to Maggie to explain:

"Maggie, I've had a call from the sheriff. Seems there has been a death, and they want me to go to talk to the family today in Etin. I wouldn't ask you to leave so soon, but it's one o'clock now and it's a three-hour trip back to Collier. I'll take you home, then back-track the eighteen miles to Etin to see the parents of the boy who died."

The attendant took the car, and Tim and his wife went on into the club.

"Wait Richard," Maggie said as Richard started to go and get his car.

Maggie stood on the steps trying to absorb what Richard had just said. She didn't want to leave before Linda and John left for their honeymoon. She was the maid of honor, and one last duty was to help Linda change for the honeymoon trip— and help decorate the car and throw the rice. She couldn't stay with Mr. and Mrs. Edwards after the couple left, because the parents had plane reservations for a trip abroad as soon as everyone was gone. As for the bus to Collier there was only a two o'clock connection that she'd already missed. She suggested with just a touch of pleading in her voice.

"We could wait long enough to help decorate the limousine and see them drive off, then I'll go to Etin with you? You don't have to take me home first."

"I'd hope you might agree to that." Richard smiled, and took her arm as they went into the club. For once, there was a tiny spark of real feeling for Richard.

Maggie left Richard and hurried to the entrance of the large reception room where she gave Linda and John quick hugs; then the Edwards, Maggie and Tim got into the receiving line with the bride and groom. When Richard came by the line, Tim delayed Richard. "I overheard you say you had to go to see a family about a death. I just received a call from the coroner about a death certificate. It seems a fourteen-year-old boy from Etin died when he was being baptized in Lake Thomlinson last night. They're listing it as an accident on the word of the minister. I've not all the details yet. Do you know what happened?" Tim was one of the state prosecutors.

Maggie had turned to talk to another guest, but when she heard Lake Thomlinson, she turned to listen to what the men were talking about. Richard was telling Tim something:

"I don't know all the particulars, but from what Sheriff Moody said on the phone, some Royal and Etin folks, as well as Collier residents, have been going to some meetings that are held on the Thomlinson property by the lake. They call themselves the Woods People, and have their own minister— I'm not sure if you'd call it a denomination, perhaps more like a cult, if you know what I mean."

A cult? Collier Thomlinson's woods? Maggie wondered what Collier knew about this. Someone interrupted further discussion by coming up to speak to Tim. After all had been greeted, Maggie went into the club with Richard and mingled among friends until Tim gave her the high sign that the couple was getting ready to leave. After Maggie had helped with last minute details for Linda, she ran outside to join the others, leaving the mother and daughter to say their good byes before the wedding couple left.

"Here they come." Tim grabbed Maggie's arm, and pulled her with him up to the front line of guests. Between laughter and more tears, Maggie caught Linda's bouquet, and the newlyweds were whisked off in a stretch limo that, for all its engineering sophistication, now sounded like a too-many-wrecks truck ready for the junk heap.

Maggie explained to the Edwards clan that she and Reverend Stevenson had to leave because of an unexpected appointment the minister had to make in Etin. The family gathered on the country club steps to wave Richard and Maggie off.

"Don't forget us. Keep in touch," The family called. Maggie looked back at the Edwards until they were out of sight.

Tim had again referred to the two men's conversation concerning the devil worship stories, and the death of one of the members of the so-called cult. Maggie wondered if Collier knew anything about the incident. He was gone a lot. Didn't she know! She'd not heard a thing from him since their dinner in Royal before Christmas, and that was almost six weeks ago. The local paper had reported that the author had gone on a short tour around the Midwest autographing his book. Then she'd heard from Letty that Collier had gone to England on business. Maggie wondered if it was writing business or woman business that took him so far from home.

Richard and Maggie had driven several miles before the minister broke the silence. "Nice of Tim Edwards to offer to help. But I won't know what's going on until I talk to the family of the boy. Tim said that he'd had a client who'd once been in a cult."

"A devil worship group in our town? I read the article in the Etin paper about the winter carnival being called off because of some sort of reports there was a devil worship group that wanted to meet some place close to our town. I ignored it as an article designed to sell papers." Maggie couldn't believe it.

"Well, there're been some fires set on the Thomlinson property." Richard sounded almost glad to be telling her the story. She listened as the minister continued.

"One pretty bad blaze destroyed a few trees before the fire department got to it. Seems there was no one around to question as to how the fire started, but later the Woods People, as they call themselves, were questioned. I wonder how Collier Thomlinson is involved?"

Maggie refused to speculate. Rather, she leaned her head back, and closed her eyes to stop the words from disturbing her thoughts about the loving family they'd just left. Maggie could understand why Linda loved John. He was so kind and funny too. She felt a momentary stab of jealous sadness at the thought that Linda and John would share a special understanding with their hearing impairment. She couldn't imagine such companionship and love. She remembered another dream of a teenager when she'd dreamed that Tim would wait until she grew up, and they would marry, and she would be Linda's sister forever. She smiled at the memory, then sobered with the thought that she hadn't changed her dreaming pattern much since that of a child. She still was a romantic, waiting for her man, even though she realized she was much too old to have such a fantasy. But on the other hand, perhaps there was nothing wrong with dreaming when one was not sure of reality.

Now and then a fence sliced through the mosaic pattern of brown earth, corn stalks, and patches of melting snow. Occasional mounds of dirty roadside snow made Maggie wish for typical March weather with its wind and rain that would clean the land.

So much had happened in the month of December. She breathed in a sigh of relief that the bazaar was over, and that there would not be another one for two years. It was by far the best bazaar their church had ever had, and much of the credit had to be given to Evelyn Murphy. Of the three hundred who attended, some had come from as far as Royal and Madison.

Evelyn's lovely needlepoint pillow had been raffled off. At first Evelyn had objected to her pillow being raffled off instead of auctioned as planned, but other committee members insisted it would make more money sold in a raffle, and Evelyn understood why it was best when the pillow raffle made over six hundred dollars.

How they had gotten the jumble of merchandise in the small room was a challenge. It had been difficult to arrange the booths so that the merchandise could be displayed without stacking, and enough aisle space had to be left for customers to browse. For lack of space, two booths of hand-carved toys had to be moved to the entrance by the stairs. They'd not sold well because of the location, and had to be sold that next week to local people and church members.

Seeing how much their church did need the new addition, Maggie had given a matching pledge for the building fund. She planned to give even more as the project got under way.

With the bazaar, her birthday and the trusteeship turned over to her on her birthday, all but for the lack of word from Mr. Thomlinson, the month of December had been very rewarding. And if her heart did trip a bit when she thought about him, why should she expect him to feel the same and call her? Perhaps she exaggerated her feelings for the man with the wild, flaming red hair. It was all right. She'd had a good holiday and a good report from her publisher. She'd spent some time in her favorite city, Chicago. The fires Richard had mentioned must have taken place while she was out of town.

Her thoughts finally settled to appreciate how cozy it was inside the warm automobile. Pleasant too to listen to the steady drone of the engine that overlaid Richard's one-sided conversation. Maggie mused on the idea that Richard reminded her of her mother, who also needed no one to listen. She smiled and turned to watch Richard's lips.

"John's an interesting man. They have a common bond with their deafness. But my, the hardships they'll have to endure." Richard finished the comment with a shake of the head as he maneuvered a curve and slowed for a patch of wet snow.

Hardships? He thought it would be an endurance contest did he? Of all the inexcusable remarks! "Oh, I don't know. I believe they'll have a very active and full life. Linda can hear you know. Not in the conventional way, but she has more instinctive listening ability than some who can hear." Her words came out clipped and cold. Maggie recalled the motto Linda and she'd made up when they'd been in school: "Being deaf is not as bad as hearing and not listening."

She remembered the feeling of hopelessness when her stepfather had ignored her attempts to talk. Bert had made her feel ignorant, but she was deaf that's why she couldn't communicate. Bert Murphy had not tried to listen to her. Hearing but not listening, that was Bert—and Richard?

"Do you ever think of marriage?" Richard asked.

The question caused surprise and some irritation. Where had that question come from? He was looking at the road ahead apparently riding on his own train of thought without a clue that her last remark had been said to open the conversation to a deeper, more meaningful level. And now, he brought up the subject of marriage, about which he was probably equally inadequate to discuss.

Maggie replied somewhat indifferently, "Richard, I'm all for the institution."

The brash remark was lost on the minister. "I'm thirty-five and a bachelor. I've often wondered, when I've counseled couples on marriage, what it would be like to share my life with a woman. At times I've even felt guilty, thinking my parishioners might want me to marry. Do you?"

This was an on-the-edge-of-the-cliff discussion. Of course, both of them had endured the church ladies' matchmaking for over a year now. Neither one of them had a shred of romantic feeling for the other. Maggie decided she wouldn't take the question personally.

"No, I've thought you hadn't met anyone whom you would want to marry. It's a very personal decision between two people," Maggie said.

"Maggie, I've started this conversation badly." Richard slowed the car to a crawl. Maggie felt like opening the door and jumping out, but compassion subdued frustration.

"What do you want to say, Richard? I can hear you." She asked.

"I admire you very much for your strength in overcoming your difficulty." He said intently looking ahead at the road.

She had been flippant, but the remark had gone over his head. Now, he was calling her hearing deficit a difficulty. What a way to phrase her hearing!

The silence was palatable until Richard continued. "I believe we get along quite nicely."

"You're quite right. We do have a nice friendship, and I like you as my minister. Oh, look, we're approaching Etin." Maggie pointed ahead where a grain elevator loomed high above a treeline. Silhouetted against an overcast sky, the building's silo looked something like a cathedral spire.

"I'll be quiet so you can concentrate on a prayer, or some helpful message with which you'll want to leave the family of the boy," she suggested.

"Of course. I'll prepare for the family. We'll discuss this at another time," Richard said.

He'd decided not to listen. "Richard, we're friends. Let's leave it at that." Maggie was sorry to be so blunt, but she sincerely hoped that her suggestion would put a stop to the conversation once and for all.

He nodded and was quiet as they entered the town. The Main Street was old and shabby. As they drove along the main street, Maggie noticed two empty brick buildings, marked as having been built in the late 1800's. Windows of another store were covered with two-by-fours. An empty corner lot was covered with weeds, and one car was parked in front of a video specialty shop. It was apparent that businesses had moved to the outskirts of town where there was room for chain stores, discount stores and mega groceries. It distressed Maggie to see how the town had let the center of its community deteriorate.

"Here's Franklin Street. We're looking for 151." Richard turned down the street, and drove to the address. It was a single story dwelling badly in need of paint. A lawnmower leaned on a patch of tall, snow-covered bushes. A battered Cadillac was parked by the curb.

"I'll stay here," Maggie offered.

"I wish you'd come with me. You're sensitive and understanding." Richard came around and opened her door.

"I don't want to interfere."

"You'll be helping me." Richard touched her arm. She quickly got out and started up to the house. The minister followed.

At Richard's knock, a man with short stubby legs opened the door halfway and peered out at the two. Maggie thought his size made the man resemble an Irish gremlin, but his unkempt overall appearance was not that of a happy little elf. His greasy hair, wary eyes, and downturned mouth denoted an unhappy and angry man. Maggie guessed his age to be about sixty.

Richard spoke first. "I'm Reverend Stevenson, and this is Miss Murphy. We've come at the request of Stan Moody, the county sheriff, to see the parents of Denny Wright. I hear there's been trouble."

With an audible grunt of disgust, the little man opened the door. "Yeah, the sheriff said we was to expect you, though why I don't rightly know. Better come in."

The long-faced man stood aside to let them enter. "I'm Clifford Wright, the boy's step-grandfather, and in there is Jessie, his mom." He pointed to a young woman, sitting on a sagging couch in the living room beyond where they stood in the short hall. "Jessie, this here's the minister from Collier."

Maggie saw the young woman in the shadows of a room filled with the clutter of newspapers, magazines, and an overflowing basket of wash that was apparently waiting to be folded. The place reeked of stale smoke.

When Richard walked into the room, Maggie waited in the hall to the side of the living room entrance. Glancing around, Maggie noticed a room to the left of her, obviously the kitchen. Through the open door she could see plates of half-eaten food on a table. The dregs from an overturned beer bottle dripped off the oilcloth, and ran down to puddle on the floor. The sink was filled with unwashed pots and pans.

At that moment, a woman with stringy brown hair, dressed in a wraparound that accentuated her thin body walked out of a room next to the kitchen. Clifford turned when she came into the hallway. "This is my wife, Thelma."

The woman acknowledged the introduction with a slight tilt of the head, and slowly walked over to the side of where Richard and Jessie sat. Maggie studied the woman with the painfully thin body, deep-set, expressionless black eyes and weathered face. She imagined that Thelma had once been a very pretty woman, but had somehow given up caring how she looked, or how to be friendly. She now stood slumped against the wall, arms folded over her breasts, with a vague expression as she looked at Jessie and the preacher.

Maggie was pretty sure that she'd guessed Clifford's age of sixty about right, and if she tried to guess, she'd say Mrs. Wright could be in her early forties. Though, at first, she had appeared much older. Maggie also presumed that the girl, Jessie with the same straggly hair as Thelma, must be the woman's daughter. Richard had said that Jessie, the mother of the fourteen-year-old boy, who had drowned, was about Maggie's age, thirty. Jessie had been fifteen when she'd had Dennis. Jessie's mother, Thelma, must have been about fifteen when she'd had Jessie. There was a generational pattern of teenage, unwed mothers in the family.

Clifford spoke up. "Jessie don't need no preacher to come and say a blessing over her. Jessie's not ever met a churchy, God-person yet that has any interest in her kind, and she don't need their interest neither. We got each other to get through grieving time. Like the sheriff said, you seen us, now ya better leave." He ended his clipped message with a grunt, and a sly grin that was more of a sneer than friendly.

Maggie felt a deep sympathy for this young woman who hurt, but was not allowed to grieve. She was pretty sure Jessie would carry guilt and rage over the death of her son for many years to come, unless she got to express her feelings to someone other than this cantankerous old man and silent mother. Completely ignoring the veiled threat, Maggie quickly walked over and sat down on the couch beside Jessie. When she sat, puffs of dust flew out of the cushions and floated in the streaks of light that quivered under the window shade. Lazy spirals of smoke from a smoldering cigarette in an overflowing ashtray assailed her nose. Through the haze of dust and smoke, Maggie noted the haphazard arrangement of stiff wooden chairs. To one side was a table with a dried-up poinsettia plant with yellowed leaves. Her glance skipped to study a floor lamp with a crooked shade that looked like a rakish clown, laughing at all of them. The whole room was bizarre, like some sort of set for an Addams family movie.

"I'm so sorry about your son. How old was he?" Maggie spoke to the mother of the boy who had drowned.

Jessie looked at Maggie and began to cry. Not sobs, but just a steady stream of tears that the young woman tried to stop by rubbing at her wet eyes. Maggie got a handkerchief from her pocket and handed it to Jessie. The mother and stepfather silently stood to the side, as did Richard. Maggie looked over at the minister to see if he had something to say, but Richard just smiled his gentle smile, and seemed content for her to comfort the woman.

"He was a goin' on fourteen. He'd been livin' with another boy's family outside town. Didn't like the way Clifford corrected him. He wasn't goin' to school, and Clifford beat him up pretty good. 'Course, I let Clifford beat him, cause I didn't know what to do." Jessie's voice trailed off. The girl looked hesitantly over at the living room entrance through a fringe of stubby lashes. Even though Maggie had her back to him, Maggie knew that Clifford Wright was staring at the young woman. Coldness skimmed up the back of her neck. The old saying that someone was walking on a grave came to Maggie. Perhaps it was a feeling of tension in the room that caused her to shiver. Somehow, she knew that she had to help the mother of the boy.

"You must be tired after all the questions that the police have no doubt had to ask. You need to rest." Hesitantly, Maggie added, "This may be a bad time to talk of your loss. Perhaps I could come back in a few days. Maybe we could go to lunch?" Maggie's eyes were filled with concern as she looked at the bowed head of Jessie. The mother's shoulders shook with sobs. Jessie couldn't or was afraid to acknowledge the invitation in front of the two relatives who stood like guards by the doorway.

The air was thick with tension and distrust that made it hard for Maggie to breathe. She was suffocating and had to get out of the room. She hurriedly pushed up from the couch, walked by Jessie's silent mother, and continued on to the front door where the grandfather stood staring at her with cold unblinking eyes. Maggie breathed in fresh air as she waited for Richard on the porch. *Please come Richard. There's something evil in this house.*

Maggie was sure Jessie was some sort of victim, but again, who was to blame, Clifford, Thelma, or both? Neither of them seemed concerned that Jessie was silently sobbing into Maggie's handkerchief.

Richard walked up and shook hands with Clifford. Maggie looked back into the living room and found Jessie's tear-filled eyes looking at her as if she wanted to speak. Maggie sensed a quiet desperation, a pleading as if Jessie would like to accept Maggie's invitation, but was too afraid or cowed to do so.

Maggie asked again, "May I take you to lunch, Jessie?"

"Naw, don't reckon that'll be necessary, miss. We're here for Jessie. You can save yourself a trip." There was an angry cadence to stepfather's words accentuated by the grim set of his mouth and the piercingly cold look he gave Maggie as he stood holding the door open.

Maggie glanced back at the silent wife, and met the stare of eyes as hard as black marbles. Though Thelma may have once been a very pretty woman, she had become an emaciated, indifferent person. Maggie hesitantly smiled to her, gave a brief nod to Mr. Wright and walked down the porch steps.

Richard had stepped back into the house to say good-bye to Jessie.

Maggie couldn't rid herself of the premonition of evil in the house. She wondered if Jessie could feel it. Perhaps it wasn't only grief that prompted the tears. The parents seemed so indifferent to the girl's suffering. She would have to find a way to talk to Jessie without Thelma and Clifford present.

The day had been emotionally charged—first with wonderful, euphoric happiness, then with deep sadness and grief and something more that felt almost like hate. It had left Maggie exhausted. As they drove toward Collier she leaned back and closed her eyes in hopes sleep would come, but Richard broke the peaceful silence.

"It seems that the girl's mother and stepfather went to the Woods People meetings. That's the group that meets in the barn on Collier Thomlinson's property. I can't understand that man." He must be referring to the mystery writer Maggie thought.

Richard huffed and continued. "Why would he allow devil worshipers to meet on his land?"

"Perhaps the Woods People aren't the same group we've been hearing about." Maggie said, wanting to defend Collier in some way. "He's been gone for several weeks. Maybe he doesn't know about the group." She again tried to relax, but Richard wanted to talk.

"Well, they've been reported to the police. Someone on the northeast side of town had noticed signs of lights, or a fire in the deep woods that borders Lake Thomlinson and called to report it to the police. I've heard that an Irishman named Derrick Evans is head of the Woods People group. Some say he's had some kind of revelation that told him to be done with conventional organized churches. He was a Presbyterian before. The Woods People group is not a church at all, and it's certainly not Christian in any sense of the word. Somewhat heathenish, I'd suspect. Probably chant mumbo jumbo like one of those cults I've been talking about in my sermons."

"There was a feeling of evil in that house. Jessie seemed terrified of something."

"Well, maybe not evil, Maggie. Your active imagination has taken over. But they are definitely not going to listen to the word of God. Why, can you imagine a Christian not letting the authorities know about the death? Apparently to them, reality is like a television program. With a flick, their conscience is turned off. They've turned off the death and all the questions concerning it," Richard said.

"Richard, what a thing to say. How can you be so sure you're right? Perhaps all was done according to the law, or the people who saw the baptism trusted their leaders to do it right." The words burst from her lips. Never once in the three years she had known Richard, had she ever contradicted him or voiced what she thought. She'd always listened to him.

Richard frowned and looked sideways at Maggie before quickly turning back to execute a curve in the road. He slowly shook his head. "Maggie, those people back there are willing to let someone else do everything for them. They do not want the responsibility of having to make a decision for themselves. And I'd guess, they'd never listen to me preach about God— I'm not the right preacher. They're not ready for real commitment. Trust me. I know." He straightened the wheel and put on a little more speed.

Maggie clamped her lips together and, back to the days when she did not want to listen, closed her eyes, and pretended to sleep. This time, there was no way that she could discuss the needs of others being best served by the church community. But she had to admit that there was some truth in what Richard had said about the people being inclined to let their leaders do the thinking for them in certain circumstances, such as this boy's death.

While the two ate at a drive-in at the edge of town, they both avoided more discussion about the boy and his family. Richard kept up a running commentary on the new addition to the church, and none too soon for Maggie, they drove up in front of the Murphy home at eight-forty.

"I'd invite you in, but I know it's been a long day. Thank you for going to the wedding, Richard," Maggie said.

"It was a lovely wedding," Richard replied.

"See you in church," Maggie called as she walked away, leaving Richard sitting in his car at the curb.

Evelyn sat in the living room waiting. Learning that Richard was not coming in for a chat, Evelyn settled for a description of the wedding. She wanted to know all the colors and what wedding gifts they received.

"Did they like my Hadley casserole? It was more practical than something silver, but I believe they'll be living a simple life."

"They loved the casserole, got many nice pieces of silver, and Linda's brother Tim and his wife gave them flatware." Maggie quickly relayed the gift list, music, ritual, and refreshments of the reception, without the added suggestion that Linda's new husband was one of the wealthiest men in the state. Their life might retain a form of simplicity, but they would never worry about money. After an hour of questions and answers, Maggie pleaded exhaustion and went to prepare for bed. She'd said nothing about the death and the family in Etin.

"Well, did Richard ask you anything?" Evelyn stood at the door of the bathroom and watched as Maggie brushed her teeth.

"No, Mother." Maggie tapped her toothbrush against the sink more firmly than necessary.

"Why, I was so sure since you attended the wedding, got into the romance of the ritual, plus you had all of that driving time together." Evelyn's raised eyebrows punctuated the unasked question.

"Richard alluded to marriage, but I stopped the conversation before he would be embarrassed. I'm sure I could never love him and his feelings for me, unsure of them as he may be, could never be about married love. "Please don't worry about me. I feel under no obligation to catch a man." Maggie walked past Evelyn and went on into her bedroom, but before she closed the door, she attempted to nullify her mother's suppositions.

"Richard is a friend, that's all. And I believe deep down that's the way he wants it."

Her mother had followed her. "You're old enough to become serious. You've had your birthday and now must manage your trust, with my help of course. But, I won't be here forever, you know."

Again the old saw twanged. Maggie could hear Evelyn Murphy's remarks—"Why don't you do such and such? What will people say? I may die before the year is over. You know about my heart condition." Maggie had no desire to have her mother start a predictable conversation and especially about Richard's virtues right now. She was tired, and much more interested in thinking about Cole Thomlinson. What in the world had happened to him?

"Good night, Mother."

"Good nightie." Evelyn sang out from across the hall.

CHAPTER 9

On the morning Collier was to leave on his promotional trip he had been in the exercise room when the police department had called. Mrs. Tuttle had taken the call, and had talked to Don Stone, the chief of police. He'd given an update on the fires that Collier had requested. Don said that it looked like some of the fires had been deliberate, not an act of nature, and that the new church group that had been using the woods without permission might have been involved. The police were investigating.

As much as he disliked supervising the policing of his property, blaming his disinterest in business affairs on his father, Collier couldn't ignore the veiled warning the police message had conveyed. Collier called the chief for details. Then, he called Derrick Evans, as the leader of the people suspected of the fires, to join him for a talk.

That afternoon, airline tickets changed for the next day, and the first stop on his tour, Border's Bookstore in Dallas, having been called to inform the public relations staff of his delay, he unwillingly put aside his work, and wheeled himself into the drawing room to await the minister. At the grandfather clock's stroke of two, Robert announced the arrival of Mr. Evans. The man was ushered into the drawing room. They exchanged greetings, and Collier suggested that Derrick should sit down on the couch by the fireplace, then proceeded to move himself to a spot where he could face the visitor. Derrick Evans ignored the invitation to sit, and instead walked to the French windows.

"Nice view." The words were squeezed out as if the man's throat were coated with sandpaper. He turned, hands behind his back, and silently eyed Collier.

Collier rolled closer to the silent figure, and studied the Irishman. Evans was a tall man with thick arms that hung out and away from his barrel chest. Faded overalls hooked over wide, beefy shoulders covered a protruding belly and thick long legs. The Irishman's heavy, gray beard rounded a thin mouth, and covered his lower face and chin. Collier's scrutiny took only seconds before he again motioned the man to the couch.

"I like to have a man at eye level when I talk to him," Collier said.

Evans slowly walked over to the couch, and sat down with an audible grunt. His round flushed face, and rolls of fat visible under the T-shirt he wore, showed a man going to fat. Blunt fingers ran through thin hair, then raked over the bushy beard. He took a cigarette from his blue workshirt pocket, and started to light it.

"Sorry, I've an allergy that won't allow smoking in my home." Collier knew that the non-smoking mandate would not help the man's nerves. "We'll get this over with as quickly as possible. I won't detain you long."

Collier leaned forward, hands on his knees. "Mr. Evans, I understand that you are the leader of a small group of twenty some people who have started a church." He stopped.

"Yes, we've named ourselves the Woods People. The suggested name of the townspeople seemed to agree with us." Derrick crossed his arms across the shelf of his chest as if prepared to defend himself, but said no more.

"I own the woods northeast of here. Around the perimeter of that area is a tall wire fence topped with barbed wire. The gate on that side of the property has a sign on it that reads, Private Property. The area hasn't been a place where people can just walk in, drop camping gear and set up camp, but the

Thomlinson family has never denied anyone the use of the area for picnics and family outings if they ask."

Collier waited a moment to see if the man had something to add. Evans stroked his beard and sat looking at Collier with a sharp, steady look that belied the rest of his languid appearance. His eyes shifted from Collier to Mrs. Tuttle who had come to leave a pot of Green tea and scones on the table that sat between them. Collier rolled his chair to the tea table, where he poured him and Derrick a cup of tea and passed the watchful man the plate of warm biscuits. They both ate for a few minutes in silence. After a long drink of tea Collier looked over the rim at the minister and again spoke about the woods' incident.

"I understand that fires have been spotted, and sections of the woods have been leveled by fires. Many small saplings coming on to replace old trees have been destroyed." Collier spoke, and watched the man take a sip of tea. Evan's eyes darted away from Collier's stare like a skittish cat ready to bolt or attack at a moment's notice.

Collier decided to be more blunt. "If the fire department had not been alerted about fires on at least two occasions, more extensive damage could have been done to the property. I can't ignore the unlawful use of my property." Collier noticed a tightening of the bearded jaw. He continued. "Recently, when the fire and police departments were alerted to still another fire in the woods, they arrived at the site too quickly for the trespassers to clean up. Around the still burning fire, the officers found candleholders, a gong, a chalice, and a short wooden staff—all materials used in destructive rituals that would indicate some kind of Satanism was being practiced on the site." Collier's penetrating blue eyes stared at Derrick.

The man put his cup back on the serving tray, and started to get up, but stopped as Collier spoke. "Mr. Evans, your religious group has been suspected of being the trespassers. Some villagers believe your group is practicing some sort of devil worship."

"I've been wonderin' what you wanted to talk about." The self-appointed minister settled back down in the chair, and tilted his head toward the heavy growth of trees to the left of the house.

"Tis strange to be sittin' in your house, offered a cup of tea, when my group is being accused of settin' a fire in your woods." The throaty voice had a snapping cadence much like that of a bullfrog's croak. He concentrated on his hands that rubbed the polished wood of the chair arms as he spoke.

"You Irish?" Collier asked.

"Yeah." The man's bearded mouth spread into a grin, and when he raised his eyes to look over at Collier there was a glint of questioning humor in them. He seemed somewhat more relaxed, but for the hands that now curled tightly over each chair arm as if ready to push up and away at a moment's notice.

"I see. How did your church start? The few Irishmen around here are usually Catholic. Is this group a spin-off from Catholicism?" Collier had sensed Evan's unease, and had deliberately moved away from the fires to talk about the man's religious background.

Derrick Evans uncrossed his leg and sat up a little straighter. "My father was an ordained Presbyterian minister in Ireland. He was also a dairy farmer. I had a brother fifteen years older than I, who'd come over, and settled and died here in Collier."

The pride in his family and Irish background was evident.

"I stayed in Ireland with my mother and father. After my parents died, I stayed on with my wife, then I lost her to a terrible virus. I couldn't see much reason to stay in the old country any longer. I loved Ireland, but not the sad memories of my loved ones. I couldn't see much reason for church and prayer either. I came to the States, stayed in the East for awhile, moved here with a restlessness, but with no thought of gettin' back to religion. I joined the police force, thought I'd given up on God, but somethin' was missin' in my life. Somethin' was still missin' when I went to a church here in Collier. So I started a church with people who were searchin', or had like beliefs. I went from policeman to preacher." He smiled after he had finished the rather sketchy background of his religion.

Collier noted that the man had a rather kind face when he smiled and found that he was genuinely interested in Reverend Evans' new religion. "What beliefs do your people have?"

"In my hometown, Sixmilebridge in County Claire, kinship and friendship were synonymous. For instance, we had a custom of 'cooring'. It comes from the Irish word comhair, which means to help—lending a boy was practiced. That's when a lad from a family without a mowing machine would work free of charge for a local farmer with the equipment to mow and stack hay. Then that farmer would pay his debt, mowing for the man whose son had helped save the hay." He seemed to relax a little, picked up a biscuit and took a large bite. Apparently speaking of what he believed in was giving him confidence.

Collier asked, "Like the bartering of labor?"

"On that order." The minister wiped his hands on a napkin, and leaned forward a little. "The sense of community means a lot to me. I wanted to help others with or without pay. I saw that organized churches here had plenty of rules to follow, and lots of money was made for the running of the church. Charity money was given to other places, but little of it was saved for the folks of the church. The kind of helping that Jesus preached seemed unimportant."

"That statement may be somewhat harsh." Collier felt obliged to defend formal religion.

"Maybe. The ritual of our new church here in Collier includes cooring."

Collier found himself beginning to like the man. Not so much because of his beliefs, but for the fact that he stood for something bigger than himself. Apparently he had a mission to help those who had fallen through the cracks of formal religion.

"Our religion is not a cult of devil worshipers. We use no chalices, gongs, or any Satan worship rituals in our church." He stated this with eyes that sparked with resentment. He rubbed the back of his neck and added, "We've met in your woods, I'll say that. We've had fires, but none unattended. We just use fires to keep warm. We didn't ask permission what with you letting the town have rights to the snowhill, the carnival and all."

He'd looked steadily at Collier. "I've got an idea about who might have let a fire get out of control and do damage to your woods." Derrick retrieved his cup from the table, and took a deep drink.

Collier knew the group had to have seen the no entrance sign, and had gone into the woods without permission. He also believed the man was telling the truth about the ritualistic fires. Perhaps Derrick could help him nail the ones who did the damage to the woods. It was a trade off worth considering. He decided he would not confront the man about illegal entry.

"I'm in hopes you can tell me about the unattended fires, for I intend that those woods be preserved. It is a request of my great-grandfather that I wish to honor. Your people are on my land and having meetings. Fires, though well-attended, may do damage to the trees and surrounding brush." Collier leaned forward and slowly set down his cup. His eyes held Evans'.

"The bottom line is, Mr. Evans, that northeast side of the lake is private property, and I shall see to it that it stays that way." Collier paused, then added, "I have a job for you if you'll help me."

Derrick stroked his beard as if somewhat skeptical of what was going to be asked of him as he waited for Collier to continue.

"Since the fire scares, I believe it best if I hire a full-time watchman at the gate to keep vandals away. You've been a policeman. Would you want the job?"

"Me?" The word was squeezed out an octave higher. "Why, you just accused my group of setting those fires." White teeth appeared in the slit of a mouth behind the beard. "Seems you're thinkin' one thing, but sayin' another."

"I need someone to watch the property and if you are the watchman, I'll give your group permission to have their meetings there in the barn that's behind that last row of pines on the far side of the woods. I'll do something about heating the barn too," Collier said.

"And while I'm watching for fires there, who will be putting out the fires of resentment you'll have started?" Derrick Evans' chuckle was accompanied by a squinting of his eyes as if to imply he was pondering his own question.

"It's my right to enforce the rules about who uses my land and barn. But I could use your help. Think about it." Somehow, Collier knew they'd come to an agreement.

CHAPTER 10

It was Sunday, the next day after Linda's and John's wedding. Denny Wright's death had seemed to go unnoticed. Today, Richard had begun a series of sermons on admonishment of unusual practices and beliefs. A continuation of the discussions on cults was no doubt inspired by the recent incident in the Thomlinson woods. The power of belief as practiced by his flock was central to the Community Church minister's theme.

As they passed by Richard on the front steps of the church, praise for the morning's message flowed from parishioners' mouths, and floated skyward in white puffs of frozen air for it was sunny but still crisply cold. Maggie walked away from the church, considering Richard's message that seemed intended for the already faithful. The Woods People must have been the ones of whom he spoke when he accused some of rejecting Jesus' teachings, and claimed that they were unchristian.

How did Richard know for sure, and how wrong were they that were trying to change? Perhaps a deeper message would address God's acceptance of the sinner as well as the righteous man. Maggie was at a loss to understand the thesis of some religious convictions.

The truth was, it was not the church, but Richard who disturbed her. Richard was a good person. He attended to his congregation in Collier, but seemed rather distant with others who were not members of his church. How could he be so intolerant of those not of his flock? What happened to empathic understanding of those who don't know or understand the wonder of God's love? The book of Luke told Jesus' story of the shepherd going to find one lost lamb when the rest of the herd was safely home. And, as a matter of fact, how tolerant was she when she criticized a man of God that was devoting his life to God's teachings?

Questions without answers disturbed her thoughts as she silently drove her mother to the Fairchild House to meet Ginny Phillips for lunch. At the end of the service, Richard had announced the Murphy's fifty-thousand-dollar gift for the new church wing. While at the restaurant, Evelyn and Ginny eagerly discussed plans for the new building with the church friends who stopped at their table to chat, and to exclaim over the wonderful thing Maggie and her mother had done. The monetary gift they'd just made would not pave the way to the Kingdom of Heaven, but it certainly drew the admiration of church members.

"I've just heard that some people believe that the fires over by the lake were set by a Satan cult. Ginny says they call themselves the Woods People. You know, the one led by that Irishman Derrick Evans."

Evelyn filled Maggie in on the latest gossip inspired by the day's sermon as they walked to their car from the restaurant. When they got to the car, Evelyn asked Maggie to drive. Getting in on the passenger side, she pulled the heavy car door closed with a few grunts and put on her seat belt.

"Remember Richard alluded to something about staying away from those who worship false gods? Well, indeed, devil worship is certainly that. Let's go around to see where the fires were set," Evelyn suggested as soon as they had driven out of the parking lot.

"I wonder if intolerance and rejection are not devil inspired?" Maggie questioned as they drove past the main part of town, and on toward the northeast side of the lake where the last fire was discovered.

Ignoring the comment, Evelyn exclaimed, "It gives me the shivers to think of the rituals they perform. Why, do you know, some Satanists actually sacrifice chickens and goats just like the heathens did in the Bible?"

As they neared the entrance of the Thomlinson mansion, Maggie lifted her foot off the accelerator to slow the car before she made a right turn at the next street corner.

"Oh, don't slow down here! That awful Collier Thomlinson is in on the devil worship!" Evelyn exclaimed.

"What in the world do you mean?" Maggie asked as she drove by the wrought iron gate and turned right toward the lake. "It's like some people to gossip about the Woods People out of fear. And, out of jealousy, they've added Mr. Thomlinson to the list of believers. He probably has had nothing to do with the group other than the fact that he owns the land where they are meeting." Maggie was indignant enough to speak up.

"Well, Thomlinson gave Derrick Evans a job as the gate keeper on the northeast side of his property." Evelyn said.

The information surprised Maggie. She did not see Cole as one who would be exceptionally tolerant or charitable. It disappointed her for some reason to think that he might have more to do with the people that she'd presumed. Aloud, she asked if her mother would like to drive over to Etin with her.

"I want to see how Jessie Wright is doing," Maggie added.

"Is she the one who lost her son?" Maggie nodded, and Evelyn continued, "There's the lake where I heard the boy was drowned." She pointed to the lake just visible through the woods that they were driving by.

"Do you suppose the boy was drowned on purpose? Maybe it was some kind of ritual that went wrong. Look! There are some people coming out of that barn. Would you ever! I do believe that's where they meet," Evelyn rambled on as they drove by the property.

"Margaret Ann, do you have to go to Etin? I hate for you to get involved with anyone who attends those meetings."

"We don't know if Jessie Wright has anything to do with the group who have been meeting in those woods. And if we did hear she attended, I would bet we would learn she is not an active participant. She just doesn't seem to be the kind that would be active in much of anything. Anyway, she can use a little Christian charity." Maggie's patience was wearing thin.

"Well, I'll go with you. I certainly don't want you to go alone. Did you know that Clifford Wright was one of the leaders of those demonstrators who picketed Thomlinson Industries three years ago? Ginny says the man resents the family because he was fired over the protests. Maybe he set the fires in the woods. Margaret Ann, I'm afraid! Why can't we just stay away from the trouble?"

"If Mr. Wright is there, I won't go in. I'm not that brave." Maggie glanced at her mother reassuringly and the two women drove on in companionable silence the rest of the way to Etin, and down the main part of town to the Wright address.

The largest employer in the town, the Thomlinson Dairy, hired 150 people and bought milk from all of the surrounding farms in the territory. Maggie recalled hearing that several years ago, a union had tried to come in to the Thomlinson Industry in Etin. Only a few dairy employees agreed to demonstrate for the union and picketed. They used scare tactics to intimidate the rest of the employees and the company with acts of violence that had the authorities forcing them to stop. The protesters were given notice by the Thomlinson group and asked to leave. The union was kept out.

So Clifford Wright, Denny's grandfather, had been one of the ringleaders of the union group that fought the Thomlinsons. As much as she hated gossip, some was worth listening to. Her mother hadn't heard the whole story about Jessie, or Maggie's intuitive feelings about the situation, and Maggie was not about to reveal it now when they were on their way to Wright's home.

The Wright house came into view, and Maggie noticed that the old Cadillac, with the dented fender which had been parked at the curb a week ago, was not there.

"I'll see if Jessie is at home," Maggie said.

"And I'll stay in the car with the doors locked. This is certainly not in a very nice neighborhood, Margaret Ann."

"Yes, you lock the doors. I'll only be there for a short time and will leave the engine running so you won't be cold." Maggie jumped out, climbed the steps to the sagging porch, and walked up to the door.

Before she could knock, Jessie opened the door, peered out beyond Maggie to the automobile in which Evelyn sat, then glanced back at Maggie.

"Hi. There's no one here but me."

"Good." Maggie opened the screen door and waited for Jessie to invite her in. Jessie was hesitant and held the door halfway closed, as she looked again at Maggie's car.

"Jessie, I've come to see you. I've wanted to take you to lunch, but maybe we can visit here without being interrupted. There's no one but my mother in that car."

Jessie seemed to weigh Maggie's words, then smiled shyly and opened the door. "Come in if you've a mind to."

Maggie walked into the dingy living room. The blinds were still down, the room was in semi-darkness and the clutter was worse than before. Maggie sat down on a Naugehide chair that had metal arms and a sleigh-style base. Jessie followed, to sit on the couch by an ashtray, and immediately lit a cigarette with shaky fingers.

"Why did you come all the way over here to see me?" Jessie asked after taking a long drag and exhaling smoke into the stuffy, unventilated room.

"I was concerned about you. The loss of a child has to be one of the worst tragedies a person must face. I care that you hurt and, though you have to live with the pain, it might bring you some kind of relief if you could talk to me about it. I'd like to help you if I can."

Jessie's large gray-blue eyes filled, and she wiped the tears away with the back of her hand, taking a swipe at the long hair that limply fell across her face. "Thanks. I guess I don't have no one to talk to about it. Denny was a good boy. Not like some that attend those meetings."

"Meetings?" It was a question Maggie hoped would encourage elaboration.

"Yeah. It's a church group that meets every week in a barn, in a wood at the edge of Collier. Eddie Tuttle attended the church meetings, and Denny went with him. Denny don't have no religion. Don't believe he knew nothin' about the people; he just went cause his friend was going. It was kinda odd 'cause my stepfather, Denny's granddad Clifford, went to the group meetings too."

"I don't quite understand. Why was that odd?" Maggie asked.

"Clifford beat Denny up pretty bad some weeks passed, and Denny moved in with his friend Eddie. Denny was livin' with Eddie Tuttle and his parents."

What must have been several minutes passed while the girl sat listlessly taking quick, short puffs on her cigarette. Maggie remained silent trying to picture the events that must have led up to the boy's baptism. Why did Denny change his mind about belonging to the church group and being baptized? Is Eddie related to the housekeeper, Mrs. Tuttle? Her heart sank at the implication. If he was Mrs. Tuttle's son, perhaps Collier Tomlinson was somehow involved.

Aloud, she asked, "What made Denny change his mind about the church?"

"He never said exactly. But he did get real interested in goin' to church there. He went to Bible studies too. He'd come most Saturdays to see me. That is, he'd come whenever Cliff and my mom weren't here. I noticed he begun to clean himself up, kept a comb handy, and fiddled with keeping his hair nice." The girl smiled and lifted her chin in a proud, wistful sort of way.

The silence gathered around the two. If Maggie had ever wondered whether Jessie had been involved in the death of her own son, the love and pride that the young woman had shown today was enough to convince Maggie that Jessie had been a loving mother who wanted the best for her boy.

Jessie ground out her cigarette in a dirty ashtray and attempted to wipe up the overflow of ash. "Guess what I told him about bein' clean sort of soaked in after he got religion. Then, couple of weeks back, he came over and said he was goin' to join the church. He didn't say nothin about being dunked to do it. They mustn't have told him that part of belongin' 'cause he was real afraid of water."

Denny had only gone to the church because of his friend Eddie. Denny was fearful of water, yet agreed to the church's ritualistic immersion. Maggie tried to imagine the night of the tragedy, but dipping someone into the lake in the act of baptism seemed too innocent an act to have caused the drowning.

"How did he drown?" Maggie immediately wished she hadn't inquired. She'd not meant to have Jessie dredge up all of the sadness of that night.

"Don't know. I didn't go to see him get baptized, 'cause I had work to do here. I..." Jessie broke off with a sob. Maggie pulled a tissue from her pocket, and handed it to the woman. "Thank you. Seems you're always ready for us teary-eyed folks." Jessie smiled shyly through a screen of lusterless hair at Maggie.

Maggie's heart went out to Jessie. The woman had a quiet dignity that seemed somewhat out of place in her surroundings. Sitting here, discussing her dead son had to be difficult. Maggie considered leaving before asking anything else, but noticing the way Jessie looked at her as if waiting to talk more about that night, Maggie hesitantly asked.

"Jessie, can you tell me what happened to Denny?"

Jessie got up, picked up the ashtray, and went out to the kitchen. In a few minutes, she returned with a clean tin ashtray and lit another cigarette. She seemed to be considering the question, then brushed back her hair, took a deep breath and looked over at Maggie:

"Like I said he was awful afraid of water, didn't ever learn to swim. He drowned when they tried to baptize him." Her voice faded with the words. Maggie read her lips. "That's all Clifford said when he got home. Eddie and his folks come over the next day, but didn't say nothin. Maybe, 'cause Thelma and Clifford were here listening to us talk. It's hurt pretty bad that Clifford and other folks buried Denny right away. They didn't say nothin' to me." She shook her bowed head back and forth.

"Jessie, where does Denny's friend Eddie live?" Maggie asked.

"Tuttles live on tuther side of town near the depot station. Their house is the two-story gray one. Mr. and Mrs. Tuttle go to the Baptist Church here in Etin, but they're probably home now, church over 'n all." The girl looked expectantly at Maggie. "You goin' go see Eddie? I'd surely appreciate it if you did. I got to know how to put Denny to rest in my mind 'cause it just seems he's floatin' out there someplace. I need to know things so he can rest somewhere."

It seemed she'd walked into a plot as complex and full of knotty details as some of Mr. Thomlinson's mystery novels. Which led her to wonder at his part in this particular Lake Thomlinson plot. Again, she wondered if Eddie's mother could be the Mrs. Tuttle who had served Maggie tea that day at the Thomlinson's. She didn't want to know for sure, so didn't ask. Picking up her coat, she started for the front door. She stopped to look back at the girl who was following her. Jessie was saying something.

"Supposin' you'd call me after you talk to Eddie?" The pleading in the woman's eyes was as profound in meaning as would have been desperate words for help. Maggie gave her a quick hug, said she'd call her as soon as she knew anything.

Getting in the car, Maggie told her mother that she had one short stop to make. "It won't take long," she said.

"Oh, dear. I believe you should turn this over to the police. It's their job to take care of these things." Her mother showed her distress in the quick gasps of air she took before each word. Evelyn Murphy did not like confrontation.

"Mother, I won't be more than half an hour. Jessie Wright needs help, which means that I must see Eddie Tuttle. I don't know if he can tell me anything of importance in connection with Denny Wright's death. If there's something, I'll turn it over to the police."

Her mother took a deep breath, and the two rode the rest of the way in silence. They went past the deserted downtown area of Etin, the railroad station, and drove on to the gray house Jessie had described.

The Tuttle home was a wood-frame house with a small yard and freshly shoveled walk. A bright red pickup truck was parked in the driveway. Maggie got out of the car with a, "won't be long," trailing behind as she hurried up the steps onto the porch. At the right side of the open porch there was an old-fashioned swing gently swaying with the sharp winter wind. The image of sitting on the porch on a lazy summer day was pleasantly peaceful.

"Hello. Are you Eddie Tuttle?" She spoke to the young man who had opened the door and stood in the doorway.

"Hi, I'm Eddie. My folks aren't here. They went to Collier today." His smile was shy. He looked to be about sixteen or seventeen, wore thick glasses, and had a mop of curly black hair that some girls would die for. He was tall, thin, and very neat in his brown corduroys and dark green pullover sweater. Maggie took only a moment to evaluate him as a nice, introverted black youngster who was in the process of becoming a man, and showing evidence of it by the light stubble of hair on his chin.

"I've just come from Jessie Wright's, and would like to speak to you for a minute." Maggie tried to explain why she had come unannounced.

He shifted his weight, head bowed. With a nod, he opened the door and led Maggie into a pleasant room that was clean and neat. A pot of ivy hung over one curtained window. A group of philodendron plants clustered on a round table on the far side of the room. A wide picture window overlooked a large backyard with a fenced off section that looked to be the plot for a summertime vegetable garden. There were only the essentials of two overstuffed chairs, a couch, and a set of dining chairs around a cardtable. Three African violet plants, which sat on the surface of the small table by the couch, had a profusion of pink flowers adorning velvet leaves. The Spartan room, with its lack of ornamentation, except for the healthy green plants, was very different from that of the Thomlinson ornately decorated drawing room, yet Maggie got the same feeling of comfort and friendliness in the room. She could well understand why Denny preferred to live here after seeing the boy's own home.

From somewhere else in the house, Maggie could make out the beat of a drum and the sliding twang of a guitar that she recognized as hard rock music. It all but drowned out her words as she tried to explain why she'd come.

"Jessie said you'd come to her house, but she didn't get a chance to talk to you. I told her I would come and see if there was anything more you wanted to tell her about her son's death." Maggie waited expectantly.

Eddie yelled something over the blaring music. Maggie indicated she couldn't hear what he said. He left, the music dimmed, and he returned to motion for Maggie to sit down in one of two swivel chairs covered in flowered chintz material. He sat down in the other one and moved the chair so he would face Maggie.

"You a relative or somethin'?"

"No, I just met Jessie the other day when I went to the house with a minister after the accident. I care and want to help her if I can. It was an accident?"

"That's what's kinda' queer. I didn't actually see Denny go under. He drowned you know." Eddie leaned forward placing his elbows on his knees, and concentrated on rubbing his hands together. He cracked his knuckles for a few seconds, glanced up, then quickly dropped his glance back down to his hands, and laced them in and out as if to clean them.

"What did you see?" Maggie hoped she wasn't pushing him back into his shell. He seemed ready to bolt if she said the wrong thing. What a lot this boy had to overcome. His best friend had been killed in front of him. Like so many of the shootings and killings around the nation, she read about them and sympathized from a distance. But this death had happened in Collier. She'd had no real comprehension of what others had had to endure, until now.

Apparently he wanted to talk, for he placed his hands palm down on each knee and looked directly at Maggie.

"I was on the back side of the clearing by the others, who were getting ready to go into the barn after Denny got baptized. Inside the barn, they'd planned to have the rest of the ceremony."

Maggie couldn't quite picture the scene, but nodded as if she understood.

"I heard Denny cry out, then he yelled at the top of his lungs. Sometimes some folks get awful emotional when they're put under water at baptism time, but this time, it sounded like he was scared or being killed. You know?" Eddie again rubbed his hands back and forth on his knees, and stared at the frayed carpeting as if reliving the scene.

"I pushed through the crowd of people to the spot where Denny was bein' held by his granddaddy, Mr. Wright. Mr. Evans was standin' by sayin' somethin' about bein' born again. Mrs. Wright stood to one side of the three, and others had backed off a little for Denny was screamin' somethin' awful."

Maggie wondered how many people were watching the scene Eddie was describing, but she said nothing. She felt her own hands go clammy. "What happened then, Eddie?"

"Mr. Wright hit Denny on the side of his head, real hard, then he grabbed Denny's shoulders and pushed him under. Seemed like longer than a minute, but Preacher Evans always says a prayer or something, and it takes just about that long and he did, and old man Wright lifted Denny up and out of the water. Denny was all limp like—his head wagged, and his arms flapped. It seemed that there was no life atol. People kinda clustered around, and before I knew it, someone yelled that Denny was dead.

"I helped hold back the crowd while Preacher and Clifford were bent over Denny. Preacher Evans was pushing on Denny's chest and giving him mouth to mouth. He kept at it for quite a while. Finally, he got up and asked us all to pray for Denny, for he was gone to the angels."

The boy sucked in a breath on a sob, rubbed his lips roughly and squared himself in the chair. "Thelma and Clifford Wright walked away and just left him. I got another guy to help, and we put him in the body bag the preacher gave us. The preacher is a deputy policeman, and he and the town cop, Don Stone, who was there for the baptism, gave me permission to take the body to the church burial place."

Eddie sat for a minute just staring at the plant on the table. The music was playing. Maggie waited. After a while, Eddie looked over at Maggie as if to ask if she understood what he was saying.

She leaned over to lay a hand on his arm. "I know this is hard for you Eddie, but it does help to know what exactly happened." She wanted Eddie to explain how he was able to move the body so quickly, but didn't feel comfortable asking. The rituals of the Woods People church had to be a lot different than the Community Church, which ruled that a body could not be buried until the coroner had been informed of the death. There were also laws of the state to be considered.

Eddie swallowed hard and continued. "With help, I got Denny in back of my pick-up truck. I was gona' take him to his mom, but old-man Wright come up and said for me to follow him and the boys—Leo Gordon and two others. I did like he said and followed along behind Leo's truck to the Gordon farm some six miles south of town. Now, I had a sinkin' feeling that they'd planned to cremate Denny 'cause that's where the other Woods People who've died were cremated, by putting the boxed-up body in a pit."

Maggie felt her face drain of color and held up her hand as if to say she didn't want to hear what he was saying. Eddie quickly added, "Or buried them in a box, all legal like. Sure, sometimes they did that too."

He seemed concerned, and asked if Maggie needed some water. Nothing would help the feeling she had in the pit of her stomach. She shook her head with a weak "No thank you."

The young man eased up from his chair. Putting his hands in his back pockets, shoulders slumped, he stood studying the toe of his shoe. "I said I thought Jessie Wright would want to say good-bye to her son. Cliff said Denny looked so bad he didn't want Jessie to see him. I said again that I felt Denny's mom would like to see her boy, but the grandfather just got the others to get the body out of the backend of my truck, and they walked away with Denny. I drove off, feelin' bad about it all. I heard later they didn't cremate, just buried Denny.

"Course I knew it was the way of the Woods People to bury quick like. The soul's gone, body's an empty shell and all that, so being the grandpa and all, I figured he knew best whichever way. But I shouldn't have gone and let 'em do it." The young man shook his bowed head squinting hard to hold back tears.

Maggie swallowed hard. Disbelief and revulsion clogged her throat so she couldn't speak. Maggie hesitantly asked, "Do you think he drowned, Eddie?"

"I don't know for sure, maybe I never will. But I believe that blow Clifford gave Denny knocked him out so's how he did drown, or else the blow killed him. I hate to think it, but that's just about the way I see it." Eddie slouched back down in his chair.

Maggie didn't know where to go from here. Surely others had seen what this boy had seen. Why didn't some others come forward with the story? Apparently the police believed it to be an accident. But why had they rushed off to bury a boy who died under suspicious circumstances?

Aloud she asked, "Have you talked to anyone about this? Your folks? A friend?"

He whispered, "No." Maggie understood the word he said by reading the boy's lips.

He looked at her. "My folks'd gone to get supplies for spring planting. I didn't bother them. They was too upset about the whole thing. Told me not to go to no more meetings. Guess they had funny feelings about the bunch, and were havin' second thoughts about me goin'. They'd felt real bad for Denny too, bein' as how he was livin' with us and all. But guess they thought it best to keep their peace—so to speak. They don't talk much to folks anyway." Eddie wiped his eyes with the back of his hand, and wiggled in his chair like a cat trying to get comfortable. "No, don't think of no one to talk to except Mrs.Wright."

"Denny's mom, Jessie?"

"Yea, the other one, Denny's grandmom is a real weird one. She never did say nothin' and she's the grandma. Guess there's somethin' wrong with her."

"And Mr. Wright?"

"Well, I couldn't go to him and say I thought somethin' 'cause maybe I was wrong and Denny did die natural like, him bein' involved and all."

Eddie had moved to sit up straight. He had a surprised look as if something had just come to him. "I didn't even talk to Preacher Evans. He did approve me taking Denny, but guess I should have talked to him after that night." The boy stood up, rammed his hands in his pockets and walked out of the room. The beat of the music changed, but was still hard rock.

He came back to stand in the doorway. She hastily got up. "I must leave." With stomach churning, she quickly went to open the door to get some fresh air, leaving Eddie to follow.

Maggie turned back to the boy. "I wish you could see Jessie Wright. She needs to know about what happened. It might help her. Do you suppose you could talk to her without her folks being around?"

"I'll try. And Ma'am, I'm glad I got this off my chest. I didn't rightly know how I'd live with it much longer." His sad smile touched her.

"Thank you," Maggie said and left.

Walking slowly back to her car, she skimmed over his story, and wondered if he may have wanted to say more. Maybe she should have pushed him to describe the scene again in more detail. But no, she couldn't stand to hear a more graphic picture of the blow Denny must have received from his step-grandfather, or a more vivid picture of the quick burial before the mother saw her boy. It had been a thoughtless and cruel act. She shuddered. How did investigative law officers do their job?

While getting into and starting the car, questions still swirled. Surely there's a law about a death certificate, and where is the father? Where does he fit in the unhappy household, and this tragic event? She drove away from the house oblivious of her mother who sat beside her.

"Well, what was that all about? Honestly, you leave me in the car where I almost freeze and now, halfway home, you still say nothing. Sometimes I get very tired of your silences, young lady." Evelyn Murphy jerked the fur collar of her coat up closer to her neck.

As if coming out of a daze, Maggie slowly noticed that Evelyn had put her needlepoint away and was waiting to hear a blow by blow description of what had taken place, but there was no way Maggie could reveal what she'd learned. Not just yet, and especially to her mother, who would go straight to the phone and call Ginny Phillips. It was too hard for her mother to resist telling news to a friend.

"I'm not sure what it was about and until I do, I can't talk about it. I'll tell you later." Maggie's voice was hushed.

"Well, that's not an answer. I'm your mother for heaven sake. If you can't tell me, whom can you tell?"

"I wish I knew, mother. I sincerely wish I knew."

Maggie turned on the wipers to sweep away the large flakes of wet snow that pelted the windshield as she guided the car through slush, and past fields with bald patches of thawing ground. This gray March day reflected the sadness of the affair—a Christian ritual that became a heathenish nightmare. Even if the Woods People group wasn't a cult, they were certainly tempting the devil with their rituals.

"Maybe this wet snow will change to rain." Maggie's words, though barely audible, were a feeble attempt to make light conversation. The effort was met with silence.

Maggie steered the car the eighteen miles until at last they were home. Driving up to the curb in front of their house, she parked, and turned to her mother. "The library is open until five. I'll go by and get a book I need."

As she watched the tiny woman walk to the house, Maggie felt a stab of regret that she couldn't share what she'd learned with the most important person in her life. But it was best to not share thoughts concerning Collier Thomlinson or the question of murder to her mother. But whom could she talk to?

Thinking of the past days, Letty had been very solicitous since the lavender book incident. It was almost embarrassing how the librarian followed Maggie around the row of stacks, asking if she could help in any way. She also seemed to enjoy talking about Reverend Richard every chance she got. Letty had even asked Maggie to have coffee at the drugstore one day so they could discuss different aspects of the building program, about which the woman had seemed very well informed—Letty and Richard? What an item that would be for the gossips. The thought brought a smile to Maggie's lips.

As soon as Maggie got into the library, Letty held up a book, and motioned for Maggie to come to the checkout desk. "Here it is. Mr. Thomlinson was very emphatic that I should hold this book for you."

Maggie took the book with a smile, and walked back to her spot with her mind still filled with echoes of Eddie's words. A piece of paper fell out of the book Letty had just given her—*Good reading! Sorry I kept it so long* and the initials, GCT. She stared at the note for a moment. Collier Thomlinson! Why not talk to him about the death? Eddie's mother worked for him. He'd hired Mr. Evans to police the grounds of his home. Her optimism surged.

"Letty, may I use your phone?"

CHAPTER 11

"Come in. Come in. See, I'm so anxious to see you that I open the front door myself." Collier Thomlinson greeted Maggie at the door of his home, laid her coat and scarf on his lap, then ushered her into the French drawing room where she had visited before.

"It's nice to have a chance to see this lovely room again." Maggie smiled at Collier as she walked over to the fireplace to warm her hands. With her back to him, she asked, "Does Derrick Evans work for you?"

"Well, so much for believing you came only to see me." A smile curved with the arching of brows. "Yes, Evans is on my payroll. Why?"

"I'm not sure." Maggie turned to look at Collier who had wheeled over to her side. "I've heard some disturbing news and, since the man involved in the report is employed by you, I thought you might be able to help me."

"Sit down. I'll get us a little something. It's Mrs. Tuttle's and her husband's day off and my valet, Robert, is away. In fact, Derrick Evans just left about a half-hour ago. He's filling in, bringing in wood, heating up food and such. Pity he's not still here." Collier stumbled through the explanation of his help, and stopped with a questioning look.

"Yes, I wish he were." She hesitated to tell the employer of the minister. Would Cole think her crazy when she told him what she'd heard, or worse, think she was pushing herself on him?

He spoke, "Please, how can I help?"

"I'd hoped you could." She hesitated not knowing how to start. When she looked up, Cole was leaving the room. Maggie watched him leave. His leaving the room was certainly a reprieve, for she was still unsure of his part in the affair, and didn't know how to pursue the conversation.

The last time she'd been here there had been a fresh arrangement of lilies and lavender in a fluted vase on the table by the door. Today, there was a stemmed arrangement in the vase and some of the fresh flowers were lavender. She smiled, remembering, "To the lovely Lavender Lady". He'd signed that in her book. The book signing and dinner evening in Royal had been such a bittersweet experience for her. Bitter, because of the lingering guilt for having drunk too much and having kissed him, almost a stranger. Sweet, because she felt such happiness remembering their conversation in the restaurant. But why hadn't he called her? It must have meant little to him. What a fool she was to think he would help her with Jessie. She walked over to the settee where he'd placed her coat.

At the same moment, Cole reappeared with a tray on his lap filled with tea biscuits, dishes, cups and a steaming pot. "The sweets were prepared yesterday by Mrs. Tuttle, and the water was heated before Mr. Evans left. As you can see, I've added a cup for you. Tea is good for the nerves. I feel nervous. Do you?"

Maggie clutched her coat. She was nervous but had no idea why he should be nervous. Perhaps it was because he had no desire to see her again. *Well, here I am in your face!*

She dropped her coat on the chair, and determinedly walked over to take the tray of biscuits and tea from his lap. Putting it on the table as Mrs. Tuttle had done the last time Maggie was there, she asked, "Is this where you want it?"

"Yes, there will do. Now, pour us some of that Jasmine tea, and tell me all about it."

She obediently poured two cups of tea, asked if he took sugar, which, at the nod of his head, she added, and handed him a cup. She then seated herself in the fireside chair across the table from his wheelchair, as if it were a daily ritual for her to preside over the tea table in this man's home.

"I've just come from Eddie Tuttle's home." Maggie waited. Cole said nothing.

"He was with the group the night that Denny Wright drowned." There was still no comment from Collier.

"There was a drowning on Sunday. Eddie Wright was being baptized in your lake and died. It was a Woods People ritual and Mr. Evans is their leader.

Now a definite response as Cole put down his cup and leaned forward with a questioning, "Yes?"

"I believe Eddie has some doubts about the death. He didn't come out and say it, but I got the impression that he thought Denny might not have drowned. The boy might have been dead before he was dunked in the lake. And to compound it, Clifford Wright, the step-grandfather and some others may have buried the body without permission from the authorities. It seems there is a ritual the Woods People perform. They must dispose of a dead person before sunset of the next day of the death, but there were only four men involved in this burial rite. The mother, Jessie Wright, wasn't even in attendance. And too, Denny Wright may have been buried before the coroner signed the report."

Collier's frown seemed to suggest that he was trying to make sense of what she had just said. His frown made Maggie question what she'd just told him. Perhaps she'd read too much into what Eddie had told her, but she did have the feeling that Eddie thought the drowning was questionable. She picked up her cup, set it back in the saucer. The pulse in her throat made it impossible for her to swallow. She darted a glance down to the rug, over to the fireplace, then to the winter snow scene outside the windows as if trying to avoid Collier's penetrating gray-blue eyes.

After a long silence, Collier spoke. "I spoke to Mr. Evans before I left on my book tour about some fires in my woods. Derrick denied it was the Woods People. I believed him, and hired him to keep trespassers out of my woods. In return, I told him that he and his group could meet on my property."

"I'd wondered why Derrick Evans' group was allowed access to the woods." Hesitantly, she continued before he could say anything. "The incident occurred just this past Friday evening. The night the boy died, Mr. Evans was there as were the grandparents of the boy. I've become involved because I went with our minister to talk to the bereaved family after Denny's death. The boy's mother, Jessie, seemed so lost somehow, as if there were no one to talk to. I took it upon myself to return to the home this afternoon."

"You saw her?"

"Yes, I visited with her. While I was there, she asked me to go and talk to Eddie, and you've heard the rest." Having thus explained herself, her tension dimmed. It was good to have shared the story with Collier. It was too much to keep to oneself, just as it had to have been too much for Jessie and Eddie to handle alone.

"I've been gone, just returned last night as a matter of fact, somewhat of a recluse anyway, don't hear or keep up with the local news. I do recall that the Devil's Backbone Winter Carnival was called off. I've never entered into any of the carnival arrangements, so didn't pay much attention to the details of that event—just glad people enjoy that old hill." He reached over for a biscuit and offered one to Maggie who refused with a shake of the head. He continued:

"Derrick Evans called me while I was gone. It seems that the town's people have been up in arms about the fires and the stories about some cult group. Some citizens were coming to Derrick threatening to burn down my barn where the Woods

People had been meeting. I could not return, but asked Derrick to go to the authorities, with my approval, and suggest there be a called meeting to talk about the situation. He told me in a later call that a bulletin was sent out, and Derrick convinced the many who attended that the Woods People was a viable group, a religious community, and most importantly, were good Collier citizens who respect the law. He told me not to worry. Anger and fear were quelled, and community spirit was revived."

"I haven't heard about the meeting. Mother and I must have been in Chicago when that took place."

Cole's gaze remained distant. He swiveled the chair to look outside almost as if he'd forgotten she was there. At last he turned back around. "I hadn't heard about the drowning until now. I'm surprised by what you've just told me, but if this questionable information gets out before the truth is known, it will be worse.

He rolled over to the table and put his cup on the tray. "Perhaps I should talk to Evans before the populace is again stirred up by suspicions. You say this happened just two nights ago?" Maggie nodded.

He asked as if to himself. "How in the world did they keep it so quiet?"

"I wondered the same, but believe the burial was not known by too many. I'm guessing that Clifford Wright and his family are somewhat shunned by the Woods People group and, being rather reclusive themselves, those that were there ignored rather than become involved." Maggie tried to explain.

She realized that there were a lot of holes in her theory about the people remaining silent. Silence-among-thieves came to mind, but maybe Derrick Evans could clear that up too. That's why she'd come, to talk to Cole before going to the police. He'd understood her concern before she could voice it. She added:

"I don't listen to gossip, but when I heard of this incident first hand from Eddie, I knew I had to do something. Is your Mrs. Tuttle related to Eddie?"

"She's Eddie's mother. I've not seen her since my return. I'm sure she'll tell me if she knows anything about this incident." With a shrug of the shoulders, Collier's smile dimmed to a frown. For a few moments he searched Maggie's face, then he leaned forward in his chair.

"You came to me thinking if I was not involved with these sorry circumstances, I might still have some ideas about procedure since I'm a mystery writer. Is that it?"

He settled back in his chair, folding his arms over his chest. "Sorry to disappoint you. The mysteries I write are strictly fiction, not based on fact, and this particular mystery has all the makings of a child abuse segment in the news-hungry papers. I'm surprised it wasn't picked up as such."

He leaned forward again. "Is that the only reason you came to me?"

The intensity of Collier's stare struck sensitive nerves, and drew her to him as if they were fellow conspirators. Should she tell him that she trusted him after that night when she'd had too much champagne and he'd remained a gentleman? Or that she'd wanted to see him again and this was an excuse to do so?

Her face flushed. She had to move, break the spell, and abruptly got up to go over to the French doors. With her back to Collier, Maggie studied the frozen lake that glistened with the same silvery shade as the penetrating blue eyes of the man behind her. A pair of enormous birds dipped and circled, looking for food in the depths of the freezing water.

Without turning, she belatedly answered his question. "I came to you because I believed I could talk to you about this. I don't have anyone to whom I can tell such a story." She could see his reflection framed in the long glass window, and was startled when his narrowed eyes locked on hers in the reflected scene.

"What about that minister who brought you to the author evening? Isn't a man of God suppose to be trustworthy?"

She lifted her chin. He raised a hand. "I'm sorry. I don't know the man. I'm glad you felt you could confide in me. Come here, please."

Maggie turned and slowly walked to him. For a moment, they looked at each other as if in challenge. Cole was the first to break the spell. "I'll talk to Derrick Evans. Would you like to be here when I talk to him?"

"Yes I would." Maggie quickly answered and sat down once more by the table across from Cole.

After a slight pause, Cole said, "Perhaps Mrs. Tuttle may be able to help Jessie in some way. I'll call you about the meeting with Evans."

Maggie was quick to answer. "No, please, let me call you," and took a last sip of tea. "It's after seven and I must go. My mother is expecting me."

He picked up the tea tray. "Now, tell me, do you know how to make scrambled eggs? I'm a hungry man. You may fix the evening meal that we'll share. Come this way."

He looked her way with a slight lift of brows, then held up a hand as if he'd just thought of something. "You'll have to excuse my style. I'm used to giving orders. Let's start again— Would you please stay so I can show you my kitchen? I believe you have an interest in that particular area of a house."

His attempt to beg pardon was awkward, but his smile was endearingly sweet. Besides she was curious to see the kitchen of such a spacious dwelling.

She nodded acceptance. He rolled out of the room with Maggie following behind. They passed through three workrooms, an open room that seemed to be a sitting room for the staff, and on into an enormous turn-of-the-century kitchen. Delft tiles bordered the sterile white room with its navy-blue and white tiled floor. A wrought-iron range, which on closer inspection was a white, most modern Aga stove trimmed with stainless steel, dominated one wall along with floor to ceiling Thermidor ovens. This state-of-the-art-in-cooking equipment was obviously new to the kitchen, as were the side-by-side Thermidor freezer and refrigerator, which gleamed from their place. Brass kettles and pans hanging above a long, wood-block table were more the mansion's vintage, and gave the spacious room a feel of solidness, of timelessness, of former days when herbs were dried from the hooks still evident above the windows. And deep metal sinks with curved faucets ornately carved to resemble swans' necks, had surely been a part of the original design.

Maggie could only imagine what tales of feasts this important room of the household could tell. It seemed almost sinful to be a kitchen in which meals were prepared for just one person.

"Please call your mother, tell her you're doing your Christian duty by helping a poor soul. You can do that can't you?" He called back to her as he proceeded to a panel on a side wall, and flipped switches that flooded the large room with tube lighting around the ceiling, and turned on spots that lit special work stations: the stove, refrigerator, salad and cutting board areas.

"They're all here." Collier made a sweep with his hand. "All the necessities for creating gastronomic delights. There's the phone too." He pointed to the telephone on the desk. "This ravenous gourmand shall await the feast the chef will prepare." He bowed his head to her.

She smiled. "It won't be a seven-course dinner, but I'd enjoy fixing those scrambled eggs you mentioned with a few of my own herb touches. But first, I'll call Mother."

Cole rolled out of the room, leaving her alone. She walked around the room, curiously touching the counters, checking the gas burners on the stove, peeking into the refrigerator which seemed very well stocked with fresh vegetables and herbs. After a quick look in the freezer, she had a plan for their meal. Eagerness to cook was dampened after she'd dialed the phone.

"You what?" Evelyn Murphy's shout vibrated in Maggie's ear. She held the phone away, but could still hear her mother's loud laments about coming home, not staying with that awful man.

"Mother, I'll be home after dinner. I'll tell you all about it when I get there."

Words poured on as Maggie held the receiver away from her ear, allowing only snippets of warning: "A cult leader...Ginny says pornographic..."

"Yes, mother." Maggie slowly lowered the phone to its cradle as she chuckled to herself. She'd never heard or read of lavender being used for devious purposes. And if Ginny Phillips thought Cole's books so pornographic, how did she know unless she'd read them? And why did she read them if she knew? The whole circle of questions came back to the same conclusion—it was all supposition, not any of it based on fact. She'd read two of Cole's books and they were not objectionable.

Before she could change her mind about staying for dinner, Maggie hurried back through the maze of rooms, and stopped at the entrance to the dimly lit drawing room where Collier sat close by the fireplace, gazing out the window. The sky was drained of light, leaving only a tinge of pink under a thin gray layer of fast moving clouds.

"Well, I'm staying." Maggie's voice shook with emotion she couldn't control.

"And did your mother approve?" He didn't wait for an answer, only shrugged his shoulders as he added, rather indifferently. "You're a lady. I promise to be a gentleman at all times."

Maggie ignored his remark and quickly described the dish she was preparing. "It's an omelet dish that can be varied to include shrimp, ham or spinach. It usually has Harvarte cheese, green pepper, curry and a touch of any health herb I might choose."

"Such as?" He interrupted.

"St.-John's-wort is for depression, Echinacea is for colds, dried blueberries may help stomach woes and is an arthritic preventative. But since your cupboards don't seem to have such additives," she grinned, "I'll make the eggs with other ingredients that I saw in the refrigerator." She lifted a brow and smiled at Cole. "Of course, herbs that have medicinal qualities are better for the individual if taken internally as a tea, which is a brew you enjoy, I've noticed."

"Yes, I do enjoy a cup of tea, and like to share one whenever possible. It's a relaxing way to visit. However, I don't know much about medicinal uses of tea."

"I'm learning about their medicinal properties and plan to plant an herb garden this spring to try different formulas." Maggie's heart jumped—that's exactly what she wanted to do.

"Don't get too carried away with those formulas — fatal attraction, you know." They both laughed.

Returning to the kitchen, Maggie continued to describe other tea herbs while Cole listened as if he were truly interested.

"Do you want to eat here in the kitchen, or in front of the fire in the drawing room?" Cole asked.

Maggie had trouble hearing his question, but guessed as he'd gestured to the other part of the house. "In the drawing room, please."

"Good, I'll set the table." Cole rolled out of the kitchen to the pantry.

With a few choice words of grumbling, he complained that his housekeeper apparently hid eating equipment in inconvenient, quite ridiculous, locations that had him using a hide and seek formula for finding silverware, plates and napkins. He finally had all assembled cutlery and dishes on a large tray and proceeded to carry all to the drawing room, calling back that he'd find a suitable wine for their meal.

***

"You made a basic meal special with your combination of herbs in the omelet. I liked the baked tomatoes layered with brie cheese—warm rolls too. And the spinach salad with herb vinaigrette dressing was most unusual and delicious. Were there dried cranberries in the salad?

"Yes, I added the cranberries to the spinach and walnuts before I found the can of Mandarin oranges—decided to use both fruits with the spinach. The herb dressing had a very light pinch of sage and cinnamon. Sage is not the usual herb used in a tart dressing, but I find just the smallest use of it enhances the flavor, without being overpowering." Maggie put a finger on her goblet before Cole could pour her more wine.

"I'm glad you liked everything. Working in your wonderful kitchen with Mrs. Tuttle's excellent selection of staples, I couldn't go wrong. I'll bring some dried herbs from my garden to replace what I used, plus a few extras that Mrs. Tuttle may enjoy using." She glanced at her watch to see that it was not yet eight.

"I didn't have time to make a dessert, but did find some chocolate mousse in the refrigerator that Mrs. Tuttle apparently made for your dinner."

"Excellent. Let me carry our dishes to the kitchen, then we can enjoy our tea and chocolate confection," Cole said and drained the rest of his white wine.

Stacking the dirty dishes on the large tray, the two went back to the kitchen. Maggie immediately began to rinse and put the dishes in the dishwasher over Cole's protest that Mrs. Tuttle could clean up in the morning.

Maggie ignored him. How could she leave such a lovely kitchen even with the small clutter of their meager meal? He reluctantly helped by putting the butter back in the refrigerator, handing her the used skillet, and rolled around in the way, until Maggie politely asked him to let her finish. At last, with counters spotlessly clean, and stainless steel gleaming, they returned to the main room of the house accompanied by the dessert, and the ever-present pot of tea and two cups. Cole placed his chair by the tea table opposite Maggie, who had chosen the damask covered couch by the fireplace.

He studied her for a moment. "Do you go to this Richard person's church?" He asked and flicked his gaze to the fire, but not before she saw a flash of irritation in his eyes, and noted the clenched jaw.

"Yes. He's the pastor of the Community Church, which I attend. And you?"

Cole glanced at her with a slight smile and quizzical lift of his eyebrows. "I don't go to church. Do you think that disqualifies me from believing in a Supreme Being?" He moved over to lift a dry log and place it on the dimming fire.

For a moment she sat listening to the crackle of logs being lapped by hot flames as she considered his question. He seemed one who had an inner strength she would call belief, but she couldn't pass up the challenge his question presented.

"It doesn't disqualify you from believing in God, but one is benefited in many ways by attending a worship service."

"How?" He moved around the small tea table to sit facing her.

She looked for the smirk, a sly smile, but the smile accompanied by raised brows seemed to imply interest in learning why anyone would take the time to go to church.

"If I don't attend church, take part in the ritual, the need to live a Christian life is dimmed."

"So the act of commitment replenishes one."

Her explanation must have seemed simplistic to a doctor of letters. No matter, her faith was much more than a commitment. Maggie felt compelled to defend her beliefs.

"Besides the need to replenish and enrich my spiritual growth, I need to be accepted. And people of my faith, in my church accept me," she said.

"That kind of need is limiting to one, I'd imagine." Cole rubbed the palms of his hands together, studying them for a moment before he resumed:

"I ramble a bit when I get into the tangle of needs one feels one must have. You say you need the acceptance of the chosen few of your particular church. Perhaps your churchgoing fulfills your need—the human need for confidence, normalcy, ease with people." He seemed to weigh each word carefully, as if trying to reach a conclusion about churchgoing.

She murmured, "I didn't hear all of what you said."

He looked at her questioningly, then repeated what he'd said in pretty much the same words.

Maggie sighed, "Well, I've not met my personal confidence goal. And normalcy is really just a term isn't it? And as for my ease with people, the occasion pretty much dictates my comfort level." She smiled at him. "You put me at ease, as does my dear friend Linda, who is totally deaf."

She shrugged, "I'm deaf too. Or, considered partially so. After years of semi-silence, I've had corrective surgery. Now, I can hear fairly well, but during the non-hearing years, I had to be very observant to understand others. I appreciated my church members being patient with me. And Linda has been my friend since we went to deaf school together."

"My dear God. How little we know. I didn't realize you were deaf." His voice soothed as he placed his hand over hers for a moment, then leaned back in his chair with an audible sigh.

"And being in the minority, different than most, if you will, could that have been the reason for your church friends' empathy? Do you think that you receive their empathy because of your difference?"

"I hope my being different, as you call it, has not been the reason people have been caring. I do know that my deafness has made me more aware of others' difficulties, and has enhanced my understanding of the differences in all people."

"I've sensed that in you," he said with conviction.

The silence they shared was filled with unheard murmurs and thoughts as the two sat gazing into the fire. Maggie thought she'd never been so attracted to a man as she was to Cole, and wondered what it was that attracted her so.

After a time, she asked the way to the powder room, Cole led her across the hall and disappeared. When she returned to the drawing room, Cole had swung his wheelchair closer to the fireplace. Since his face was averted, Maggie enjoyed watching the play of firelight sharpen the angles of his cheekbone and jaw and throw a wavering shadow beneath his wide-set eyes. She imagined the fire's glow in those eyes.

Her smile became a frown as she watched the silent figure suddenly throw aside the coverlet, and saw the steel-braced legs. He grabbed two ski-like poles from the wall at the side of the fireplace, slipped his heavily muscled arms into their metal straps, and tightly gripping the padded handles of the poles, he pulled himself up and out of the wheelchair. With a grunt of satisfaction, he adjusted the straps on each arm, then maneuvered the rods so he could swing his body back toward Maggie. The amazing, mercurial procedure of lifting his body from the chair had taken only seconds to perform.

Watching a six-foot-three man rise from a wheelchair was much like watching the miracle of a butterfly slipping out of its cocoon. Maggie was awed. She could not tear her gaze from the powerfully built, lean and handsome man, who stood so proudly in front of her.

"My dear, I don't mean to startle you. This is a daily ritual of a different sort that I perform." He chortled, apparently at his play on the word ritual. A lingering soft smile and gentle look over his brows were directed to Maggie.

"It is a commitment that has meaning for me, because it shows me how I've progressed."

Lifting his shoulders, and gripping the stabilizing canes, he adjusted his stance just a bit before he added, "I received a spinal cord injury in a bicycle-truck collision that resulted in paralysis. The lumbar vertebra level was affected, which is the upper motor neuron lesion. Lesion refers to the injured area of the spine."

"But you're standing." Her voice was hushed.

"I suppose this does call for an explanation." Cole chewed on his lower lip.

"My injury is associated with the Brown-Sequard lesion syndrome. I do have some use of parts of my anatomy." He paused for a moment, avoiding eye contact, then continued:

"Since central cord lesions have a high probability of recovery in the lower extremities, I've been encouraged to not give up hope of change for the better. But so far, I can't sustain the use of my muscles long enough to pleasurably or even laboriously walk. I use leg braces for stability so I can twice daily do this exercise. It upsets my angular parts, and encourages the gravitational flow of blood. It gives my body a chance to stretch, and me the chance to show off in front of a beautiful woman.

"Now, back to the subject at hand." Cole braced himself more firmly on the metal canes. "I'm flawed. So, like you, I recognize those who are kind. But I do wonder why we flawed ones receive empathic understanding, while others who are whole may not?"

His question belied the strength and determination he displayed. Maggie answered quietly, "You're not flawed, but beautifully whole. There's something deep about you, and subtle."

Again he wore that cryptic look with the one-sided grin. Maggie ignored the look and added, "I've wondered at times why I receive so much attention. I suppose, partially anyway, that I somehow fulfill that need of people to be kind."

Cole looked doubtful as he asked, "So those of us with disabilities are the sponges that absorb that need of the physically sound?" Before she could reply he added with a note of irony, "They're either overly kind, or reject us."

As if to himself he continued, "I learned rejection at an early age. My parents, other relatives, and their friends idolized me. I was a good athlete and a precious, only child, so they turned me into some sort of super person. But after the accident, I was no longer praised or pursued by others than my parents. I'd had my time in the sun, and was cast aside before I was given a chance to show that I could possibly be even more. No, others did not want to think about my kind of difference. I was not the vehicle for kind treatment. I must have seemed as foreign to them as this idea of a cult in Collier is to me. Embarrassment has something to do with it I imagine."

After a period of silence, tightly holding his weight on the strong columns of steel, Collier carefully turned away from the fire, and stood looking out at the lake with his back to Maggie. She wanted to go over and wrap her arms around the waist of this proud man. What determination and discipline it had taken for him to become the person he was.

He spoke loudly, for her benefit she realized, as his back was still to her. "At school in England, the word practical was capitalized. All of my schooling and philosophical studies were based on the PRACTICAL. It is a form of perfectionism, I should think, and possibly only a peculiarity of English schooling. I guess that's why I enjoy adding a little whimsy to the stories I write. The silliness or fun included in my writing takes away my fear of intense practicality." Collier slowly turned back toward her, lifting his shoulders as if to question his method of coping.

Maggie remained silent and watched as he propelled himself hand over hand back to his wheelchair. Sitting down, he took the supports from his arms, lifted his legs so he could put his feet on the footrest, and covered his metal-braced limbs with the lap robe. Smoothing the robe with his hands, eyes down, he spoke barely loud enough for Maggie to hear:

"I studied, then taught. What an ego I had to feed. I might add that it was nourished by frustration, for I did attempt the impossible at times. 'Sooner strangle an infant in its cradle than nurse unacted desires'. William Blake wrote that. What trivia I've learned."

Snips of sound—sizzling wood, short breaths, the moving wheels as Collier rolled himself over to pour himself more tea—broke the silence. He raised an eyebrow questioningly to

Maggie. She nodded yes, and he moved to fill her cup, then lifted his cup in a kind of salute before taking a long drink.

His mood changed with a smile. "Well, I found the scraps to throw to my unquenchable ego. I have my writing and it fulfills me." He grinned at her. "How did you choose a career?"

His mood-switch from serious, to light and back to her had Maggie confused. "Why do I write cookbooks?" He nodded. She thought for a moment, then slowly explained, "I write because of a need to be productive, but I'm not sure that writing cookbooks is what I really would like to do. I've wanted to do more with my writing, but I've not done it. In that way, I've let myself down I suppose."

She smiled with a shrug as she set her cup back on the tray and proceeded to fold her napkin as a clue to the fact that she would be leaving soon. "I must seem indecisive to you."

"It's necessary to be productive." Cole smiled. "Actually, Maggie, I find you enchanting the way you are."

He cleared his throat and swung around to move to the end of the room close by the piano. Flipping a light switch, he moved to the side so Maggie could get the full view of the small painting on the piano top.

"This is my favorite painting of my mother. The one of her in the hall is quite stiff I believe." He gazed at the painting. "I loved her completely. My father was the disciplinarian, she and I the ones to obey. We laughed at times, behind Father's back, at the foolishness of his rules."

Collier cleared his throat and lowered his voice until it sounded very deep and as if recorded at slow speed:

"While I'm gone your mother is in charge."

Cole continued in his normal voice, "I had no desire to have it otherwise. She was wise in the way she handled her discipline, for she had me thinking what I was to do was my idea."

He rode back to stop beside Maggie. "'Always stand when a lady comes into a room.' Well, as you see, I got around that command." A rueful chuckle accompanied the remark.

Maggie caught herself smiling with him. "You seem to take your handicap for granted. I've never been able to do that, though I've learned to live with it. I thank God every day that I can be independent."

"Yes, I can tell." His lips curved into a smile.

Maggie didn't catch his remark. "Others have often said I talk, enunciate words, differently, but I don't hear inflection in speech."

"You have a charming accent. What else is hard for you to pick up on in your hearing, if you don't mind my asking."

"I have difficulty in the airport when flights are announced. I wish the announcements were written on a screen. Then too, I know I don't catch all the words to a song. At times, I make up my own words to go with the music, for I love to sing. It must sound awful to others when I do that."

"My form of dancing is equally awful to others I'm sure. But I have an active imagination. Shall we dance?"

Maggie arched a brow in question.

"You sit on my lap thus." He patted his legs and Maggie cautiously moved to sit on his lap on which he'd supplied a soft pillow. Placing one arm around his neck, and the other awkwardly on the arm of the chair, she held on while Cole pushed the wheelchair. "Now, we glide around listening to the music." He closed his eyes as he hummed "Fascination" and moved them slowly around the large room. Maggie cuddled nearer to place her head and a hand on his shoulder, closed her eyes and enjoyed the ride.

When at last he stopped and she stood up, she noted his tight smile. There was a distancing in his look as if he were closing himself off from her again. The keyed-up excitement she'd been feeling plummeted. She was, after all, just a plain person who could never hope to be glamorous or mysterious. Her vivid imaginings had made her feel special—that was all. She walked over to the vase of flowers, and reached out a hand to touch the blossoms of lavender. A murmur of his voice made her turn and walk closer to hear him.

"You have your religion to keep you from being so self-focused." He pushed the wheels of his chair over to the fireplace, and lifted logs to let the flames lick their undersides. "I must seem very self-centered to you." He continued to poke and rearrange the burning logs.

"No," Maggie protested. "You've had to work to overcome your disability. Just as I've had to work to overcome my deafness. If we were chosen by God to be an example of overcoming weakness, then God has also given us the strength to be what we can be."

She knelt down by Cole's chair. "Perhaps you can understand my feeling of having a strength that is bigger than me. It's like going outside of myself to another dimension." She looked questioningly at Cole.

"A place where you can house your mind against all storms." With a nod of understanding, he finished. Maggie agreed with a nod as she eased to her feet.

He took hold of her hand to keep her close. "Thank you for sharing. Now, tell me just a little about your cookbooks using herbs."

"We've now moved from the philosophical to the practical, I see," she teased as she pulled up a small bench and sat down next to him. "My cookbooks are much too practical. I must introduce some whimsy in them." She laughed remembering his description of practical.

"Take the Candytuft plant that's used in cake baking. Its seeds can also be chewed for arthritic complaints. Not too fanciful is it?" she asked.

She gazed into the fire recalling how diligently she'd read about different herbs. How interested she'd been in delving back in the history of the plants.

"My study is rather boring I'm afraid. Perhaps I shouldn't write that herb cookbook after all."

"Why?" he questioned.

She looked at him. "Well, the first reason is that the substance in some herbs, though good to taste, might be toxic—too risky to suggest for cooking—might be cause for that fatal attraction of which you spoke."

His look was of concern. "What kind of plant could be toxic?"

"The tansy plant that I researched. It's a member of the perennial daisy family that can be used to flavor cakes and puddings, especially those eaten at Easter. And it's a flavoring agent in certain alcoholic beverages, including Chartreuse. But some tansy has a toxic chemical used for an insect repellent. That toxin can induce convulsions and psychotic effects in human beings. It's just too unreliable to recommend, and too difficult for the reader to distinguish between the toxic and non-toxic tansy."

"What about summer savory? Have you researched it?" Cole leaned back, making a tent of his hands over curved lips as he waited for her answer.

"Yes, it's used as a spice in bean and other legume dishes, and in various kinds of sausage."

A small smile played at the edges of Cole's mouth. "I recall reading that in former days it was used as an aphrodisiac. It was believed to stimulate the sex drive."

Straight-faced, Maggie countered, "In earlier times yes, just as winter savory was thought to decrease the sex drive."

Maggie, noting his exaggerated look of disappointment, smiled primly. "Take the Passion Flower. You might suppose it's named for something to do with human passion."

"It's not?" Cole's eye brows raised.

"No, it's not. It derived its name from the imagined resemblance of its floral parts to the elements surrounding the crucifixion of Christ. And the symbolic name was given after Biblical times had come into existence. It's used in Europe as a sedative, but hasn't been recognized as safe or effective in the United States."

He grinned. "Any other plant with a suggestive name?"

"Well…" Maggie thought for a minute, then grinned back at him. "There's the Lovage plant that contains no love potion chemical. Its leaves can be used as a seasoning, especially for soups, also in liqueurs, herb bitters and sauces."

"Too bad, I do like imagining what the name implies."

"Umm—you've given me an idea." Maggie tapped a finger on her cheek. "Perhaps my next book should be on the history of herbs and their use early-on in society for medicinal purposes. That would certainly be a practical subject. Of course, the additional use of the herbs we've just mentioned would be added for a bit of whimsy. Yes, I could add a few edible delights as well, like lavender bread." Maggie's laugh was filled with teasing.

Cole laugh, echoing hers, suddenly faded. His eyes became serious. "I admire you and your work. I wish I'd asked you for information on herbs with killing properties, instead of taking that herb book out, causing you such worry."

His mood seemed to ease. A slight glimmer of challenge flashed in very blue eyes. "Of course, maybe we wouldn't have met had I not been so thoughtless." Leaning forward, he took her hand.

She wrapped her fingers around his, and with a mischievous grin suggested, "I'd be glad to list some herbs for your next thriller that are deadly for humans if taken internally."

"I'll take you up on that. I'd much rather listen to you explain herbs than read a research book."

An hour later—chocolate eaten, tea cold, sitting in the shadowed room—their words were mixed with metaphors.

She pushed herself up and out of the chair. "I must go. It's been a wonderful evening." She turned and quickly walked over to pick up her coat, and looked back him. "Thank you."

"Is that all I get for being the perfect host who opened the wine, toasted your beauty, bared my pock-marked soul?" In a more serious tone, of voice, Collier added, "Thank you for the delightful evening you've given me. And now, please come here."

Maggie slowly went back to him, took the hand he held out, and was drawn down to his face so close she could see the reflection of embers flicker in his blue-black eyes—eyes that steadily looked into hers.

In a soft voice she couldn't hear, but did understand, he said, "I've wanted to kiss you for hours. Can you bend to me?" And Maggie did.

It was raining when Maggie drove home at midnight. Driving into the garage, quietly slipping into the house, going to her bedroom, she held her breath, hoping that the creak she heard was really the old house adjusting to the lowered thermostat instead of footsteps on creaking floor boards. Getting into bed with a deep sigh, she pulled the warm blanket up under her chin and relived the evening. She'd not wanted to leave Cole this evening. She'd never had anyone, not even

Linda, to whom she'd confided her deepest beliefs, her doubts, until this lonely man.

CHAPTER 12

The lake was as black as freshly poured tar. Its surface was flat and smooth, but for one ribbon of glistening moonbeams that scattered before an object that slowly moved toward shore with snake-like grace. Maggie stood with Collier and watched its progress. The low insistent moan, which accompanied its slow advance toward them, made her shiver. She leaned back into Collier's arms and he whispered into her ear, "I'm here. Don't be afraid."

Again, the moan—it became louder—then a voice. Maggie awoke with a start, her heart pounding against her rib cage.

"Margaret Ann. It's after nine o'clock." Her mother's voice drifted through the door.

"Yes," Maggie mumbled. Turning over on her side, knees to chest under the comforter, she snuggled in for a few more minutes. Cold air touched her face as she listened to the sweep of wind that beat against the windowpanes and slipped past weather stripping with a low rumbling hum. She covered her head from the cold and noise. No wonder she'd dreamed of monsters on the lake. The dear, drafty old house was complaining about the chilling rain.

After a few warm, comforting minutes, she threw back the covers and jumped to the cold floor. Slippers on, robe zipped, she hurried to the hall to turn up the thermostat. The sixty-two degree setting had her fully awake and worrying. Either the furnace was not working, or she was in for a lecture about the night before from her mother. If it were an ordinary morning, Evelyn would have turned up the heat before going to the kitchen to make breakfast. Funny how she knew all the signs of her mother's moods. Well, forewarned is to be forearmed—or something like that.

Throwing off robe and slippers, Maggie ran for a hot shower. In record time, she was dressed in a pair of gray tweed slacks, a bright red pullover sweater with a matching cardigan for layered warmth. For a moment, she studied herself in the mirror, amazed that the only clue of the happiness felt inside was the extra sparkle in dark-smudged eyes. Quickly applying some cover-up and lipstick, she sailed out of the room.

"Good morning, Mother." There was a smiling lilt in Maggie's voice as she headed for the kitchen.

Evelyn came into the kitchen tugging on gloves. "Ginny is picking me up for our trip to Royal in a few minutes. Before I leave, I think we should talk about last night, Margaret Ann."

Maggie had poured herself a cup of coffee and carried it out of the kitchen past her mother. She'd heard the command, but this time Maggie was determined that last night would not be discussed. "Sorry, I've a phone call to make." She called over her shoulder on the way to the hall phone.

"Margaret Ann, you come back here this instant." Her mother flung the order. Ignoring the woman, Maggie hurriedly looked up the Thomlinson number and dialed.

"Hello. Mr. Thomlinson please. Thank you. Yes, hello. This is Maggie. Have you heard anything? Fine, I'll be there." Maggie hung up the phone, and hurriedly drained her coffee cup. Her mother was standing at the kitchen door.

"Who were you talking to?" The clatter of rain pelting the house with unnerving persistence all but smothered Evelyn's question, but Maggie heard.

With her arm halfway in the sleeve of her coat, Maggie stopped and gave her mother a steady look. "Collier Thomlinson is going to talk to someone about Denny Wright's death, and has asked me to be there." She shrugged into the coat and grabbed her hat from a peg on the wall. "So I'll take the car since Ginny is picking you up."

"I'd rather you didn't go." Evelyn's words followed after Maggie who was already to the garage, where she quickly punched the door opener, slipped into the car, and drove out toward the Thomlinson mansion.

The heavy downpour that had grayed the morning, had diminished to a fine drizzle by the time she arrived at the Thomlinson entrance, where the wrought iron gate slowly opened for her. In the distance, she caught a quick glimpse of the old barn as she drove down the avenue of rain-soaked trees, and wondered what was the reason that the Woods People might have felt compelled to start a new type of spiritual quest. What was missing in structured Christianity?

CHAPTER 13

Robert greeted her at the door. "Mr. Thomlinson is in the library."

"Thank you, Robert. I can find my way," Maggie suggested.

"Yes, Madam." A smile softened Robert's usual aloofness.

Maggie hurried down the wide hall glancing at the portraits and wondered if those smiles held secrets of past impropriety. She was smiling at the thought as she entered the walnut-paneled room.

"Have you heard anything more about a coroner's report or the death certificate?" Cole smiled a greeting and asked.

Maggie shook her head. "Perhaps Mr. Evans can explain."

"Come over here, Maggie, I want to show you something." Cole indicated a straight-back chair that was pulled up beside a table that was covered with pamphlets and magazines. "All of this is the devil worship material I have sorted through."

Maggie sat down, and picked up one of the magazines. Cole came to her side. "I want some straight answers from Mr. Evans as to just what his group is about."

"I'll be glad to tell you, Sir." Derrick Evans had entered. "What do you wish to know?"

Collier wheeled around. Apparently Robert had ushered the man to the library without the usual introduction. Collier quickly covered his surprise. "First let me introduce you two— Maggie this is Derrick Evans, Derrick—Maggie Murphy."

Without waiting for either to speak Collier continued, "I've asked you once before, are you a devil worshiper?"

"Certainly not! We don't worship the devil nor do we worship Satan. We're people of Christ and other great

169

prophets." Derrick Evans, seeming to be undisturbed by the abruptness of Collier's question, added:

"I helped start our religion of transcendence. There are those who've never felt a part of denominational faith, yet have needed something higher than themselves in which to believe. The people of my flock may appear rough around the edges, but I assure you that they are as faithful or more so than some others of this community."

Mr. Evans' firm-set mouth slowly eased as he looked at Maggie with a nod and slight smile. "Miss Murphy is it?" Choosing a mint from the candy dish on an end table, he sat down in one of the large leather chairs facing Collier and Maggie.

There had been a significant change in the man. An open-necked flannel shirt and brown corduroys had replaced the faded T-shirt and overalls he usually wore. Mud spattered boots were clean, and his clean, long hair had been trimmed. The Irishman looked presentable, but he still had a defensive manner.

"My flock have become friends who are interested in helping each other. When they're together in worship, they're learning to set aside differences and aspire to unconditional love." He stopped talking apparently waiting for a response.

"That is certainly commendable, but I also see that in denominational churches." Maggie said.

"Yes, I'm sure." Derrick leaned forward in his chair. "It's hard to explain, Miss Murphy, for so much of religion is a feeling that peels away the materialistic self and feeds the soul. I believe my people are trying to rely on God rather than themselves for guidance in their life's journey. They've never felt comfortable in other churches, but I believe all of our members feel a part of God's earthly community in our church."

Maggie nodded.   Collier remained silent, listening, as Derrick continued.

"We have Eucharist, but it's spiritual. We kneel and receive the person of Christ. There is no bread and wine. We worship out of doors or in the barn so architecture and symbolism don't get in the way. And baptism is central."

From the pamphlet-strewn table, Derrick Evans picked up a magazine with a cover that displayed a Dali-like surreal painting of a misshapen silver chalice and a twisted cross on a crimson background slashed with bright orange. He studied it, and laid it down.

"No, we're not Satan worshipers. And I truly believe that we may understand what Christ was trying to show his people more than do some of those in more formal religious settings." The minister sat back in the chair.

Maggie wanted to divert the conversation from church differences. It was one thing for her to ponder differences to herself, but she wasn't versed enough in all denominational practices to converse with this man on such a level.

"How do you stay warm in the barn this time of year?" she asked.

"The barn was originally the milking barn, and there are blowers which were used to keep the cattle and milkers warm. With permission from Mr. Thomlinson here, we added more heaters and two large fans to keep the warm air circulating in the large barn. It works very well. Especially after Mr. Thomlinson suggested he'd pay for insulation if we parishioners would do the work. We finally have the barn ready for this next winter. It's really quite warm."

"I'm glad to hear that, Mr. Evans." Maggie smiled at Evans and moved to the other leather chair opposite Evans as she thought about what the minister had explained about his church. She could understand how he might have needed to start a new church. She'd thought of changes that might be needed in her own church, hadn't she?

"How did Denny Wright die?" Collier asked bluntly.

"There are those who might suggest that the blow from his stepfather somehow was the cause, but I don't believe that to be true. Don Stone, the chief of police, was there that night and ruled it an accidental drowning. And as for the people, who were present, they too thought it was an accident. They would never condone a deliberate drowning." Evans looked at Collier and Maggie, seeming to wait for their next question.

"Was a report signed by the coroner? I believe he's the next in line to sign the death certificate in Dane County?" Collier asked.

Maggie watched Derrick shift in his chair and ball one hand over the other as he replied, "The corner did not come to the scene of the drowning that night. Don Stone and I signed the death certificate declaring it accidental. I notified the coroner of the incident that same night, and the next day, Saturday, I personally took the certificate to Royal for the coroner to sign. You have to understand that the coroner and I trust each other. It was a long drive for him..." Derrick's voice dimmed. He cleared his throat and added:

"Proceedings were done in a legal manner. The behavior of Clifford Wright is another matter that greatly disturbs me. He and some others took it upon themselves to bury Denny's body that night before the coroner's signature was affixed to the certificate."

Mrs. Tuttle had entered while Derrick was talking. Collier beckoned for her to come in and sit down. She seemed hesitant to speak, sat down and, apparently mustering courage, she spoke.

"Guess you should know what's being said. About two months ago, Eddie stopped going to our Baptist Church and started to go to the Woods People Church. I never did much approve of my Eddie going to that new church. Edward told me to just stop badgering the boy. He'd go to church if he wanted to, and that no persuasion on my part would help. I finally agreed. After all, we'd been a church-going family. My son went to church as a child. He just got away from it somehow. Well, anyway Edward told me to not insist anymore—Eddie going to the Baptist church you know."

The woman's eyes filled with tears. "I didn't want to bother you with any of this, Mr. Collier."

"Please, Mrs. Tuttle. I need to hear what you have to say." Cole moved over and took his housekeeper's hand for a moment. "I have to know details if I'm to help." He smiled and moved over by Maggie.

"Yes, well, Eddie told me and Edward about the yelling, the hit, and the dunking. I believe that Mrs. Wright, regardless of how useless she seems, would have spoken out if she had any doubt about the cause of Denny's death. She's not dumb, you know. She's just resigned to life with a bully. And as for Clifford Wright, I can't believe he would deliberately kill his grandson. Like I said, I don't belong to the Woods Peoples' church, but I do know several members who were there, and they thought it was an accident. They don't like Clifford Wright, but they don't want to accuse an innocent man of murder either. Well, I guess you'll do what's best. I don't know what else I can do. It's so sad." She pushed up and out of the chair.

Before she could leave, Collier stopped her. "Mrs. Tuttle. I wish you'd told me about this group."

Even though he'd confronted her, Collier seemed uncomfortable to be sharing confidences with Mrs. Tuttle. At least it seemed so to Maggie, who had been watching the interchange between the two. She wondered if it had something to do with the help and the lord-of-the-manner attitude. But looking at the kind expression on Collier's face, the concern on the housekeeper's, she presumed that the two were just not used to exchanging confidences. Perhaps Collier's complicated schedule was a part of the reason. Like Mrs. Tuttle had said, she didn't want to bother him.

Mrs. Tuttle's eyes clouded, her mouth tightened. "Religion is a choice. Like I said, Eddie was going to church, for which I'm grateful to you, Mr. Evans."

Eddie's mother had turned to speak to the minister. "He seemed to get something special from your sermons. Always a good boy mind you, but just more considerate, kinder to me it seemed, after he'd been to your services." Her voice quivered with emotion.

Then, eyes bright with unshed tears and a proud lift to her chin, Mrs. Tuttle looked steadily at Collier. "Mr. Thomlinson, I was glad when you let the Woods People use your land. I didn't have any quarrel with the group until the sad death of Denny. I really would have told you had you been here." Collier nodded as if he understood. She excused herself and left the room.

Collier turned back to Evans. "The grandfather performed an illegal act which might be termed a misdemeanor or even a felony." The three were silent, apparently considering the ramifications of Clifford Wright's actions.

Mr. Evans leaned forward, hands on knees, and looked at first Maggie then Collier before dropping his eyes to his hands. "Our church requires that the body be sealed in an airtight wooden coffin with burial the day after death. Since we do not believe in expensive trappings for the dead, an inexpensive welfare coffin is used. And there is no embalming, and no service before burial day. We believe the body is the discarded garment of life on earth. The soul has gone to Jesus. It was wrong of Mr. Wright's group to bury the body before the family could say their good-byes, and before the death certificate was signed, but the rest of what they did is within the guidelines our parishioners are to follow."

"And Jack Donnegar, the coroner, didn't object?"

Derrick looked up quickly. "I told you that he trusted my explanation. He had the flu so was not up to driving to Collier Friday night to take custody of the body and sign the release for us to bury the body. He suggested that I bring the certificate to his home the next day, Saturday, so he could sign the death certificate. He and I respect each other. He attends our church once in a while, so we've become pretty close."

The man hesitated before adding, "I presumed that Clifford Wright and Eddie were taking the boy's body to the Wright's home, then to the farm for the usual burial procedure. I should have gone with them. I didn't realize..." He shook his bent head. White-knuckled hands pressed tightly on his knees.

Collier rolled his chair to the windows and looked outside. Slate-gray sky and a sweeping wind to clean the remains of snow from the land were the usual accompaniments of such a March day. Would that the stiff wind could brush away human desolation as well, Collier thought.

Without turning back to Maggie and Evans, Collier said, "I'd like to see the death papers. Also, I believe it would be wise to ask others in your group about that night, and about the religious practice of dunking in the lake, matters like that."

He rolled around to face them, and gave a sigh of resignation before adding, "I've become involved because this terrible deed happened on my property. I must take responsibility too. Before going to the police about this matter, I've asked Clifford Wright to come here about four-thirty, and he's kindly consented to come. He told me he resents some people's questioning his involvement in Denny's death, and wants to clear up some things. You're welcome to stay, Derrick."

"No thank you. I believe you might have a better understanding of the man if I'm not here. He's not one of our regular parishioners, comes sporadically. We're going to the Wright's at five-thirty and have a prayer time for Jessie. Then, our members will meet at the barn. We'll break bread together, and afterward discuss Clifford's actions on that tragic night as well as on other occasions."

Derrick didn't mention anything about a felony charge. But the little Maggie knew about the law told her Clifford Wright would have a day in court regardless of what the Woods People decided.

The minister turned to Maggie. "You want to come? Jessie seems to like and trust you."

"I'm sorry. Maggie hesitated. "I have a meeting. I can't come." Maggie's eyes pleaded for Cole to say he could be there.

Apparently, Collier interpreted her wish. "Guess I can make it. What time did you say?" His voice was low and gruff. He cleared his throat with an over-the-eyebrow glance at Maggie.

"We'll meet in the barn at seven, if it's still O.K. for us to use the barn for our meetings?" Derrick got up, and took the coat Robert had silently come in and handed him.

"Yes, of course. I'll be there about eight-fifteen. I suppose the meal will be over by then?" The minister nodded a yes and slowly ambled toward the door.

"Derrick," Collier said. Without turning toward Collier, Derrick stopped, straightened his back and stuffed his thick hands into the pockets of his pants. His stance seemed defiant.

Collier moved closer to the man. "It'll be interesting to meet your group. Sometimes a splintering off of a more formal religion becomes more of a club than a religious order. A kind of support system that I believe can be a good thing even though it tries legal limits. But it sounds like you're after real meaning."

Derrick Evans met Collier's steady gaze. His mouth slowly curled into a tight smile. "I know what you mean. This situation has given me a turn, that's for sure. We'll have to get past it, and talk about some changes, but carry on God's work. We're outsiders that have become insiders with each other. Good folks, Mr. Thomlinson. Good folks." Derrick looked at Maggie. "Nice to meet you, Miss Murphy."

She smiled and remained silent. Maggie respected the man. His congregation was learning how to share in their own way. After all, love of God, whatever the path to Him, should be the ultimate concern.

Collier moved over to Derrick and shook the man's outstretched hand. "Thank you. I appreciate your taking the time to explain things to us. Good luck." He rode beside Evans to the front door.

As if she'd been listening to the conversation, and had waited until the men had left the room, Mrs. Tuttle came in from the galley. Hesitantly, the woman brushed her hands on her apron and looked at Maggie. "I do thank you, Miss Murphy, for going to see Eddie. You can trust what he says. He's a good boy. And I thank you too for talking to him. I did try to see Jessie Wright, but her folks hung up on me. I feel sorry for that woman..." She stood silently for a minute. "I know your mother."

Maggie watched the cook leave the room, wondering why Mrs. Tuttle would mention those grocery store chance encounters.

"Well, that's that." Collier had returned to the room. "Maggie, what do you think about what Derrick said about the Woods People?"

"I don't know, but I believe they may be a God-centered group with certain rituals in the baptism of individuals and burial that they may wish to revise." Maggie smiled. "Thanks for asking my opinion."

Slowly brushing back his fiery halo of hair, Collier looked over his bushy eyebrows. "It's true, I don't often ask the opinion of others. Apparently, you've noticed that about me." He tilted his head with a questioning raise of the eyebrows. "Won't you stay for awhile even though you can't stay and eat?"

"I can stay a short while."

"Good, good. Are you comfortable? Warm enough? Could I call Mrs. Tuttle for more tea? No? It's a habit I've kept since England—tea that is."

He rode over to her. "Let's go into the drawing room where there's a fire going." Without waiting for an answer, he swung his chair across the hall to the formal room, and on over to the Steinway piano. "Do you play?" He glanced back at Maggie who had followed.

"No, We've never had a piano. I enjoy music, but have no talent for playing any instrument. It's a little hard anyway, Beethoven notwithstanding." It was quiet. The faint sound of a cupboard door being closed and the hum of a blender in the distance told of Mrs. Tuttle's presence. Logs crackled and sputtered on the fire. Neither spoke for a time.

"Have you heard why they're called The Woods People?" Maggie had walked past the piano to look out the window. Swirls of snow left ripples of white on the frozen lake.

Collier moved up beside her. "They've adopted the name the town gossips coined. I heard that the group had considered naming their church, The Dispensable Church. The Woods People name is more permanent, don't you think?"

The first name seemed appropriate somehow when one considered how unorganized the group really was. Yet, in a way, Maggie thought the group was something like she'd envisioned a church could be. The Dispensable Church—yes, she liked the title even if they hadn't chosen it.

"Will you find something of this situation to use in your book?" Maggie inquired. She'd moved to sit on the arm of the fireside couch like a bird perched for flight, not knowing if it was safe to stay.

He moved nearer. "Well, the storyline of my present manuscript is far removed from this incident. But I'm not above saving parcels of this true event for another story I'm beginning to put together."

"Oh? I've recently stayed up nights to read three of your books. Are others about the same detective, Bertram Strand?"

"Bertram Strand, the protagonist in all my mystery stories, never gets the heroine, if indeed there is a sweet female morsel he can enjoy during an adventure. He always ends up alone—a detective solving crimes."

Collier's expressive face was sober. He leaned toward Maggie and looked deeply into her eyes. "Bertram is a very cynical, self-contained fellow who is admired but seldom loved. Perhaps it's because he appears distant. If so, it's a bluff." He moved away again.

"Anything beyond the detective thrillers?" Maggie quickly changed the subject. She had the feeling that they leaned toward each other, then backed away before anything like intimate thoughts could be shared. She recognized her own reluctance to become involved. Linda had once mentioned that Maggie would be opening up to let others in. At times, she felt she and Cole had crossed that barrier—were more open. He was a disturbing man. She slipped off the chair arm and down into the soft-cushioned couch.

"I usually have two or more mystery manuscripts going at the same time. I don't know if that is the way most writers do it, but when I tire of the one, run out of ideas to keep the plot thick, I turn to another plot that is cooking on the back burner. Gets my juices going so to speak."

"I couldn't possibly do that." Maggie ran a finger over the embossed gold leaves on the satin fabric of the love seat for a moment, then glanced up. "I've been trying to write some non-fiction about things pertaining to life. Inspired I must admit, by our last lengthy conversation. And I've started a history of herbs book." Her green eyes sought his with a smile.

Collier's eyes held hers. "Writing is a rewarding task. The writer creates for the enjoyment of the reader, and in the process can enhance his or her own self-awareness."

"I hope writing will enhance my self-awareness. Heaven only knows I need to assert myself and rely on myself more."

"Why do you believe yourself to be incapable? You have stood up to my authoritative commands well enough."

"I feel I can disagree with you and you'll not necessarily agree with me, but will listen to my opinion. Lately, I've compared myself with my friend Linda Edwards. She's independent, though totally deaf. She's completely self-confident, kind but not condescending and not afraid if someone's opinion differs from her own. The comparison makes me see myself as I am. I'm afraid to make any decision without the help of my mother. It's been easier to ask for help rather than try to make a decision. I've done it again by asking you to help me with this Jessie thing."

"I value you for yourself. I know if you ask me for help there is a good reason. As for asking my advice, it hasn't been self-serving. It's added a dimension to my life. For that, I thank you." His smile invited more.

"Me too." Breathlessly, she held out her hand as if to say she was going.

Collier placed a gentle kiss in the palm of her hand. "I like to talk to you. Thank you for seeing past my abrupt demeanor. I'm English-educated you know."

Maggie caught the words, if not the British accent, and laughed with him as they went to the door and said good-bye.

CHAPTER 14

It was not yet five o'clock and already the sky had dimmed. Lights of the distant town cast shimmers on the velvet-covered lake, while small electric spot- lights in the trees tried to imitate the glow of the lost moon. Collier gazed out for a moment, thinking how he wished he was at the computer writing down descriptions. Writing was like a void in time. His thoughts dissolved as the voice of the unpleasant man got louder.

"And then, I gave him a slap to make him stop the hysterics." Clifford Wright sat in Collier's drawing room. A small man in coveralls, plaid shirt and work boots overrun at the heels, had a putty-like face, soft and pouchy, that rested atop a long neck with an Adam's apple stopper. Collier had turned away when Wright had begun his vivid description of the beating. Now, he again faced the molester. Clifford's features were molded into the placid, smiling face of a man who would never think of beating his grandson.

"Was it your habit, to hit Denny when he didn't do your bidding?"

Clifford rubbed the back of his hand over his mouth, and studied the toe of his boot for a moment before replying. "Like I say, if a kid don't listen, you've got to pound some sense into him. Denny never did listen good." Wright shifted in the large chair.

Collier could feel his own face getting warm. "And you believe this tactic worked."

"Well like I told you. He was a willful one and needed a hand now and then to keep him steady on."

Collier chilled at the suggestive grin and sadistic undertones of the man's remark. Apparently, he hit and yelled at Denny to make the boy mind. How can one reach a man who thinks like this?

"Mr. Wright, how did Jessie act when you administered your corrective measures?" Collier's eyes were blue ice as he stared at the man.

With a grunt, Wright rubbed a hand over his mouth, but Collier caught the smirk. "I never much cared about what Jessie thought. Guess she's lucky to have a roof over her head, and to have someone to learn the boy some things he'll need to know to get on in this world. She didn't ever do it for him."

"I fail to see how hitting and yelling at a child has any educational value." Collier's words were clipped.

Clifford Wright's jaw clenched. His mouth turned down and was tightly closed. He rose slowly from the chair, yanked up his pants with a gesture of disgust and swaggered over to Collier. "Seems you have mighty fancy ideas about education. Course, being lame makes you have time for all that book learn'n. Suppose if you don't have kids and read a lot you can be an expert on the subject of raising 'em. 'Course some can be brats and I say they need a heavy hand to straighten out." Clifford's defiant stance—short legs planted far apart, shoulders hunched, hands in front pockets, was accompanied by a sneering face.

Collier took a deep breath and rubbed his hands back and forth over his numb limbs. This man is a replica of a gargoyle that Goudè might have sculpted. Would that this man were only a statue atop the barn roof to ward off non-believers, Collier thought.

Repulsed by the ignorant man, Collier rode over, pulled open the door to the hall, and firmly said, "Good day."

Grim-faced, Collier eyed the swaggering man as he went by, then watched as Clifford Wright continued down the hall toward Robert who waited, door open, at the main entrance.

Midway down the hall, Wright turned back toward Collier. "You're pretty nosy about folks and their offsprings in this town. Maybe the folks around here could be tell'n you a secret or two." With a tip of a hand to his uncovered head and a wry smile, Clifford Wright walked out of the door.

As Robert went passed Collier on the way to the back of the house, he murmured, "A bad one, Mr. Thomlinson."

Collier felt heaviness across his shoulders as if someone had just laid a load of bricks on his back. What did Wright mean talking about offspring and secrets? There'd been a sinister quality to the veiled threat. How could that man possibly be a part a church of God? Perhaps the Woods People were a cult after all.

***

At 8:10, Collier was driven to the north end of his property, through an open gate, to a cleared area where some twenty cars were parked. With Robert's help, he got out, and leaving Robert with the van, Collier pushed himself the short distance to the barn. He started to go up the rise to the barn entrance, but abruptly clamped down on the brakes of his wheelchair, and slid to a stop at the foot of the ramp. Notes from a fiddle drifted out of the barn, accompanied by voices talking and laughing. It sounded more like a party than a hearing. Collier wondered if the inquiry the Woods People were suppose to be having was being taken seriously and, if so, would it make any difference in Denny Wright's death? After all, Clifford Wright went to the church.

What am I doing here? An image of Maggie Murphy flashed before his eyes. I told her I'd come to this trial, or whatever it is. He realized that it was also his responsibility. With a heavy intake of breath, Collier pushed himself up and into the barn.

Derrick Evans nodded over to Collier while others, noting Mr. Thomlinson's arrival, began to quickly move tables to the side of the room. The music stopped, and all quickly took their seats, facing the makeshift stage where the defendant and the preacher had taken their seats. Collier placed himself and his wheelchair at the back of the room not far from Mrs. Wright and Jessie.

The meeting was brought to order by the minister. Witnesses began to review the night of Denny Wright's baptism. Some, who had been close to the scene, described how the grandfather had tried to stop the boy's yells by hitting him. Others described how Clifford had pushed Denny under the water for the baptismal submersion. And they also reiterated what most attending the meeting knew, that no one was sure if the boy was breathing when he was pulled up out of the water, and that the minister had performed mouth to mouth resuscitation for quite a while.

Not all of the people so readily testified. They shuffled away from actually speaking as if somewhat uneasy to describe their part in the affair as they glanced back at Collier. Leo Gordon came forward to testify about the burial:

"After he was dead, Minister Evans and Don Stone signed papers say'en that it was an accident—the drowning. A little later, after the preacher said the coroner had been notified and would sign the papers the next day, me and Eddie Tuttle put the body in Eddie's truck. Cliff told Eddie to follow us. And Cliff, Roy Smith, Jake Story and me, drove in Cliff's car to my place outside town. We took out the body, Eddie left, and Cliff said it'd help his daughter if we just dug her boy in. He said she prob'ly couldn't face it."

The skinny man with the shiny bald pate rubbed his hands over the knees of his blue jeans, and looked at the floor for a few moments before he added in a hushed tone, "And we four buried Denny quick and quiet like." Leo looked at the other men sitting in the front row who remained silent. "We've been friends for a long time and stick together."

A person in the back of the room yelled. "Yeah, you four are good at getting our group into trouble. You're the ones who caused all the ruckus by starting those fires before we got organized as a church."

A woman sitting to the right of Collier jumped up and shouted in a high pitched voice, "We didn't want to have those fire rituals in our new church worship. If it hadn't been for Reverend Evans taking a stand and stopping the fires and sacrifices of animals, our holy church would never have made it. We don't want devil worship. We want to worship Jesus Christ and God."

Others shouted in agreement, "Yes! Right! We believe in God not the devil!" Another yelled, "What about burying Denny Wright?" Like thunder after lightning, the airing of the offenses the four men had committed when they tried to infuse devil worship into the Woods Peoples' service, and their questionable burial of Denny Wright, sparked protest and anger so intense that Collier felt the heat and rumble of a commencing brawl.

So those four men started the fires, Collier thought. He'd wondered why Derrick Evans had been silent about who started them, though he did tell the truth when he said his group didn't condone it. Apparently, Collier noted, more than one type of worshipper had joined to make up the Woods People. The smoldering truth had at last erupted.

Shoving and pushing had begun. Grunts and yells filled the barn with expletives. The minister stood, raised his arms toward the people and said, "Stop! This is a holy place. We'll not desecrate it with fighting."

The group's burst of anger was dampened. All settled down and were quiet. It surprised Collier that the members of the church were so quickly calmed, yet he too had felt the pull of Derrick Evans' commanding presence. The minister continued:

"We've come here to find out about Denny Wright's death. The fires are another matter, which will be reviewed later. For those of you who didn't attend the ceremony that night, I did call a police officer, Don Stone, to the scene. He questioned those present, and seemed satisfied that the death was by drowning. I had no reason to doubt that the death was an accidental drowning. It's true that Mr. Stone and I signed the death certificate as police officers. I called and explained the situation to the coroner. The next day, I personally took the certificate to the coroner for his signature. The coroner read and signed it because he trusted Don and me." A satisfied murmur stirred the air as Evans continued:

"The body was to be sealed in a welfare box and buried in our burial plot out on Leo Gordon's farm the next day which was Saturday after I'd gotten the coroner's signed report. I got the report, but Clifford and the others had already buried the body. The wake for the boy was this evening at Jessie's house." His voice shook for a moment, then he again spoke firmly:

"This meeting has been called at the request of some who believe further investigation into Denny Wright's death is needed. What we decide tonight will be relayed to the police."

The witnessing ended with Clifford Wright defending himself by denying that he had hit the boy hard enough to kill him. "Hell, I'd hit him harder than that plenty of times," he said glumly.

Five men and three women walked out of the barn with the minister. Collier surmised that the group was the governing body who would decide Clifford Wright's fate. The remaining people silently began to gather up the remains of food and dishes on the tables. Some thirty minutes later, swishes of chilled air from the cold March night accompanied the committee when they came back inside the warm barn. The minister walked over to talk to a man who was apparently taking the part of a bailiff. The man took Clifford's arm and led him to the center of the stage facing the congregation. Derrick Evans walked forward and stood at the front of the stage beside the accused man. The committee of eight took up a stance behind the minister.

Derrick Evans held up his hand. "I'm too involved to give the verdict of the committee. Mr. Cartwright, as bailiff, will read the findings of the committee." He moved back.

A murmur again resonated through the assemblage as people protested, "No, you would have stopped Cliff. You're not to blame." He stepped to the front, held up his hand, and the muttering stopped.

Evans voice was firm and unwavering. "I beg you to listen. I need to do this. I've asked the committee to meet tomorrow without my presence so they can judge me for my part in this tragic incident. I am responsible as your minister for the conduct of our church members. I pray to God to forgive me for not going with Eddie Tuttle that night. I failed you as an officer of the law and as your minister. Mr. Cartwright will read the committee's decision." With bowed head, the minister left the stage.

Cartwright read from a paper that a committee member had handed him. "Members of the Woods People Church Committee have heard the evidence in regards to the death of Denny Wright. They have voted that Denny Wright's death could have been accidental. We believe that it is possible that the thought of being submerged for the baptism could have made Denny Wright panic, therefore, he ingested water and drowned. If this is true, Clifford Wright's blows, though vicious, were not the cause of the boy's death."

The bailiff read from a second sheet. "Though it is the policy of our church to have burial the next day after death, and the papers were signed by the police to that effect, the burial was untimely. The coroner had not signed the formal papers, and the family did not get to say their last good-byes to Denny. Clifford Wright, Leo Gordon, Roy Smith, and Jake Story will be turned over to the police as participants in the unlawful burial of Denny Wright. The Woods People Church's Administrative Committee will be accountable for turning over to the authorities the record of tonight's meeting, which has been duly recorded by Mrs. Clara Biggs." The murmurs were subdued, signifying satisfaction.

Derrick Evans stepped forward in front of the group. "I'm proud of all of you for coming to this meeting. You did well. Thank you for being a part of this heartfelt group decision. We will be able to answer any questions people may ask. God go with you."

Collier considered the decision. Perhaps, absolving Clifford Wright of guilt, extending understanding love to him might cause the man's behavior to change. Maybe that would be the one positive thing to come from the tragedy. Collier felt ambivalent about the decision made by the Woods People. There was still a chance the man would be proven guilty when the police reviewed the case. The authorities might even choose to exhume the body for evidence. He silently nodded to people as he pushed himself to the wide entrance of the barn.

"Thank you for coming, Mr. Thomlinson." Derrick had followed Collier outside, where they stopped by the barn ramp.

"I found the meeting interesting," Collier said. He was not too sure he approved of the minister's method of administering justice, and did not approve of the church rituals, but he was impressed with the way Evans controlled the angry group.

The minister nodded in agreement. "I think most of these people believe Cliff was wrong in hitting Denny, but it's not much different than they have done to theirs at times. I try to preach kindness, but the way they were raised is all they know. They correct their children the way they were corrected, and usually that's by hitting, yelling or both." Derrick shrugged with a sigh as he looked back into the barn at the people milling about.

Collier looked at him searchingly. "Self-restraint is a moral truth that is supposedly a part of the fabric of a religious group. Surely this man's conduct doesn't represent what you want in your group?"

Rubbing his chin with the back of his hand as if he were considering what Collier had just said, Derrick looked over at Collier. "These are simple country folk. Clifford lost his head. He was not wholly responsible. The boy was screaming, and it was embarrassing for the grandfather as well as irritating for those who were present. Guess he was just trying to quiet the boy."

Collier retorted, "Someone once said that morality can only be consistently observed when there is self-control, and truth-telling, and trust in a group." Collier looked steadily at Evans. "Your church group live up to all that? Can you honestly say that Wright's actions demonstrated self-control? Can there be any trust or truth-telling when such actions are condoned?"

Mr. Evans stood and looked over Collier's head at some of his congregation who were going home. "Mr. Thomlinson, I'm ashamed of the way I've handled this tragic incident. I've been a part of it. You can't possibly know the torture it is for me to admit that the premise we've established as to the burial of the dead may be flawed. I even doubt that I should be the leader of this group, but I do know their hearts and prayers will help them decide the final blame." He nodded rather sadly, and walked back into the barn.

"How complicated life becomes when we haul everything over our own inadequacies," Collier mumbled to himself as he rode toward the van.

Clifford Wright had come up behind Collier. "Seen you leav'n. 'Spect you have better things to do. Like seein' that Miss Murphy?"

Collier ignored the man and rode on, but Cliff's sneering voice followed him. "Well, you and the others give me advice tonight. Maybe I'll give you a bit."

Collier wheeled around and stopped to observe the man. Clifford stood in the dim glow of the parking lot lights. He didn't seem contrite. Rather, with shoulders hunched, head cocked, he wore the smug look of the gambler who'd just put down a royal flush as he sneered.

"You have it all don't ya? You've a rich, fancy house, you're a famous writer, a helpless cripple 'nd all. Tell us poor folks how to run our families huh? If'n you see Miss Murphy, better be know'n before you git involved. She might be a pretty nice piece to play with, but there's more to it than meets the eye. Somethin' a little rotten there." Wright licked his lips and let out a knowing laugh.

Collier's head felt as if it would explode. He closed his eyes to steady himself, but could not blot out the leering grin on the man's face. He clenched his fist, and half pushed himself from his chair, "I'll kill the son of a bitch." Then reality clamped him back down in his seat as Robert appeared by his side. Without a word, Collier allowed his chauffeur to wheel him, a helpless cripple, to the van.

He would have killed the man had he the means. That alone made him no better than Cliff Wright. He'd always been fairly indifferent to others, being so intent on his work and his life. He wouldn't have helped with this questionable death had it not been for Maggie. Yet right now, he felt a roaring need to smash in the man's leering face. The man had made innuendoes about Maggie. What in the world had the man meant?

He rolled down the car window and sucked in deep gulps of fresh, clean air. Stiff pines loomed out of the darkness of the curving drive as the headlights beamed on the thick stand of trees. Carriage lights blinked, welcoming him to his home. He thought of the Wright household, and wondered what the home-life of Jessie Wright was like.

Collier pictured the barn scene he'd just left, and could see Denny's mom sitting to the side of the group. Hunched over, with arms on knees, Jessie seemed preoccupied with biting her fingernails, and glancing over at Thelma Wright, who sat beside her. He could not imagine how the young woman had allowed such treatment of her son. Or how her mother, the older woman who had sat stoically with arms folded over her ample breasts and stared down at the floor during the entire proceedings of the evening, could live with such a man.

They'd arrived at the house. With Robert's help, Collier got out of the van and proceeded up to his bedroom. A little later, Robert came in with a mug of buttered rum, and helped Collier prepare for the night. "Will that be all sir?" The valet asked.

"Yes. Thank you, Robert, do you realize how little control we have over events that happen to us? Shakespeare's Hamlet had it about right when he said we all are in some sort of production, learning our lines and our part in the theme of the whole as the play proceeds, without knowing a damn thing about the outcome."

"Sir, I believe man has some say in the events of his life. He's given choices he can make. Choice is what makes life interesting and worthwhile." Robert smiled. "Good night, Sir."

"Good night, Robert, and thank you." Collier leaned over and picked up the mug of hot rum Robert had set down on the bedside table. He watched the melted butter swirl on the surface of the hot liquor, and breathed in the sweet, warm steam. He mused for a moment. Perhaps humans need counsel from something higher than themselves when choices are to be made in response to events. Maggie had suggested as much.

The rum burned the inside of his mouth, much as thoughts about human need burned in his mind. Putting down the drained cup, he switched off the reading lamp as he visualized a need—his finger tips touching Maggie's full red lips, a hand skimming down the soft column of her throat to her breasts. His heart thudded in his chest as he imagined all the soft, warm intimate places he could touch, and how he could pleasure her. Somewhere inside of himself, Collier knew he could feel— could command his body. The many specialists who had examined him through the years had told him he might have the means to experience a man's arousal. He'd had women—knew how to please them—even had times, not often, when he'd thought he might be able to perform the sex act after his fashion. Sleep ended disturbingly erotic thoughts.

CHAPTER 15

"There were sounds of silence floating in the crisp month of May—murmurs and scratches of nature still unseen but warming, stretching, preparing to appear dressed in colors of spring." Maggie had written to Collier by E-mail sending him an idea for a short introduction to be used in her new herb book.

He had E-mailed back immediately. Now that's whimsical!

Maggie laughed aloud. She wondered how the meetings were going in New York with the producer from England. The possibility of his latest novel being made into stage play was exciting, but he'd been gone much too long for Maggie.

What filler for loneliness the FAX machine and E-mail had become. Even the before-bedtime calls had helped, but she missed him.

It had been eight days since Cole had gone to New York. He and Maggie had met briefly before he left, and he'd told her about the Woods People meeting, how Jessie had seemed timid, unsure and fearful through the terrible trial. Though they'd argued a bit about the church members' verdict—Cole blaming, Maggie forgiving—they both had agreed that it was best for the law to decide the outcome of Clifford Wright's fate.

Yesterday, she'd heard about the charges brought against Clifford Wright and had sent a FAX to Cole at the Plaza Hotel. She again skimmed through the sheet she'd sent:

"The police weren't satisfied with the Woods People verdict that the Denny Wright's death was an accident, and have booked Cliff for the death of his step-grandson on reckless homicide charges. The grandfather is in jail waiting for his trial. The defense team is demanding that the body be exhumed for evidence.

"Derrick Evans is back in the good graces of his church. The people have stood behind him, and have insisted that their minister did nothing wrong the night of Denny's death. The Woods People are going to church as usual, but some sweeping changes have been made in church procedure, and in their Book of Discipline. I outline here:

1) Baptismal submersion is to be used only with the permission of those being baptized. If the person being baptized does not want to be submerged, he/she may be exempt from the ritualistic procedure and sprinkled with holy water. A committee has been designated to decide in such cases.

2) Burial will be held before sunset on the day after death. The coroner, one policeman and a family member must sign the release for the burial.

3) A wake will take place before burial."

A door closed, foot steps sounded down the hall. "Maggie, I'm home." The lilt in her mother's voice was almost audible to Maggie. Before she could answer, Evelyn breezed in out of breath.

"I just heard that Letty Levert and our pastor are seeing each other." Evelyn proceeded to sit down beside the desk where Maggie was working on the computer.

"Where did you hear that?"

Her mother leaned closer. "Remember, I told you not long ago that Lettie was taking books over to Richard's house, and some of us have wondered what was going on?" Without waiting for an answer, Evelyn continued. "Well, Ginny just asked him when she went to his office to help fold some mailers, and he said he was quite fond of Lavitia. She'd come to his house for advice."

"Mother, how could Mrs. Phillips ask? And even so, that hardly means that they're having an affair or that their meeting was romantic." Maggie almost choked on the word.

"Honestly, not only does television saturate the viewing audience with romance, liaisons, intrigue—so do the church do-gooders of the community." Maggie's voice rose in spite of herself. "Why don't the gossips let the poor couple alone?"

Maggie pushed up out of the chair, and paced back and forth. Why did she feel so invaded over the news concerning Letty and Richard?

Suddenly, a thought slammed into her thinking—*I'm jealous of them! I'd like to have an affair with Collier Thomlinson! Wow! What would happen if Ginny told Mother that?*

Maggie's thoughts were not on the Richard and Letty subject that her mother was still discussing. Her glance strayed to the living room where spring-weather changes had been made. A pink parchment fan now covered the fireplace opening, which signaled no more gas-fed fires. Her thoughts drifted to that one special evening in February when snow was on the ground—a huge fireplace ablaze, casting shadows on a portrait of Cole as a small child. She remembered every thing that she and he had discussed that night she had fallen in love.

Evelyn still chatted on. "I wonder how serious it is? What if he should decide to marry her?"

The question interrupted Maggie's daydreams. "Well, would that be so bad? If the story is true, I admire the couple. Letty is a fine woman and Richard needs someone." Maggie got up to turn on the lamp on her desk.

"But she's Catholic," Evelyn gasped almost shuddering.

"Mother, I've always liked Letty. When we were young, she was one of the few girls my age that attempted to communicate with me, even though it must have been difficult.

She cared enough to ask me to her home to play when I was home for some holidays. Who else did that?"

Maggie looked over at her mother, who sat busying her hands with ripping the wrapper off a new skein of yarn. "And who took me to lunch not too long ago wanting to know about the building program of the church, and gave a thousand dollars to our building fund? She may be a Catholic, but she's a Christian and interested in Community Church."

"Yes, I suppose she is." Evelyn Murphy nodded absently as she handed Maggie the yarn to hold, and began to roll up the pink wool strands.

Maggie watched Evelyn roll the yarn into a ball, but her mind was still on Richard. "I've wondered at times who Richard is. Is he truly a humble disciple of God, or is the self-image he portrays of his own creation that was fashioned from theological concepts of what a minister of God should be? I hope he's good enough for Letty. He doesn't seem fully honest somehow."

"Maggie, if we were all completely honest, nobody could live in this world."

Maggie silently agreed. Complete honesty was hard to share. That's why Maggie hadn't shared her feelings for Cole with her mother. It was too personal. How could she tell the woman that she missed being with Collier?

It was not necessarily sexual closeness she desired with Cole, but the need to have him in her everyday life. Once, they'd talked about togetherness. He'd told her that his greatest fear of commitment was that the person he loved would take away his privacy. Cole had said that Maggie was his greatest challenge, and she'd asked him why…

"Well, I can see you've decided to not listen." Evelyn Murphy's voice broke through Maggie's reverie. Her mother was through winding the yarn, and had needles filled with the pink yarn starting the shawl she'd promised a friend.

Maggie quickly glanced at her watch to see it was almost six. She picked up discarded pieces of wrapper strewn on the floor, and turned on more lights as she went to her room, calling back to her mother. "I've got to get ready. Collier is back from New York, and is coming to pick me up for dinner."

"Oh, dear. That man has simply ruined our companionship. I can't even get a conversation going with you. It's always Collier. He calls and you two talk for hours. I like to talk to you too you know." Evelyn looked after the retreating figure, hands poised with knitting needles like a conductor ready to give the musical signal for a crescendo as her voice escalated to a whine. "You know how I feel about that man." Her voice rang loudly.

Maggie came back to the door of the den. "Mother stop! Collier is a good friend, and I think too much of him to allow you to say ugly things about him." Quickly going back to her bedroom, she didn't or couldn't hear her mother's last opinion thrust.

Later, when the doorbell rang, Maggie, dressed in a green linen skirt and white silk blouse, with a lightweight sweater thrown around her shoulders, quickly went to answer the doorbell, as her mother called from the living room, "Margaret Ann, get the door please."

"Bye, Mother."

With a happy smile of welcome for Robert at the door, she hurried on to the car, leaving the chauffeur to follow closely behind. Inside the car she leaned over and gave Collier a kiss on the cheek. "Hi!" She said.

"Is that as good as you can do?" He growled and pulled her to him to give her a long, deep kiss that lingered with longing.

Breathlessly Maggie moved away as Robert got in the car.

Cole took her hand, "Would you mind very much if we went back to my house? Mrs. T has left what she calls a light supper, likely it is a full dinner menu, for us on the verandah."

Maggie squeezed his hand, "I love Mrs. Tuttle's cooking. I'll be bringing her some fresh herbs soon. Did I tell you that my herb plants are peeking through?"

"You haven't told me all of the happenings in Collier since I've been gone. I've noticed that the daffodils have started to bloom—tulips too. You've made me aware of so many things, Maggie." A thoughtful smile lingered on his lips as he kissed the hand he held.

"Ah, my Maggie. It will be a magical garden I've no doubt." With a lingering look, he gently pulled Maggie to him and murmured in her ear. "It's been eight days my girl, much too long." She lay her head on his shoulder, and they rode in silence the rest of the short distance to his house.

The house was alive with a bright greeting of lights as Maggie walked ahead of Collier down the long hall to the drawing room. As they entered the inviting room, Maggie suddenly stopped, leaned over to cup Cole's face between her hands and gave him a quick lingering kiss.

"Oh, Collier. It's so good to be with you; I feel foolishly happy."

"And you think I don't? Just because I'm a cynic and live vicariously through my books?" Maggie gasped as Cole lifted her up and onto his knees, made a turn of the wheels, and moved the chair through the drawing room, out to the open verandah, and gave the chair a quick spin before stopping.

"Ah, Maggie mine, I too can be happy with a real person."

"What a wonderful way to get someplace in a hurry." She kissed his cheek.

Slipping off his lap, Maggie walked over to the patio table where a circle of tiny tapers gave wavering light to the table set for two. Over by the French doors, was a long serving cart filled with Mrs. Tuttle's gourmet specialties: roast duckling with plum sauce, rice, assorted vegetables, crisp greens for salad. Robert stood by ready to help Maggie with her chair.

"Thank you, Robert," Maggie smiled up at the quiet man as she took the seat he offered.

Collier moved to sit beside Maggie. "Let us enjoy the wine for awhile, Robert. Don't tell Mrs. T. She'll expect us to eat right away while her delicious meal is hot," Cole chuckled to the departing Robert.

He turned to Maggie, silently watching the flickering candle light reflect off her ebony hair, dance in her emerald eyes, and breathed in deeply of the fresh, crisp fragrance that she wore. Gently, he touched the hair that lay on her shoulder, soothed a finger down her cheek. Leaning forward, looking deep into her eyes, he whispered. "I remember the first time I saw you. I thought you had the most exquisite pearl-like skin. I wanted to touch it, touch you."

Maggie opened her mouth to speak, but he touched a finger to her lips. "You were—are—perfection, my dear Maggie."

His gaze shifted away as he added with a chuckle, "You had on that ridiculous red tam-o'-shanter." He leaned back in his chair. Picking up his glass of wine, he took a long sip while staring out at the lake as if lost in thought.

She noticed the change in his eyes, that subtle but distinct distancing she'd seen before. The silence lengthened. It was as if he hadn't spoken.

"Collier," Maggie said hesitantly, "What is love to you? We've skirted the issue many times."

Collier sighed. He leaned forward and looked at her with steel-blue eyes. "My dear, shared meals, conversations about the weather and our writing, while commendable, is not the kind of intimacy I'd wish for us." He gaze shifted back to the lake.

"If we had no other kind of intimacy but that which you describe, I'd be content because, before you, I've had no wish to share any of my thoughts, dreams—or my life."

Maggie watched him pour more wine into his glass from the decanter on the table. Then he slumped back in his chair, and again stared out at the shining lake.

"Blind innocence speaks with no real knowledge of true intimacy," he said.

The depth of his cynicism shocked her. "Do you care for me?"

"Oh, I care. I care very much, but a celibate friendship is not what I'd wish for us. And I don't know if anything else is possible." His voice was flat.

"So I'm only an object, not a real, live, breathing person to you?" Maggie's voice hitched at the end.

"You're more than that, and I think you know it." Cole skimmed a hand over his eyes and started again:

"You are the sum of all my parts, my best, my other me. I can no longer say I can live without you, yet, it would be torture to live with you without the intimacy I want for both of us."

Maggie whispered, "Intimacy can be so many shared experiences—like talking, eating, and listening to lovely music."

"That isn't everything." He ground out the words, hesitated a moment, then quickly added, "It's true that the happiness I've felt when I've been alone is not the same rewarding feeling I have when I share my thoughts, my hopes and dreams with you, Maggie. You enhance my life by sharing my dreams, though I've doubts about some obstacles." He tipped back his head and gulped down the remaining wine in his goblet.

"You really don't care for me enough." Her whispered words hung in the air.

He stared out past her toward the lake. "Oh, my dear, how much I wish I could be as you wish me to be."

Maggie leaned toward him, forcing him to look at her as she took both of his hands in hers. "You are what I wish you to be for you are yourself. That's all I'll ever need. If it's me you doubt, I know I can't hea...r..." She broke the word on a sob, scooped up her glass of wine, and walked to the edge of the terrace. Breathing gulps of fresh, cool air, between sips of wine, she watched the ripple of velvet waves lap against the shore. Though the sounds of nighttime were lost to her, she knew the moment he came up beside her.

"Maggie, please look at me." She turned. "I do love you completely and forever." The words came out raspy and heavy with emotion.

Tears rolled down Maggie's cheeks as she knelt by his wheelchair. "You know—you must know that I love you."

He smoothed away her tears with his fingers, then cupped her face between his hands. "Ah, Maggie, if I asked you to spend the night, would you?"

"Yes," Maggie whispered and lay her head on his lap.

Stroking her hair, he gazed down at her and asked, "Whatever the night may bring?"

She kissed the palm of his hand and looked up at him. "Whatever it may bring, it will be with you."

"Then let's get this meal over with." Cole called, "Robert, we're ready to eat."

CHAPTER 16

They rode up in Cole's private elevator to his bedroom suite. Cole wheeled over to an armoire, pulled a silk shirt from a hanger, and gave it to Maggie with the suggestion that the bathroom was back to the right side of the room. Robert knocked, came in, and the two men disappeared into what seemed to be a dressing room leaving Maggie alone. Heart pounding, mouth dry, Maggie slowly advanced into the large bedroom, eyes flicking over the high-ceilinged, huge room, decorated in shades of burgundy, beige and brown. There were chairs by a fireplace, flowers on a bedside stand. At the far side of the room she could see a massage table, weights, treadmill, walking ramp. The best of stainless steel equipment for body building was there. Her glance slipped over the large mahogany bed then flitted back to notice the smooth sheets turned down, large pillows fluffed, and others stacked against the brown velvet corduroy bolster at the head of the ornately carved headboard.

She sidled toward the outer door, and heard voices— mumbles of Cole's and Robert's voices reached from the other room to her as she stood trembling. I can't—I don't know what to do. She again started for the door clutching the nightshirt in her hand.

Cole came out of the adjoining room alone. He had on silk pajamas and the lap robe was draped on the back of the wheelchair. She noticed that he was bare foot. His hair was combed, but still unruly. She was silent—questioning.

"Maggie?" He moved to her, and held out a hand for her to sit on his lap. She curled up in his arms, and was held close against his chest.

"I was too abrupt with you, Maggie. There's a second entrance to my dressing room and bath that Robert uses to come and help me prepare for bed. He has also prepared the bathroom over here for you," he explained.

"It's separate from the one I use," he said as he wheeled them over to the other dressing room and bath. He stopped by the bathroom door and waited. "Maggie?" She lay in his arms, trembling—afraid to stay, but not wanting to leave.

"It will be all right. I'll be gentle. I love you." He whispered in her ear.

With a wavering smile, Maggie kissed his cheek, and slowly, slipped from his lap to walk into the bathroom. Gently closing the door, she leaned against it—eyes closed, heart racing with fear and excitement. She knew it would be all right. She trusted and loved this man with all of her heart. She prayed that she would find the way to show him that she cared.

The bathroom's small sitting room had a white linen couch, and an organdy skirted antique vanity with matching bench. A silver hairbrush and mirror were placed on the glass top of the vanity. On through an archway was a hand painted wash bowl with gold faucets, a commode, and a built-in shower. Toothpaste and a toothbrush in its new wrapper lay on the glass shelf above the wash bowl. Pristine white monogrammed towels hung on warming racks. There seemed to be all of the essentials for a lady's toilette—for an over-night rendezvous.

She took off her clothes, and carefully laid them on the couch. After shaking fingers had buttoned Cole's silk shirt, she slowly brushed her hair, while studying the reflection of the small woman in an oversized nightshirt, who was framed in the gilded mirror.

All of her past life seemed to have led up to this moment. All of her dreams that had been illusions, had become expectations and fears. This was reality with Cole. Maggie pushed back her hair, and walked back into the bedroom where she found Cole sitting up in bed cushioned with pillows.

"Come here, Maggie-mine." He held out a hand, she climbed up beside him on the bed, and poised on her knees looking at him with large emerald eyes.

"I wish we had some champagne," she whispered.

"We can have some if you wish, Maggie, but it does not enhance the libido."

"I—thought it might give me..."

"Courage? No, Maggie-mine. It would only give you vague recall of what you may enjoy if you let yourself." He made room, and she scooted up to lay in the crook of his arm. He brushed back her hair and gently kissed her cheek, her neck to savor the scent of her. Then skimmed his tongue over her lips, feeling their softness open as his lips met hers in a kiss, breathlessly demanding.

"Please..." Her soft whisper on his lips released all hesitancy, and he pulled her closer in a still deeper kiss.

Against her lips he whispered, "It's us, Maggie. It's now, it's a new dawning of something vaguely imagined never fully attained—let's be together in this—just we two..."

Dazed, drugged with desire, she arched to let his hands glide over her face, her breasts, down her satin body. With whispered murmurs on tender swollen lips, strong gentle hands explored, soothed and teased feather touches over her body. Breath-catching, pleasure-fought moments were filled with stroking, nibbling, probing and moans of selfish need. Vulnerable passion spiraled in waves so intense that she could not stop the spears of hot explosive release. Warm glistening bodies were soothed and empowered.

A quiet time then with her arms around him, while her hands stroked his hair. "Tell me what to do," she whispered to her love.

At his bidding, her soft hesitant hands slowly, lingeringly explored, wandered, and smoothed over his muscled chest, strong arms, to parts unmoved by touch. Wanting to give what was asked, her soft lips and tongue explored—a faint movement, another, then imagined dreams experienced.

Cole sighed, "Maggie-mine," and laid a hand on the head that rested on his chest.

The night was heavy with discovery. They talked, tasted, explored in a tangle of sheets. At last, happily satiated, they slept.

The room was filled with a tinge of early morning light. Birdsong announced a beautiful day had arrived. Cole lay quietly, and looked at Maggie in bed beside him. They had shared beauty that humbled him.

His voice husky with sleep, eyes still closed, Cole gathered Maggie to him until her small warm body was curled on his chest and her face was close to his. "Thank you God for giving me feelings." He whispered, and placed a kiss on Maggie's soft cheek as if to seal the pronouncement.

Maggie snaked an arm around his neck, and wiggled closer so her breasts were pressed to his muscled chest. "I should go," she murmured, but made no effort to move.

He chuckled, smoothing her hair away so he could see her face. "Afraid of what people will say?" He asked.

She mewed when he smoothed a hand over her—lifted up so she could look into his eyes. "I'm angered by gossip."

"Why do you suppose that is?" Collier leaned down to kiss her on the nose.

Maggie leaned toward him for a nibble of lips, and shifted off him to sit up and rest her chin on her raised knees. "Because gossip is not always true. Some can be vicious rumors."

"Gossip that proves to be correct information can be constructive learning material." He thoughtfully rubbed a hand down her leg.

"How?" Shivers of pleasure made her voice quiver.

"Perhaps people will gossip about us. But could they not also come to understand how right we are for each other?" There was no sarcasm, only a trace of questioning concern as he lightly caressed her.

Maggie moved to encircle him with both arms, and laid her head on his chest. "Oh, Collier, I don't care what others say. I know I've been loved." She pushed up to look at him. "You made it beautiful for me."

"I'm glad, my dear." Cole moved so they faced each other. Gently, he laid the palm of his hand on her cheek. "You made it beautiful for me."

Then with a pat, he added, "Now go before the ego-pleasers are out and about. I'll call for Robert after you've gone."

"Can I do something for you?" Maggie was made brave by love.

"No, my dear, but thank you for asking. I'm afraid I'll always be helplessly in need of Robert when it comes to my preparations for the day."

Robert did come and help Collier prepare for the day after Maggie had left. Cole went to the library to work, but could concentrate on nothing but the picture of Maggie and their night together. He wasn't sure he'd be able to repeat the performance, or whatever it was. Still, the doctors had been right; there was hope. Lovely Margaret Ann Murphy had satisfied his quest for wholeness.

For a moment he felt a weightless joy, which plunged to despair. Damn! He had to leave Saturday. His agent in New York had confirmed that the National Theater in London had accepted the stage adaptation for his latest book, <u>Forbidden</u>

<u>Glory</u>. He was to leave for England in two days to help with the polishing of the script he'd presented. Bertram Strand, the character that Collier had given life, would become a stage personality. He would be a person readers would be able to see. He would be the Pygmalion of detectives, while Collier would be the character's Mr. Higgins.

Cole hadn't told Maggie about the London trip. He hadn't wanted to dim the afterglow of their night together. The play scheduling fit into Collier's trip abroad that had been planned before Cole knew Maggie. Robert and Collier were to go to England for the months of May and June. For the first part of the stay abroad, the valet would visit his family in Greenwich, and Collier would enjoy a favorite place close by, at his cottage where he could refine the play, swim and get some sun. Also later in the year, Collier was committed to lead a lecture series at Cambridge. That commitment had been fine before Margaret Ann Murphy.

CHAPTER 17

The planning and overseeing of the construction of the new addition had delayed her book publishing, but the church project had seemed more important at the time. Now, final preparations were being made for the dedication of the new wing to be held on the first Sunday in June. Maggie had just driven her mother to the church where Evelyn, Ginny and other building committee members would go over last-minute plans. After dropping her mother off, she'd returned home to work on some of the final sheets for her book. The artist had done delicious renderings of some of the herbs. It looked as if they could be picked right from the paper itself. She stopped working for a while, and sat idly looking out the window of the den. It had been four weeks since the night with Collier. Maggie had gone over and over the wonder of their discovery of each other. Different, yet the same as those long ago discussions with Linda.

Maggie frowned, recalling her mother's hysterics the morning-after the night Maggie had spent with Cole.

"Mother, I called and told you I was staying with Collier."

"Yes, and the blatancy of it. What do you mean? Why the whole town will know you spent the night with that man."

"Not if you don't tell them."

At the time, something about Evelyn's expression had made Maggie wonder if the woman had called her friend Ginny in a frenzy of what to do about her wayward daughter? Her mother was incensed about the man.

Now, Collier was in England, helping to write the play with a lecture series to do in July. The lecture was in his plan long before they had met, plus time for Robert to visit his family.

Although Collier called almost every night, Maggie found the ritual unsatisfactory, partially because of her hearing difficulty, and mainly because she could not touch that mop of red hair, run a finger over the generous mouth, touch and feel the man. Once they'd experienced each other, how could they go back to before?

The phone rang. Maggie eagerly grabbed for the phone as she glanced at her watch. Why now? It's 6 PM in Greenwich, England.

"Hello?"

"Hello, Miss Maggie?" It was Jessie Wright's voice.

The voice had a breathless quality as if she were afraid. Maggie knew that Clifford Wright hadn't been able to post bail, and was in jail waiting to be tried. "Yes, Jessie. What's wrong?"

"I need to see you, Miss Maggie. Please, could you come over today? Thelma has gone to take some things to the jail for Cliff, so I'm alone."

Maggie heard the fear and desperation in Jessie's tone of voice. She inwardly recoiled from becoming involved any further in the Wright family's lives, then felt a sense of guilt for being so self-centered.

"I'll be there within the hour."

Maggie drove to Etin and the Wright's house. The old car was gone. A lawn mower rested against the porch, as if prepared to trim the grass as soon as the thin stubble got thicker. As she carefully climbed the splintered steps, she could hear music playing and voices. Believing Thelma might have returned Maggie hesitated to knock, but Jessie opened the door. The voices and music were from a radio in the background.

"Hello. Come in." Jessie led Maggie into the house. "Would you like a cup of coffee? I just made some," she asked over her shoulder, already heading into the kitchen.

Maggie hesitated, as she remembered how filthy the kitchen had been on the last visit. But noting Jessie's shy, anxious look as if she wanted to please, Maggie nodded, yes, with a smile.

Jessie, who'd waited in the kitchen entry for Maggie's answer, smiled broadly, and motioned with her head toward the living room. "Go sit yourself down and I'll bring it in."

Maggie glanced past Jessie into the kitchen and saw a clean table. The sink was cleared of dirty dishes, and even the floor appeared to be scrubbed. She smelled freshly brewed coffee. She breathed in the welcoming smell, which mixed with some sort of lemon scent, as she continued on the short distance to the main room of the house.

Maggie gasped with pleasurable surprise. The living room window, which had been a smudged pane of glass, was clean. Freshly laundered curtains were pulled back, and sunshine streamed into the room, highlighting dusted tabletops and the waxed, wooden floor. What a change! Maggie could not believe this neat and tidy room was the same dark and unkempt dungeon she'd entered not long ago.

There were no dirty ashtrays sitting about. No dust motes floated up when she sat down on the sagging couch that was now covered with a long strip of clean cloth. Maggie was amazed at the difference good old-fashioned house cleaning could make.

"The home looks so nice and that sunshine coming through the window is wonderful," Maggie said to Jessie as the woman entered with a coffee tray.

Maggie observed that, like the house, Jessie Wright looked freshly scrubbed too. The denim blouse and jeans were clean and pressed. Her gleaming reddish blond hair was smoothed back from her pale oval face in a ponytail. She was too thin, and still ducked her head in a shy manner, but Maggie noticed that there was a sparkle in the depths of her deep-set blue eyes.

"I cleaned the place from top to bottom after Clifford left, and Mom went to her sister's for a stay. I like to clean and it kept me busy." Jessie set the tray down on the table by the couch and looked around the room. "Don't do much good." She shrugged and scratched her nose as she sank down in the chair opposite Maggie. "Dust just keeps building up again."

Maggie wondered if it wasn't just dust Jessie tried to wipe clean. Why did she call me?

Jessie leaned forward, holding Maggie's attention with her clear blue eyes. Maggie felt a chill run up her spine. What was it about Jessie's eyes?

"I asked you here because I have to tell someone something before I burst inside." A horn beeped. Jessie jumped up. The car passed by. Slowly, she sank back down in the chair, and stared at the floor. Silently, she ran the palms of her hands over the knees of her jeans as if trying to decide how to begin.

Maggie waited. Finally, with a sigh, Jessie looked up pleadingly. "You see, Eddie really believes Clifford hit Denny hard enough to knock him out. If that is so, wouldn't that mean Clifford killed Denny?"

Maggie caught the anxious note in Jessie's tone. "I'm not sure how the law works. Clifford is in jail on reckless homicide charges." The look of the mother's hurt bewilderment stopped Maggie from adding that the defense was demanding that the boy's body be exhumed to examine the cause of death.

She did add, "If the jury finds him guilty, the judge will have to decide the sentence Clifford must serve. If the jury doesn't believe there's enough evidence to convict him, he'll go free."

She saw the look of panic on Jessie's face, and leaned over to touch her hand. "Listen to me, Jessie. If Eddie really believes your stepfather hit your boy so hard that it killed Denny, Eddie should tell the police. Other witnesses might come forward too. It could make a difference in the trial."

"It's all my fault," Jessie moaned. "I should've left here long ago with Denny. I've been too scared of making it on my own. Ma always told me I was not too bright." Jessie choked on a sob. "I know I'm not, but I'm not dumb neither, and I could've gone and made a livin' for Denny and me." Jessie slumped down, and held her chin with her hands. Wrenching tears shook her frail body.

Maggie started to touch Jessie's shoulder, hesitated, then leaned back and waited for the young woman to pour out all of her self-hate and anguish in tears.

Gasping sobs with words, "I'm bad, no good," came out while Jessie struggled with the pain of what had happened to her son.

Hot tears began to form behind her own eyes as Maggie considered the woman's life. At the age of fifteen Jessie had borne a child, had to leave school, no skills for work, and, apparently, had no skills in rearing a child either. Now thirty, just Maggie's age, Jessie was a mother, and had lived a life Maggie could not imagine. Maggie wished there were words to express her sympathy to the mother of the dead boy.

Jessie slowly pushed out of her chair, and moved to the window. "Clifford was always tellin' Denny that he was a shitpoke." Jessie darted a glance at Maggie.

To Maggie, Jessie's word seemed an appropriate one for Clifford Wright from what Maggie had seen and heard about the man. Maggie nodded in agreement.

"Clifford always got plenty mad that Denny was not a daredevil like Cliff wanted the boy to be. It was hard for Cliff to understand a boy who didn't like sports, and scared of water too." Jessie still stood, shoulders drooped, arms wrapped tightly around herself as if to hold everything together.

Perhaps it helped to keep her thoughts from spilling out too fast, tears too, Maggie thought.

Jessie spoke as if to herself. "I was only fifteen when my baby came. Ma said she'd train me to rear him."

Her voice broke. She wiped at her nose and then, sitting a little straighter, she spoke up firmly. "My Denny was a good boy—gentle-like. Wouldn't let nobody hurt an animal if he was around, much less go huntin' for em."

"...seems he's floatin' out there someplace. I need to know things so he can rest." Jessie's words that day in the Wright home came back to Maggie. It's hard for her to talk about her son's death, Maggie thought. But perhaps it was best that the mother talk it through so she could put her boy and herself to rest.

Maggie asked, "Have you heard all about the burial?" and waited.

Jessie smoothed at her skirt. "They said it was because he looked too bad for me to see him. Just buried him after they got permission from that policemen who come to check out everything."

She'd avoided the word death. Returning to her chair, she hunched over trance-like. With arms on knees, she rubbed her hands together, and stared into space as if she were miles away in thought, speaking of some story she'd heard, about somebody else.

"And Denny's father? Where is he?" Maggie interjected. It was apparent that Denny's father had no part in the boy's life, but it was a question that Jessie would be asked.

"Clifford was my son's father." Jessie breathed in heavy gulps of air, and looked at Maggie with dull saddened eyes, then shifted her gaze to listlessly twist the cuff of her sleeve.

At first Maggie thought Jessie was saying that Denny was not her son. Then, the shock hit. Maggie clutched at the couch cover to stop the room from spinning. *Please God I don't want to hear this. What can I possibly do?* Somewhere from inside Maggie heard, "You can listen."

Sitting up straighter, Maggie hesitantly whispered, "How did it happen?"

"I was just a kid. Thelma and Clifford had been livin' together, but I'd been with my grandma. She'd raised me from the start, 'cause my mom didn't want to be bothered too much. Well, when my grandma died, I came to live with Clifford and my ma. They got married and all, and it was fine for awhile 'till Clifford started to drink again. Seems he'd had a drinkin' problem, quit, and somethin' triggered his need for the bottle agin." Jessie's run-on story stopped.

All Maggie could hear was the loud thumps and grinds of the rock band's drums and horns blaring out from the kitchen radio. After several minutes, Jessie got up, went into the other room, and turned off the radio. She returned to the living room to slump back down in her chair.

The heat of embarrassment for Jessie flooded Maggie's cheeks. She and Jessie were close to the same age, but what different lives they'd lived.

"I know this is a shock to you." Jessie spoke, and Maggie felt momentary panic that somehow her thoughts had been uttered aloud. "I'm not proud of what happened. I didn't willingly pleasure Clifford—no way."

Jessie cleared her throat and began to pluck at a small hole in the knee of her jeans. "I fought him off, but he just laughed and got into me anyway."

The moments dragged on. The best way to listen is to keep silent. Maggie remembered that from an article she'd read. At the time, it seemed a reasonable thing to have suggested. And now, listening to Jessie's confession, Maggie realized she was incapable of doing anything else. She waited. At the moment, her hearing was extremely sensitive to sounds; a faucet dripped heavily in the kitchen with a steady beat like a clock pendulum moving back and forth, a car screeched around a corner, a siren screamed in the distance. Each sound reverberated in Maggie's muffled hearing.

Jessie finally spoke. "I knowed—knew Thelma didn't know what was going on 'cause she worked at the New Cafe bar at night from six till two and Clifford would come home from work at the plant, start drinkin' and come find me 'fore ten o'clock. I got so I'd sneak out, and hid behind a barn on the other side of town 'till I thought he'd passed out. It worked for awhile, then one day, he got home earlier. I expect he passed up stoppin' at some bar on the way home, and surprised me. He locked me in my bedroom till he was ready to do it to me. There was no windows in my room. I had no where I could go."

Jessie moved to get up at the sound of another car slowly climbing the hill behind the house. The car went by and the sound dimmed to nothing. Jessie relaxed, and shrugged her shoulders. Maggie watched her. It was incredible the way the young woman was able to control herself after the initial crying spell. The need to share her tragic story was stronger than her shame.

"Guess that was about the time I figured I missed my period. Thelma took me to the doc and I was pregnant. I always let her think it was one of the Palmer boys, who lived on the other side of town on the farm where I done hid, but I knew it was Clifford 'cause I never laid with nobody else."

Jessie leaned forward, hands clasped between her knees, and looked pleadingly at Maggie. "I want you to know, Miss Maggie. I didn't never like for him to bed me. I hated it, and swore I would kill him one day. He left me alone after I was pregnant. Guess his conscience," Jessie leaned back and snorted in disgust, "got to him. Anyways, he hasn't touched me since, and I knowed part of it's cause my ma has had an inkling, but never talked about it, that Denny got born 'cause of Clifford. She's never said nothin'. We don't talk much.

"I stayed here cause, like I said, my ma thought I couldn't make a living for me and Denny, and she sure as hell—excuse me—wasn't goin' to be saddled with a kid while I worked. Anyways, she hadn't even wanted me had she?"

Jessie looked up and Maggie saw a spark of defiance dim to despair before the woman lowered her eyes to study the floor. Maggie knew she had to say something, anything to get Jessie to get it all out. "Was Clifford kind to you after Denny's birth?"

Jessie looked up at Maggie. "Yes, but 'ornery to my Denny. I protected my boy best I could, but guess being raised with the strap for punishment, I didn't think as much of it as folks do nowadays. I just thought that was the way a kid learned to mind and respect his elders." Jessie's eyes never left Maggie's. She seemed to beg for forgiveness, but the lost look in her eyes seemed to suggest that she'd already decided what Maggie was thinking.

Maggie leaned forward in her chair, desperately wanting to say something to help. "Jessie, it doesn't matter what other people think. You must have felt trapped, wanting to raise your child, but not having enough money or skills to leave this house. How could you have left?"

Jessie slowly pushed up from her chair, walked over to the window. Sunbeams turned the young woman's hair to a halo of fiery orange as she stood looking out at the bright summer day. She turned back to face Maggie. "I felt sorry for myself, yet did nothin'. Don't you see that is what keeps eating at me since Denny's death? Why wasn't I strong enough to get out? I killed my son!" The last words ended in a strangled shriek as Jessie covered her face with her hands and sobbed uncontrollably.

Maggie quickly went to Jessie, put an arm around the woman's shoulders, and pulled her back to sit in a chair.

"Come on, sit down." With a soothing voice, Maggie coaxed Jessie to sit down.

Kneeling by Jessie's chair, Maggie took the young woman's hands. "Jessie, look at me." Jessie pushed her hair back from her face, and looked at Maggie with listless, tear-filled eyes.

Maggie took a deep breath, and spoke slowly and firmly. "The past is over. You cannot change it. You must try and forgive yourself so you can make changes in your future." Seeing she had Jessie's attention, she added, "Will you please come home with me. I can find some way to help." Maggie stood up and waited. She was not sure how she could help, or if she wanted to expose Jessie to the shock and disgust Evelyn Murphy was sure to show, but she had to give the woman some kind of hope.

"I be thanking you, but I can't leave my ma right now, with Clifford in jail and all. She's to come home tonight." Jessie stopped explaining and sat up straighter. "I would appreciate it, though, if you'd help me find work soon as this is over. Because as soon as I can, I want to move, and please, Miss Murphy, don't tell no one about this. I reckon it would about kill my mom."

Maggie's heart went out to Jessie, who was still faithful to her mother after all that had happened. The devotion to her mother said something—any kind of love is better than no love.

But Maggie knew that the woman deserved a better existence than she had in this house.

Maggie said aloud, "I'll not say a word, and Jessie, I'll call you tomorrow after I've made some inquiries about a possible job for you."

As she drove away from the house, Maggie knew she'd sounded more confident than she felt. How could she give the girl hope? Suddenly, she remembered a recent conversation with her dear, well-off friend. Linda had said, "I have a cook, and intend to take care of our baby myself, but I'll need someone to take care of the house after the baby comes."

Of course, Linda! Maggie exclaimed aloud, "Yes!" The speedometer hit eighty before she eased on the brake.

Of everything Jessie had told her, the one thought that clung to the edge of Maggie's mind was that Jessie'd had a child. Horrible as the conception had been, the fact that the young woman was a mother touched a hidden longing. An unwanted bubble of loss made Maggie's throat ache as thoughts of Collier flashed in her mind. She and Cole had shared intimate love, after their own fashion. He'd found ways to satisfy her—she to encourage and arouse him, but he was sterile. She would never bear a child by him.

Reaching her house, but reluctant to go in, Maggie sat in the car recalling times in high school when she and Linda had talked. She smiled at their naiveté. How trusting the two had been of each other to share secrets that Maggie had never shared with her mother. A more recent time they'd talked was the night before Linda's wedding, when Linda and she had discussed love and sex.

"It's as if all those stars out there are blinking inside of you, making you ache with a longing that isn't satisfied. You can't get close enough. Kisses don't satisfy. So you talk, and share your feelings, and get to know what it is about the other that really makes the difference. You anticipate, are crazy with desire, but you wait because you've got a lifetime to enjoy each other. You'll know when it's love, Maggie." Maggie smiled. She knew.

She felt a warmth flow through her as she recalled the conversation she and Cole had shared the night before when he'd called from Greenwich, England. He'd alluded to the fact that he liked visiting on the phone, but that he'd rather have her across from him where he could see her, watching her different expressions, touching her hand. She leaned her chin on the steering wheel, smiling dreamily to herself as she imagined smoothing back that fiery red mass of hair, kissing his cheek, his mouth. Maybe we should have waited. Maybe I should have been the stronger and gone home. Guilt began to build, but an overwhelming surge of love eased the tightness in her chest.

CHAPTER 18

"And we want to thank Mrs. Evelyn Murphy and her daughter, Margaret Ann for their generous contribution. They made this day possible." Richard turned to Maggie and Evelyn who sat on the stage with him along with the other leaders of the church. Waves of clapping resounded in the new auditorium as some 200 people thanked the Murphys.

Most of the crowd of people who had attended the dedication ceremony had gone home by the time Evelyn and Maggie came out of the church. Ginny Phillips had waited, and Evelyn walked toward the car with her friend who still gushed about Evelyn's and Maggie's wonderful gift to the church. Maggie walked a little behind, inwardly smiling at the way the congregation had gushed over her mother and her when just last week the same people had been whispering about the affair that Maggie must be having with that awful Mr. Thomlinson. Aversion had again been overcome by avarice. *I must remember that line for my book.* Maggie smiled. Her dream to write about love was possible now that Cole was in her life, and a rough draft of a love story was almost ready for Cole to read when he got back from England.

Glancing back at the church, Maggie thought of Nonnie Green. Without that dear woman's generous gift none of the beautiful changes in her life and new additions to their church would have been possible. Neither would she and her mother have been the center of such appreciative attention. It was sad that a church was inclined to welcome with greater enthusiasm those who gave the most. Derrick Evans had made a point when he'd said some people were allowed to fall through the cracks of an overly ambitious church.

"Miss Murphy," a muffled voice called out. Questioningly, Maggie hesitated, and looked back toward the church. Richard was still visiting with Letty on the church steps. She glanced ahead, where her mother and Ginny Phillips were just entering the parking lot. She could see no one else. Then a movement caught her eye, and she looked closer at a car parked across the street just ahead of her. A man was leaning against the hood of the car. It was Clifford Wright!

Maggie's heart skipped a beat. Where had he come from? He must have gotten out on bail. Frantic, she looked around. No one was close by. Her mother and Ginny were out of hearing range. Richard and Letty stood far away. She hurried on.

"Maggie Murphy," Wright called out in a louder voice.

Maggie ignored the man and kept moving.

"They're about to dig up Denny's remains to see what caused his death. I got out on bail, my wife's left me, and I thought you'd be glad to know, Jessie's moved. Seems she got a job with one of your friends. But I 'spose you know'd that." Clifford called loud enough for Maggie to hear.

She stopped, and looked over at the man, now directly across the street from her. He stood propped against the old Cadillac, arms crossed over his chest, grinning at her. It was not a friendly look. It frightened her. Maggie's heart beat quickened, her voice was not too steady, but she stopped.

"Mr. Wright, I like Jessie. I'm happy to have been of help. There's no reason for you to threaten me." She fought the impulse to cry for help and took mincing steps forward on trembling legs.

"I'm not threaten', I'm tellin' ya." He called out. Maggie continued to walk.

"Hey, listen to me! Don't know what Jessie told you, but don't matter. It's our family business and nobody else's.

Seein's how you fix in other people's business, suppose I should do the same. Your mommy's got some secrets."

Clifford Wright's voice was mockingly loud and bitter as he took long strides across the street, and grabbed Maggie's arm. She tried to pull away. With a vice-like grip he jerked her closer, and stuck his unshaved face up close to Maggie's. His squinted eyes flickered like flaming candles glinting from deep caverns. His breath reeked of liquor.

"You don't know what that stepfather of yours did, do you?" His feted breath whispered in her ear. She leaned back, face turned away, tried to move, but he clamped down harder on her arm.

"It came to me, when I noticed again that dent I have in my right front fender of my old Cadillac over yonder. Seems like we stepdads have things in common. Ask yer mom about Bert and another Irishman." A slow demonic grin spread over his face as he moved back, easing up on the tight hold of her arm.

Maggie jerked her arm from the man's grasp, and raced away, and down the street toward the parking lot. What in the name of God did the man mean?

"Won't do no good to run away from it. Ask your mom." His voice trailed off as Maggie reached the ladies that had turned in astonishment when they heard Wright's yell.

Maggie stopped, heart pumping wildly, and looked back at Clifford, who still stood where she had left him. Leaning over with arms wrapped around her waist, Maggie gasped for air, as his words, stepdads, Bert, Irishman, bent fender, pounded in her ears.

"What on earth, Margaret Ann." Evelyn Murphy had turned, and saw Clifford Wright. Her face went deathly white.

"What did that awful man say to you?" With a quick intake of breath, the woman clasped her head with both hands and swayed against Maggie, who quickly wrapped her arms around her mother's waist.

Rushing the trembling woman to their car, Maggie called back over her shoulder, "Mrs. Phillips, would you please tell Richard that mother has a migraine? We can't come to eat with Letty and him? We'll call later." Maggie drove home.

Once they were home and in the house, Maggie led her mother into the living room, where she helped her to the couch.

"Now, Mother, what could Clifford Wright have meant, when he said for me to ask you about my stepfather, another Irishman, and a bent fender?" Maggie's voice quivered.

Evelyn Murphy covered her face with her hands. "Oh dear, I do feel faint. Margaret Ann please get me a cold cloth."

"Not until you tell me." Maggie folded her arms tightly around her waist and waited.

"Margaret Ann, please." Evelyn held her head and rocked back and forth. Finally, she lay down on the couch, and curled into herself. Her body twitched and trembled as if she were having a seizure.

Maggie had watched her mother as she had retched and gagged to control migraine pain, but this pain seemed to be different. She panicked. Rushing to the kitchen, Maggie turned on the faucet and let the cold water run over a towel she'd grabbed.

Maggie shuddered at the thought of Clifford Wright's face up close to hers. She closed her eyes and Clifford's face became the face of her stepfather Bert mingling with the black spots that danced in front of her eyes. Leaning on the sink, feeling nauseous, water running in a steady stream down the drain, a childhood scene was triggered:

The water was running, Evelyn Murphy's head was bowed as she leaned over the kitchen sink. She was crying, and holding on to the edge of the counter as if to steady herself.

Bert stood in the doorway of the kitchen. His open mouth was moving fast. His arms were waving. He was gesturing with his hands.

The child threw an alphabet block out of the playpen. Bert picked up the block, and shoved it in front of the child's face. The child cried. Bert picked the toddler up and shook her hard.

Maggie felt vibrations pound in her head. Coldness gathered behind her eyes. She felt as if she was suffocating, and tightly held onto the rim of the sink for support. Gradually, the memory dimmed and was gone. She rubbed at the tightness behind her eyes with short jerky movements of hands gone dead, and knew she was feeling the same way she had felt so long ago when she'd been in the playpen and wanted out, or when Bert had closed her in her room. She must have been about two years old then. She knew now that her parents had thought she was retarded when she had been that age. They hadn't known that she was different because she was deaf.

She remembered how reticent her mother had been about speaking up to Bert, or about defending Maggie. Now, looking back on those scenes of childhood, Maggie wondered if her mother had been afraid of her husband. Perhaps back then, Evelyn's migraines had been caused by the tension between the two of them—but why did she have a migraine now? Did Clifford Wright have anything to do with the sick headache today?

The cloth she'd been cooling lay in a puddle of water under the open faucet. Maggie turned off the tap, squeezed excess water from the cloth, and hurried back to the living room. She lay the cool cloth on her mother's closed eyes, then sat close by, anxiously watching the suffering woman. Finally, with a sigh, her mother seemed to relax, and lay quietly.

Maggie asked in a hushed voice. "Mother, I know that Bert is not my father, but was my father an Irishman and not James Bonner?" Maggie's voice broke. "Am I the product of an affair?" Where the question had come from Maggie didn't know, yet the face of Irishman Clifford Wright flitted in her mind for an instant.

Her mother sat up, still holding the wet cloth to the side of her face. Slowly moving to her favorite chair, she sat down with a thud. Her little feet could not reach the floor, so dangled at the end of plump legs, listlessly swaying like those of a rag doll. She leaned back and covered her face with the cloth as if to close herself off from Maggie.

"I never wanted you to know, Margaret Ann." Evelyn Murphy mumbled something about regrets.

"Mother, I can't hear what you're saying."

Evelyn pulled away the cloth, and laid it on her lap oblivious to the wetness that began to form a ring on her dress. Maggie got up, took the cloth from her mother's lap, and carried it out to put in the kitchen sink. A few minutes later, when she turned from the sink, she found that Evelyn had followed her, and was seated at the table.

The woman's lips formed whispered words so Maggie could understand. "Please, could I have a glass of water. I must take my pill."

Maggie gave her mother a glass of water and a Migral tablet. Evelyn swallowed the pill and thanked Maggie. The cloth had smeared the woman's mascara and robbed her chalk-white face of its rouge-tinted cheeks.

"You say that Clifford Wright referred to a dented fender?" Evelyn asked.

"Yes." Maggie poured herself a cup of coffee left from the morning's breakfast, and sank down in the chair across the table from her mother.

"Clifford Wright said his car had a bent fender and it reminded him of the time when Bert Murphy had one. Clifford also suggested that stepfathers with bent fenders had something in common." Maggie said.

Evelyn Murphy shook her head and let out a moan. The outburst was so unlike her mother that it frightened Maggie.

"Could Cliff Wright have been referring to Collier Thomlinson's accident over thirty years ago? Did Bert have an accident about the time of Cole's accident?" Maggie's voice caught, and she quickly sipped some coffee to relieve the dryness of her throat.

"It's like a knitted scarf. If one stitch is pulled, the whole piece may unravel." Evelyn spoke slowly and distinctly, while staring into the glass held tightly between her hands as if looking for words to say.

"I never knew for sure. I suspected, because Bert went into Etin that very next day telling me the car needed a tune-up." The woman sighed and sat back, eyes distant with memories.

"Bert had a temper. He might have run the child down in anger, wanting to hurt the father, George Thomlinson. Bert must have presumed George had hurt me. I had pleaded with Bert over and over that there had never been anything between George Thomlinson and me."

She looked up at Maggie with leaded eyes. "That very day, I told him again the same story I've told you—your father was an Englishman named Bonner."

Evelyn closed her eyes, and covered her mouth with her hands. She sat that way for a moment, then lowered her hands, and looked directly at Maggie and whispered:

"I lied to you and Bert, Maggie. Your father was not James Bonner, but was Liam Evans, Derrick Evans' older brother."

Maggie slowly sat forward in her chair, never taking her eyes from Evelyn's lips for fear she would miss something the woman was saying as Evelyn continued:

"Bert kept insisting that Thomlinson was a womanizer. He said I couldn't have resisted George Thomlinson. It wasn't true." Evelyn nodded her head back and forth as she looked pleadingly at Maggie with an extended hand. Maggie didn't respond, just sat staring at the woman, expressionless.

Evelyn clasped her hands, and bowed her head. "At first, I told the lie about your father to avoid any jealousy Bert might harbor for Liam's family." The woman hesitated then added. "I don't know why I've never been able to share this with you. I believe I told the lie for so long that it became real."

Questions swirled in Maggie's mind. Who was James Bonner? How had Mother met Liam Evans?

"Why did Bert even consider that George Thomlinson was my father?" She whispered through numb lips.

"Well, let me start at the beginning." With a sigh, Evelyn Murphy pushed aside the water glass and folded her hands on the tabletop.

"By 1942 we English had endured the Battle of Britain, and the Blitz. Bombings were not as frequent during that year. The Second World War was still on, and the Germans had switched mainly to nighttime bombing raids. People were attempting to go about business as usual.

I was sixteen, living with my parents in Lambeth, a borough of London. Having given up my formal education, I was working as a nanny for the Rogers' family in Mayfair. That particular Thursday, my day off, I'd spent with my parents. To go back to work that evening, I took the train as usual. When we arrived at Waterloo Station, the air raid warning went off, and we passengers stayed in the station until the ALL CLEAR sounded. Upon my arrival at my employer's home, I learned that Lambeth had suffered some bombing. When I could get through, I went to find my parents. Our house and several neighboring ones had been destroyed. My parents, Margaret and James Bonner, were dead." Evelyn's voice was flat, devoid of emotion, but the eyes glistened with unshed tears.

Maggie closed her eyes and heart against the pity she felt for the young girl, who had lost her parents. That was another woman in England—not the woman Maggie knew. She started with the realization that her mother had buried events of her life much as had the Woods People buried events of Denny Wright's death. Maggie heard Evelyn's voice.

"I was an only child. We had relatives, but they were scattered about the United Kingdom. I didn't even know some of them. Anyway, I didn't know any of them well enough to inquire or go to live with them. I stayed on with the Rogers' family, who had hired me when I was fifteen.

"Two years later, with the help of Mr. Rogers, who had connections, I came to America with a shipload of refugees, and had a job waiting for me. My job was to be a nanny for a one-year-old in Collier, Wisconsin. The child was George Collier Thomlinson the Fourth. My employer was his father, George Thomlinson. And that was what he was, my employer, nothing more. I was his employee. I was good at my nanny's job. He praised me, but that was all."

Words swirled in Maggie's head—*nanny, Collier, Pastor Derrick Evans' older brother, my father*. Maggie studied her cup. It was as empty as she felt. All she could hear was the warning her mother had repeated so many times. 'Don't do anything to bring shame to the family.' Maggie covered her face with her hands to stop the words that pounded in her head, and slowly pushed up from the table.

"I'm going to my room. We'll talk later." With leaden feet, she forced herself to walk out of the kitchen to her room, where she closed the bedroom door against the continuing drone of her mother's voice. She collapsed on the bed, laying an arm over her eyes.

She'd never been close to Bert Murphy. She'd never questioned why he didn't love her. As a child, fear of the unknown and hopelessness had blocked all questions she might have asked. Why hadn't her mother told her about her love affair with Liam Evans? Why had she let her daughter believe the father was a dead Englishman named James Patrick Bonner? Her mother had even used that name, Evelyn Bonner Murphy. James Bonner was Evelyn's father—Maggie's grandfather. Did it never occur to the woman that her daughter would like to know about her real father and grandparents?

Maggie's throat tightened until it felt as if she would choke. Lies! My life has been built on lies! Everyone has thought my father was an English gentleman! I've told Collier what James Patrick Bonner looked like from Mother's description, and that he'd lived in Dover. We've talked about the beauty of that part of England where my mother and father met and loved! She curled up, holding a blanket tightly against her mouth to silence the convulsive tears, and mourned the love of a parent that she'd never known.

Dark thoughts dimmed the beauty of the day as Maggie lay motionless staring at the ceiling streaked with silver beams of sunlight. There was a taste of bile as Maggie considered that Evelyn Bonner had been free to live her life without constraints. The woman had endured sadness to be sure, but she'd made her own choices, and loved. I've avoided intimate relationships and constantly worry about what others think of me. Are my fears caused by my mother's fear that I would repeat her sin? Maggie sat up and laid her head on her knees.

Evelyn Bonner, the young girl, had come to the United States. Alone, in a new country, no relatives, nothing but a few possessions and the promise of a job taking care of the Thomlinsons' child in the small town of Collier, Wisconsin. What a lonely existence those first years must have been. Perhaps Liam Evans was the one person who was kind to her. Maggie's eyes filled with tears for that young immigrant.

Rising from the bed, Maggie absently walked around her bedroom. She touched a bit of dried corsage hanging on her vanity mirror. It was a reminder of a blue organdy dress she'd had when she was six. Bert had insisted that they couldn't afford a new dress for Easter. Evelyn had told him that she would make a dress for her daughter. She ran a finger over the row upon row of good books in the low bookcase that had sat in the corner of the room by the window for as long as Maggie could remember. The books had been bought for her from Evelyn's meager shoe factory salary. And there was the old fashioned rocker, where her mother had rocked her when she was sick. The pain around her heart diminished as she sat down and rocked and considered her mother's many thoughtful acts.

Just a few hours ago at the dedication of the new addition for their church that she and her mother had given, she'd felt so close to her mother. She'd felt love and pride in their relationship. It was like the two were in tune for the first time.

Mother has always cared for me. Perhaps she has been a little too sheltering at times. She shrugged at the thought. There was no way she could dismiss the time and caring of the years and walk away as if there was nothing left of the love her mother had shown her, or the love that she'd had for her mother. It would be like taking a garden in full bloom and plowing under the blossoms.

Daylight dimmed into darkness. Too tired to change her dress for a gown, Maggie listlessly lay back down on her bed. The grandfather clock in the hall ticked and chimed each hour of the long night as she lay dried-eyed, staring at the play of shadows on the ceiling and thinking of another night when Collier and she had loved.

CHAPTER 19

Morning came and she struggled with thoughts of the gossip. Soon everyone would know about her mother. What was it Collier had said about gossip being a learning experience? What could this story do but hurt those involved? Regardless of what happened, how could she walk away from her mother?

Sounds and smells of perking coffee seeped through deep questions. Slowly, she slipped into her robe and slippers and made her way to the kitchen. Her mother had been setting out dishes for their breakfast, but turned from the table when Maggie entered. The older woman's eyes were red rimmed. Her hands shook as she tried to set down the creamer on the table. Without a morning greeting, they both sat down, and the morning ritual of pouring coffee, popping toast into the toaster, sharing the jellies and butter began.

"All night I've lain awake and tried to think of a way to explain to you, Maggie." Evelyn glanced over at Maggie, then quickly looked down at her coffee cup. "I buried the past, gave no thought of sharing it with you." Evelyn's blotched, tear-burned face was cleansed of its familiar mask of makeup, and naked as the truth she'd shared the night before.

Maggie took a few sips of coffee, set down the cup, sickened by its bitterness and her own. She wanted to ask what three-year-old Cole had been like. Was he a shy child, or was he tumbly and rowdy? What did he eat? When did he talk? So many memories her mother could share with her. Maggie's eyes filled. She wiped them with the back of her hand and quickly got up, rinsed the coffeepot to make a fresh pot of coffee.

With her back to her mother, Maggie asked, "When you were at the Thomlinsons, what was it like?"

"I worked for that family for three years. It was a lonely time." Evelyn stared into space.

"Mr. Thomlinson was good to me. Mrs. Thomlinson was not a warm person, did not really like me, but I liked my work keeping the child. I had no friends, but Nora Green who occasionally helped Bessie Hart, the fourteen-year-black girl, who helped with the cooking. Bessie married Edward Tuttle later."

"You knew Mrs. Tuttle back then?" Maggie asked as she returned to the table.

"Yes, I knew Bessie Hart Tuttle. She was younger than I was. Besides, the help was not to mingle. I went along well enough with what I was supposed to be as a servant, but it was not who I was. Since I left that employment, I've never seen Bessie, except for the few times we've happened to meet in the local stores."

Maggie's heart ached when she thought of her mother caring for Cole when he was a little boy. How she longed to ask what he was like as a child. She wanted to know if he'd been a happy child, and what had been his favorite toy.

"How long were you Collier's nanny?" Maggie asked and jumped up to get a glass of cold water from the refrigerator. Her throat was so dry. Returning to the table, she again listened to the saga of an English girl alone in America.

"After three years, Mrs. Thomlinson fired me without cause. I stayed with Nora Green for a few weeks trying to find employment, but there was nothing. After that, Nora gave me money so I could go back to England. I suppose nostalgia pulled me back more than anything, but there was nothing for me in London either."

Evelyn paused, slowly tracing a finger over the veins on one hand as if reviewing the intricate path of her life. Maggie waited patiently. It was like fiction. This life of the young woman described was so different from the life of the mother Maggie knew.

"I came back to Collier, and back to Nora's house with a one-year permit to work at the shoe factory. For the first weeks, I lived like a hermit, going to work, and returning to Nora's quiet lifestyle. Then about a month after my return from England, when I was walking by the Thomlinson estate, I saw a man coming out the front entrance. He wasn't a tall man, but seemed so with his head held high, and his straight lean body. I noticed that his corduroy jacket had a button off for the bottom half of the coat flapped away from his bone-thin body when the wind whipped at it. His shirt was sparkling white and stiff with starch. And the blue twill pants he wore, though clean, were faded and thin at the knees from constant wear and washing—I presumed at the time.

"I don't know why I stopped. Perhaps out of pity. Then he spoke, 'Hello, a pleasant day isn't it?' And the Irish lilt of his words so gaily shared touched me deeply. The greeting and his sparkling green eyes with their thick black lashes enchanted me. You have his beautiful eyes, Maggie." Tears softly traced the smile on her mother's lips. *This is my father my mother is describing!* Maggie eagerly waited for her to continue.

"We stood there saying nothing, and there was such an aura of joy, such a happiness for life that emanated from the man. I wanted to share it. I fell in love with Liam Evans at that moment." Her voice was hushed, eyes distant, as if she were reliving that day.

"He'd just come from Ireland and was working for the Thomlinson Dairy, but had been called to the Thomlinson home to help with some gardening that needed doing. I can't describe the feeling I had for that man. He was like a savior. He understood. He too had come from another land, and was trying to make a place for himself in this country. He was kind, understanding, ah so much like you, my dear."

She again looked over at Maggie as if pleading for understanding. "Yes, we loved." There was a silent plea in the look, and sadness too. "We conceived you out of that love, Maggie."

Evelyn lowered her eyes. Her voice sounded weary. "We wanted to marry, but couldn't because his wages at the dairy wouldn't support a home and wife, not yet anyway. I would have married him, but his Irish pride did get in the way of his happy outlook on life at times."

She wiped at her wet cheeks. A dreamy expression suggested she was telling a story that had been spindled in her mind for a very long time and was now slowly unwinding. She got up, poured herself a cup of the fresh coffee, and shuffled back to the table.

"I continued to stay with Nora Green. Liam lived at the dairy farm not far outside town, and we met at his lodging whenever we had free time.

"I learned I was pregnant about the same time Liam got promoted to a manager's position in the Thomlinson dairy farm operation. He was so proud of his job, and so happy about you. We wanted to marry as quickly as possible for Liam was sure to lose his job if Mr. Thomlinson learned he'd gotten me pregnant. We immigrants were not to do that sort of thing. The double standard was Mr. Thomlinson's motto all right." Bitterness laced the decided English accent.

"One week before the wedding, which was to be at the Community Church, Liam was attaching a milking machine to a cow when it kicked him in the head. He died instantly. Right after his death, before I was showing, I took another trip to

England with the little bit of money Liam and I had saved, and came back with the made-up story about the Englishman that I'd married while in England. And that I'd come back to finish my work permit, but my husband had stayed in England. Later, before you were born, I told those interested enough to ask that James had died. My make-believe husband, James Patrick Bonner, had died. That was my father's name." She smiled sadly as she gazed at Maggie. "Your grandfather, Maggie.

"Your real father, Liam Evans, died eight months before you were born. Your make-believe father, James Bonner, died one month before you were born. You were born, and I was the widow of a phantom English gentleman. Evelyn shrugged, as if to say that was the end of the story.

Maggie started to push away from the table, but was stopped by her mother's next words, "When Liam's brother, Derrick Evans, came to Collier, I'd been married to Bert for over five years and you were six. I truly believe that Derrick has never heard of Liam's and my relationship. Nora Green, Ginny Phillips and the Community Church minister at that time, Reverend William Jones, were the only ones who knew the whole story. And Reverend Jones, who helped me so much after Liam's death, died a year later." The two sat silently for quite a while.

Maggie leaned her elbows on the table, closed her eyes, and covered her mouth with both hands to hold back the sobs as tears flowed unchecked down her cheeks. How could she not know this about the woman who had given her life? The life her mother described could be that of a character in one of Collier's books. Glimpses of the past reoccurred in quick sequence, and a swirl of insightful images began to play in Maggie's mind—Bert's surly attitude toward Maggie, his bursts of anger, that Maggie could not hear, and other anger that brought tears to her mother's eyes.

Maggie was tired. It was stressful to listen and to learn about the past. She felt a tap on her hand, and looked up. Evelyn Bonner Murphy was again describing former days. It was as if, once the seal of the past had been removed, the whole truth poured out like a rush of water from a broken dam.

"After your birth, I was alone with little money and the full responsibility of a new baby. Nora Green was wonderful, but it was not her place to take care of you and me. I met Bert Murphy. He was a man with little vision, but a man who loved me. I never loved him like I did your father, Maggie. But he was there for me, and I appreciated him, liked him. Bert married me, a woman with a six months old girl-child who'd been conceived by another man. Bert didn't believe the story I'd fabricated about the Englishman. He was a stubborn man who had his own ideas of whom the father was. He kept insisting that George Thomlinson had been my lover, though I argued otherwise. I didn't tell him about Liam for he wasn't going to believe anything I said. Lies do build upon lies, and Bert had too much pride to ever have you know of his suspicions." Evelyn slumped back in her chair and concentrated on slowly stirring the contents in her cup.

"I didn't dwell on the past. I never wanted to see the Thomlinsons again. I avoided them. That's why you never knew Collier. His father and mother were dead. Let the dead bury the dead." She shook her head staring at the cup.

Still withdrawn, as if speaking in a dream, she continued. "I kept busy with my church, thank God for it, endured Bert, and loved you. There were times I would have lost my sanity if I hadn't had you to care for."

She seemed to come alive with that confession, and smiled. "I was blessed to have a child with such goodness—goodness that I'd never had. It's sad for me to admit, but I lived your accomplishments as my own." With the admission, her mother's voice became so faint that Maggie was again forced to read her lips.

"I admire you, your work ethic, your cook books, and your having overcome your hearing difficulties."

Maggie wasn't used to Evelyn's praise. It embarrassed her. She wanted to change the subject. "What about the crumpled fender? Clifford Wright talked about there being a crumpled fender." Maggie tried to put that piece of the puzzle into their lives as she tightly squeezed the cold glass of water until moisture drops seeped through her fingers.

"I don't know." It came out a moan. Evelyn leaned over, grabbed Maggie's hand and held it tightly. Evelyn looked at Maggie with a frantic look as if pleading for understanding.

"I've thought about the time of the accident all night. When the accident happened to Collier Thomlinson, that fourteen-year-old boy, I wouldn't let myself think about it. But now, Bert was hot-tempered. He could have done it. He could have hit that poor boy on his bicycle. He went to Etin to get his truck fixed that next day."

She got up and started pacing back and forth. "I remember that day so vividly. Bert came in saying he had to go to Etin. I'd heard about the hit and run from Ginny. She knew about Liam, Bert's doubts, and she point blank asked me if Bert could have been the driver of the truck. I stoutly denied it. I couldn't face it of course. Perhaps it was an accident. I've prayed so." Evelyn got up to walk back and forth, wringing her hands with bowed head.

"Oh, I know he wasn't always good to you, Maggie. That's one reason I kept you away from him as much as possible. He was obsessed with the idea that George Thomlinson was your father, and he hated the truth of it. He might have deliberately stalked the boy, and hit him with his truck. Deep down, I just don't believe Bert was capable of that."

"Why have you so disliked Collier? What did he ever do to you?"

Evelyn stopped her pacing and stared at Maggie. Her eyes became large, her mouth opened and a hesitant look changed to one of incredulity. "I believe I must have hated Valerie Thomlinson. I wanted to have nothing more to do with that family."

"Mother, how could you carry so much hate for people who helped you to come to the United States and gave you work?"

"I paid my own way, make no mistake about that. I worked for the Thomlinsons for some three years and not a day went by that Mrs. Thomlinson didn't accuse me of stealing, eating too much, being mean to her precious son. Valerie was a very unkind woman to me, and I had to put up with it. I needed the work. I suppose she was jealous of George, for he was a womanizer. There was always gossip about him and his latest woman. Maybe she was afraid I was bait for the roving dog.

"The day I was called into the library, and told my services were no longer needed, Mrs. Thomlinson offered no explanation. She did not give me a reference to help me obtain another job.

"Later, when Bert took on so about George Thomlinson, I began to realize that Valerie had believed I'd been with her husband. I had a lot of pride, Maggie. I was a good girl. Liam and I loved each other. He died before we could marry."

She sat, leaned her elbows on the table, and cradled her face in her hands. "I never told Bert about Liam. If Bert had known, he'd have told Derrick Evans. I didn't want to share you, and have to live with the gossip. But I've always kept Liam in my heart. I..." Sobs stopped the words.

When she finally looked up, Maggie ignored the ache of sympathy she had for the pathetic person across the table from her and asked, "Where did you and Bert live back then?"

Trance-like, Evelyn answered. "We moved into Bert's house right next door to this house—Mrs. Green's. You were raised right next door to your friend, Nonnie."

Maggie could make out only a few of the woman's muffled words, but it seemed her mother had deep regrets about her past. Maybe Evelyn had felt it her Christian duty to suffer the insults of Bert because of her own deceitfulness. The full disclosure had given Maggie insight into her own past. It explained why Bert was like he was. Maybe the circumstances that had made her mother distant. Yet too, some of the neglect Maggie had felt might have come from her mother's English family. They'd sent their only daughter out into the world to work at an early age. But trying to solve this complex puzzle was an example of why she so disliked gossip—not all of the facts were known before the results was decided.

The hall phone rang, and Maggie got up to answer it. She was gone for some time, then came back into the kitchen where her mother sat.

"Well, that was Linda's brother, Tim Edwards. He's been on the Wright case and has kept me informed. The defense attorney's line of defense for Clifford Wright was that the blow Clifford gave Denny was not hard enough to kill the boy before he was dunked into the water for baptism. The defense claimed that at the first gulp of water the boy took when he was submerged, his heart stopped. The exhumed body confirmed that there had been water in the lungs, which proved he was alive when he was submerged for baptism." Maggie sat down, sighed, and continued.

"When Derrick Evans was called to testify, he told of the boy's hysterics, the grandfather's blows, the submersion for baptism, the limp body when they pulled Denny from the water. Derrick said he hadn't felt a heart beat, but that sometimes it's hard to detect one. He said that he had quickly performed mouth to mouth resuscitation for twenty minutes or so with no sign of change before he gave up, and pronounced the boy dead."

"I don't understand. Why was Derrick the only one to speak?" Evelyn asked as if she'd listened, but wasn't really connecting with what Maggie was saying.

"Several witnesses at the scene verified Derrick Evans' testimony." Maggie said, adding, "The defense summary claimed that Denny was alive when he was submerged for baptism for the autopsy found water in the exhumed body's lungs—proof that he was breathing when he was put under water. Therefore, the blow from the grandfather did not kill Denny. The boy's heart stopped either before Derrick Evans had tried to resuscitate him, or during the minister's attempts to revive the boy. The boy was paralyzed with fear of water."

Maggie's eyes filled with unshed tears. She shook her head and signed the words, too choked up to speak: "The jury came back with a verdict of Not Guilty. Denny Wright died of heart failure—not from the blow he received, nor from the ingestion of water. Wright was acquitted." Maggie covered her face with her hands, and cried for the senseless injustice of it all.

"That poor, poor mother." Evelyn moved to gather Maggie to her.

CHAPTER 20

In Greenwich, England a gentle breeze lazily lifted the white organdy curtains at the open windows, and playfully carried the sheer fabric back and forth across the windowpane. Out in the garden of the Thomlinson cottage a rabbit lifted its head to sniff out danger, then greedily nibbled on a daisy. Collier watched the rabbit, and the gently swaying flowers that seemed to nibble on each other. Perhaps flowers had their own language, and talked of the delights of blossoming. He'd have to share that whimsical thought with Maggie when they talked today. He felt a sudden surge of happiness recalling their last conversation.

He'd said, "I'm afraid our happiness won't last."

She'd countered, "A moment's happiness never lasts. How can it?"

Then he'd asked, "What about what we've felt for each other?"

And she explained, "I believe passion is what we have, and passion is much deeper than happiness. It's the thrill of being alive. If the passion is with another individual, a family, a profession, a job, it can be whatever a person recognizes as the deepest level of satisfaction or joy. And it can change within the confines of relationships." He could hear her voice, smell the scent of her that lingered in his memory.

My Maggie, I see playful images in nature, experience such joy all because of you. The reverie ended with a knock on the door. At Collier's suggestion, Robert came in.

"Sir, my apologies for interrupting, but this special delivery came from the States." The man laid down a letter and started to leave the bedroom Collier used as his study.

"Robert, you weren't interrupting. I'm having one deuce of a time trying to capture this damn murderer." And Maggie takes center stage in my mind, pushing aside make-believe characters.

Collier moved away from the computer center and flexed his hands, then his shoulders. "Perhaps you've helped by taking my mind away from Bertrum and his pals. I was getting fanciful anyway. Thank you."

Collier absently ripped open the envelope with a thumb and read, as he licked a small cut caused by the sharp edge of the paper.

June 5, 1984

Dear Mr. Thomlinson,

I am Clifford Wright, and I have a buddy write this so I have a witness to what I am about to tell you. First let me say, I enjoyed prison life very much. Thank you and Miss Murphy for helping me have that experience, and for the chance to let everybody know the truth about my grandson's death and me. Guess you heard I got off. The boy had heart failure. I did not kill Denny. So you were wrong.

Collier started to throw the letter in the wastebasket, but a sickening curiosity made him read on.

Now I got another bit of news you ought to know. It's about my stepdaughter Jessie. She is the child of your father, George Thomlinson. The pillar of society as we know it in Collier, Wisconsin. Yes, Thelma had an affair with old

244

George. He couldn't marry her because he had a wife who was of his class of people. He also had a thirteen-year-old son, George Collier Thomlinson. I married Thelma and gave Jessie my name. I always knew no good would come of keeping it all a deep secret, but Thelma pleaded, and I went along with the lie that told others she'd had an affair with one of those bugger Irishmen who had moved into our town. So you see, your dad was a busy womanizer.

He also got Evelyn Murphy pregnant about four months before Thelma, so they say. Didn't know you had two sisters did you?

Bit of news to chew on isn't it?

Sincerely yours,

Clifford Wright.

Collier crushed the letter between clenched fingers. His heart raced. Damn the man. What lies! Maggie and Jessie Wright his sisters? It was unthinkable, horrible accusations, and impossible to imagine! He knew his father. He was a moral man—wasn't he?

In the back of his mind, he recalled an incident when he was still in the hospital after that fateful accident. He was awake, but not able to communicate. His parents were in his hospital room.

"Is this our punishment? I forgave you. Has God taken our boy for your sins?"

"Hush, Valerie. We've gone over all of that. Leave it as a past chapter in my life I will never repeat. So help me God."

The memory faded, but a sickening suspicion lingered. He rang for Robert.

"Robert, I must ask you to do something for me. It will require you to return to the States."

***

The daisies and tulips had faded in the heat when Robert returned from the States. Collier had just finished with the chore of dressing when Robert knocked and entered the bedroom. The man raised the shades in Collier's bedroom, and picked up garments in the bath and bedroom as Collier impatiently waited for the report concerning Clifford Wright's letter. Never had ten days seemed so long and now the man was puttering around straightening the room. Collier impatiently rolled over to stop Robert's fussing.

"Robert, what did you learn?" Sleepless concern showed in Cole's dark-circled eyes as he stared at Robert.

"I looked into the affair, Sir. The stories were well suppressed. Derrick Evans did not wish to talk about the births and parentage, but after I explained that you had learned of the discrepancies in lineage..." Cole interrupted:

"Yes, yes, get on with it man!"

"Mr. Evans admitted that he had heard that George Thomlinson fathered Thelma Wright's child.

"Sir," Robert hesitated before he continued, "I also learned that Derrick Evans came from Ireland to this country long after Jessie Wright was born. She is almost thirty, and Derrick came to Collier just three years ago. Mrs. Tuttle and several others say Derrick's older brother, Liam, who had immigrated earlier, had fathered a child before he died of a farm accident. Some thought the child was Jessie Wright, but Derrick thought not. That remains a muddle."

Collier swung his chair around and stared out the window. It took more than a little control for Collier not to yell at Robert. Every damn Englishman Collier knew had to draw out information. It was like getting the last of the toothpaste out of a rolled-up tube. Patience, patience. After all the man had gone all the way to Wisconsin to get the facts.

"There's another unanswered question, Sir. It seems that Evelyn Bonner Murphy had a child before she married Bert Murphy. Preacher Evans knew nothing. Mrs. Tuttle said Mrs. Thomlinson dismissed Miss Bonner without giving any reason, but some thought it was because of Mr. Thomlinson."

Collier's face bleached of all color. "Yes, yes. I quite understand." He held up a hand indicating that he'd heard enough. Trembling hands laced through his unruly hair. He took several deep breaths.

"Thank you, Robert. I appreciate your time and your dedication." Robert stood as if waiting to say something more.

Collier gripped the wheels of his chair and started to move out of the room then turned back with a sigh. "Is that all Robert?"

"Mrs. Tuttle was also of the opinion that your father made sure the stories were buried. She wasn't sure how."

"I've never realized the depth of my father's power. How could my father have possibly stopped the gossip?" Collier mused.

"Robert, it would seem stories were in abundance back then. I vaguely remember a woman I called Miss Eve. That woman must have been Evelyn Murphy—Maggie Murphy's mother." At the realization of what he'd just said, Collier stared with glazed eyes at his hands with thoughts focused on his past. He spoke in a whisper.

"I didn't know my nursemaid's last name. I was so into myself for all of those years after my parents died." He covered his face with his hands. Robert quietly left the room.

The room's hushed silence was disturbed by rolling wheels as Collier pushed over to the bedroom window, and looked out over the English garden with its grasses, iris, and hollyhocks. He'd always believed a garden was not a thing of beauty unless it was an English garden—a profusion of bright flowers, haphazardly interspersed with feathers of green to please the eye and touch the soul. How he'd looked forward to showing off his garden to Maggie.

Sometimes Collier imagined that the wide expanse of lawn just beyond the garden was Lake Thomlinson reflecting the green of overhanging trees at the water's edge. Like a mirage on a windless day the image brought back happy memories of playing leapfrog and diving off his father's shoulders into the lake.

His father had taught him to swim, sail a boat, and bait a hook. After the accident the memories of those adventures kept him sane. He'd always thanked his father for the good times, and for giving him those pleasant memories of the time when he'd been a strong, healthy boy.

Considering what he'd just learned of his father's sexual exploits, maybe things hadn't been right between Valerie and George Thomlinson, but Collier hadn't known about it. In his memory his father was a saint, and his mother was next to the mother of Jesus. He would always remember them as perfect parents. Why not? As a child, that was how they were for him. Tragic for sadness to cause death, but unrelenting sorrow had taken them both.

A spasm hit his stomach and bile came up in his throat. Collier rushed to the bathroom where he retched over the sink. Afterward, wiping his face with a cold cloth, he studied his features in the mirror. There was a family resemblance. Jessie could indeed be his half-sister with her strawberry blond hair that was lighter, but had the same red tint. Collier winced as he recalled the flash of questioning recognition he'd experienced when he'd first seen the girl at the Woods People trial. Yes, the eyes were the same grey-blue as his.

The color of Maggie's eyes and her hair didn't seem to fit the genetic family pattern. But the pale skin could be the pigmentation of a redhead like his father. Maggie, that beautiful, gentle human being, how could she be his sister, even his half-sister? Wouldn't he have known?

"That which is imprinted upon the spirit of man by an inward instinct." The Francis Bacon quote he'd once used surfaced. How could he love her in the way he did if it were true?

His father was gone—Maggie's mother? He could never ask the one living person who could tell him the truth. His chest tightened. What if Maggie found out? She'd told him that her father was an Englishman. All of her life she'd believed that, took pride in that handsome father. It would devastate her to learn of her mother's affair, regardless of the man. Dear Maggie and her struggle to hear had at last realized contentment.

"The people of my church accept me." She'd said that. Would they accept her if the story about her mother were learned? Collier would not allow her to endure any more pain if he could help it. His mind stumbled on a quote of his own:

"We know what we want to hear and that it must be honest, yet we persist in taking the pathway of subversion. Honesty is too harsh. We cannot stand to live in its glare. So we retreat to the shadows one way or another."

Retreat to the shadows? Was there any other way? He prayed that there was a presence housed in the depths of his being that listened and would give him guidance.

With a great effort of will, he pushed the heavy wheelchair out of his bedroom and into the study. There on the desk lay the final pages of the script for his play. He felt no sudden jolt of joy now, no eager excitement to create daring escapades on paper. Reality, twisted threads of pulsing life, could be far more bizarre than anything he could create. Best to cut short his stay in England the first moment he could, and go back to face reality.

CHAPTER 21

Collier was at the door. Maggie opened it and looked past him for Robert. Collier didn't push forward, but interrupted any greeting she was about to utter.

"Invite me in. I hate to wait." The words were clipped, the tone curt, his voice grating to his own ears.

Maggie stood back and followed him down the small hall. He turned into the living room that he'd never seen. Funny, how close he felt to her, yet had never been in her home. He turned to face Maggie, who stood by the living room entrance. Her beauty caught at his throat.

He cleared his throat, hesitated before he spoke. "I found out you were back from Chicago. I know your mother is out. I saw her leave in the car to go to her Canasta Club."

"Why didn't you just call me?" Maggie asked softly with a half smile as she advanced to stand before him.

"You've been gone. I've been gone." He turned from her, and moved farther into the brightly decorated living room. Maggie followed him into the room and stood by the entrance.

He stopped, rolled around, and gazed at her for a moment. Looking down at the rug, he rubbed a fist over his chin.

"Look Maggie, sit down please. I have something to say. It won't take long."

"Collier, I'm not going anywhere. I'm glad to see you." She moved to the couch, pushed off the mound of needlepoint pillows, and sat down.

"I'm going away, Maggie." How much easier it was to write words than say them aloud, especially to one who sat waiting patiently with questioning, beautiful eyes.

"Where? Back to England?" Maggie leaned forward, eagerly waiting.

He nodded. "Yes, for my part, the play is almost finished. They hope to start production at the London Cottesloe Theater next month. I came in such a hurry to finish up a few things that I didn't have time to write."

His confused explanation was not on purpose. He was feeling frustrated and uncomfortable. He'd no idea how to finish this conversation. *Please give me the words to be strong.*

Maggie leaned back more relaxed as if his explanation had satisfied her worry. "Wonderful! I'm so glad. You don't have to explain. I knew you were busy, and I've been in Chicago to speak with my publisher about a new idea I have for a book." She tilted her head and shyly added, "I've been anxious to get your opinion."

"Maggie!" He bellowed, lifting himself up from his wheelchair. Slowly he sank back down, and said in a firm, slow voice, "I'm leaving. I'm not coming back."

Her face was white. Her eyes went wide. "What do you mean?"

"While I was in England, I had a letter from Clifford Wright," he said.

Blazingly loud, the phone crushed the silence. Maggie got up to stop its insistent ringing.

Collier raised a hand, "No, let it ring. I can't stay." She sat back down and waited, her arms tightly clutched around her waist. The ringing stopped.

"Clifford wrote that my father had an affair with Thelma Wright before Clifford married her. My father fathered Jessie Wright. She's my half-sister."

Maggie blurted, "That's absurd. You'd have known wouldn't you? And besides, Clifford Wright doesn't like you for his own reasons. Maybe the Thomlinson Dairy incident with the union, when he lost his job, was a reason, or your part in the Woods People's hearing about Denny Wright's death. He was trying to hurt you."

He warmed at the thought that she was trying to protect him from the gossipmongers, but he did know the stories were correct. Robert had checked on stories about Evelyn Murphy too.

"How can you be sure?" Maggie asked. He held up a hand to stop her.

"Maggie, I've been to see Thelma Wright. She tells me it's true." He turned his back on Maggie and rode over to the window. "There's too much past to deal with here. I have to leave."

"What about us? Surely the fact that Clifford Wright revealed the past doesn't affect you and me today. I can see how it would hurt but, I thought we..." she hesitated, groping for words, "...had a future." Her words ended in a whisper.

Collier turned from the window, rode back to stop in front of Maggie, and looked deeply into her eyes for a long moment. "I imagine we did have something special that one night, but don't get sex mixed up with love." He hurried on.

"Maggie, being in England, getting the letter, has just made me see things as they are. There's no future for us. I can't give you the gay life of dancing, walking in the moonlight, and church on Sundays—no children."

"I don't believe we have ever discussed any of that," she said, then added, "I'm not very sophisticated, Collier, but I do understand that two people sharing one night together are not bound by traditional values to make it a lifetime commitment. You owe nothing to me really. But I do love you."

There was a burning ache behind his eyes, a tightness that he tried to pinch away. He had to cut these ties. She was his sister.

He moved to face the window, and spoke louder so she could hear. "When one lives alone, there is a rhythm learned, required. I'm a confirmed old bachelor with a handicap." He heard her gasp but, with real pain on his own part, he turned the knife in deeper.

"The change of life style would be hard to learn, even frightening. Possibly, I'm afraid of failure. I, for one, believe I'm incapable of accommodating another person in my life."

Still turned from her, he heard her approach, and looked over to see her standing close by. Silently, looking at him as if trying to comprehend what he'd just said, she waited.

He shrugged, and rubbed a hand over his quivering lips, "I don't want you hurt, Maggie. I care about you. I care for you."

"Then why...?" She licked her lips, cleared her throat. "We both have learned to survive without another person. We are accustomed to doing things a certain way. Isn't that what you're saying, Collier?" Her voice was laced with frustration. She lifted her chin and clamped her lips tightly together all the while keeping her eyes glued on him.

He stared back at her. *Doing things a certain way.* Had it only been six months since they'd had that conversation? The thought made him sad. Then the remembered joy of their one night together blotted out all thought but to hold her. One touch and all would be lost. His eyes flashed, then narrowed.

"Exactly. Guess you understand." He grunted out the words. A long moment passed. "I'll be going. Robert is waiting outside." Collier turned and quickly wheeled out of the room.

"Cole." Maggie stopped him with a word.

"Yes?"

"I'm sorry about your father. It must be awful to have learned things about the past, after all these years. Even though we try, the shadows of the past fall across our present and future. It seems as if we can't get away." Maggie's voice shook. She stood, back straight, chin up, looking down the hall at Collier.

Sunlight from the living room touched her hair and the side of her face leaving the rest of her in the shadows of the dark hall. Collier wanted to go to her, touch her lovely face. In a half whisper he thanked her, turned, and wheeled toward the door. There he stopped, and turned back as she'd done that day at the library. But this time, her face showed unspoken anguish. He turned and left.

***

It was early evening when she awakened. The room was dark. Fumbling for the light, she knocked a basket of yarn to the floor, groped for, and snapped on the Tiffany table lamp. What time was it? Where was her mother? Then Collier's words flashed in her brain. "I'm leaving." And the afternoons visit with all the hurt and loss came flooding back.

She'd dreaded having to confront Cole with the truth. Hadn't she wondered how she would tell him that her stepfather might be responsible for his crippling accident? And shouldn't she have told him that Liam Evans was her father? Now he would never know.

Perhaps it was best. He'd made it easy for her hadn't he? Like pieces fitting into a puzzle, questions were being answered. "But not like this, God. Please, I don't want them answered like this." She whispered, holding her hands over her face.

How could she go on living here, in this house, ignoring the fact that her stepfather might have crippled Collier? Staring blindly at the spot where Collier had been, she was aware of a deep emptiness. What would fill it? When would her work and

255

her life again motivate her? She heard a rustle close by, and realized that Evelyn had entered the living room.

"Hello." Evelyn extended the greeting rather hesitantly. "Richard has come with me, dear. I hope you don't mind. I've something to do, and he wanted to talk to you. He'll stay with you until I return."

"Richard?" she heard herself ask. Wondering why he had come, yet not much caring, Maggie slowly stood and watched the minister approach.

"I'll stay, Maggie. I promised your mother."

"Richard, it's really not necessary. Please go." Maggie slumped back down on the couch. Absently, she leaned over to pick up some magazines she'd thrown aside.

"Maggie, it's about Lavitia."

Maggie stopped and sat back. Robert had sat down on the chair across from her. Through thick lenses, he looked at her with smiling eyes. He seemed happy for what reason she couldn't imagine. But why did he have to be unhappy because she was?

Listlessly, she asked. "What about Letty?"

"I've asked Lavitia to marry me. You and your mother are the first to know."

Maggie didn't want to hear this. She didn't want to feel their happiness for it reminded her of her love for Cole. Richard and Letty would have what she and Cole would never have. Why didn't he just go away! She started to ask him to leave, but when she saw the smile on his face that conveyed so much happiness, she couldn't be rude to him. He was not a part of her unhappiness. He'd come with good news about his life.

Forcing a smile, she looked at him. "I'm so glad for you and Letty. Congratulations." Her struggle for enthusiasm ended. She sat not caring to talk.

"Maggie, your mother has told me about Liam. I can imagine how shocked and hurt you must be."

For a moment Maggie's eyes went wide with indignation. How can you possibly know what I feel, Richard? Do you have a direct line to God? Her silent outburst ended. There was nothing she could say that would come out right.

"Would you like to talk about it?" Richard had moved to sit beside her on the couch.

Not looking at him, she shook her head and whispered, "Richard, I appreciate your concern, I really do, but I just can't talk about it yet." She wiped at tears that filled her eyes.

"Well, the news of your real father has cleared up one bit of gossip that Letty heard at the library."

He had such a lilt in his voice. It was as if he were glad to be talking to her about her mother's deceit. Maggie didn't want to be rude, but more gossip she couldn't take right now.

"Richard, I'd rather not hear."

"The story is that Clifford Wright has started some mean gossip about Collier's father, Jessie's mother, and your mother."

"My mother?" Maggie jumped up when he spoke of her mother. "What does my mother have to do with Clifford Wright?"

"Clifford Wright told some of the Woods People that his wife, Thelma, had an affair with George Thomlinson, and so had your mother. He said you and Jessie are Collier Thomlinson's sisters. I know it's preposterous. Cliff Wright is doing it, no doubt, to hurt you and Collier. And now, Letty told me that Collier Thomlinson brought back books to the library, and told her he was leaving our town for good."

Maggie was already running from the room before Richard finished. She slammed out of the house, and raced down the street praying that Cole was still at home. She knew now that Cole hadn't told her everything he had learned. He was trying to protect her from the story about her mother and his father. That's why he was leaving. *He thinks I'm his sister.* She shuddered at the thought.

"Please, please be there," Maggie gasped as she continued to run toward Collier's house.

"Margaret Ann? Where are you going?" Evelyn had stopped her car at the curb.

"Running to Collier's." Frustrated, winded and much too keyed up to give long explanations, Maggie stopped long enough to catch her breath. She stared fixedly at her mother as if to dare her to object.

"Get in. I'll take you." Her mother opened the car door.

Maggie ran to the driver's side. "I'll drive, Mother."

The car lunged forward as Maggie explained. "I just talked to Richard. I believe Cole thinks George Thomlinson is my father. Something about the rumor Clifford Wright started."

"Yes, I know. I just checked that story with Thelma Wright." Evelyn cast a worried glance at Maggie. "And you want to tell him it's not true?"

"Yes. Mother, I love Cole. That's why he left me so abruptly, don't you see? He didn't want to tell me we were brother and sister. I must let him know we're not related."

They reached the mansion. Tires squealing, Maggie drove through the Thomlinson entrance, and on to the front of the house. As soon as the car stopped, Maggie was out, and running up to knock on the massive mahogany door.

"Mr. Thomlinson is in the library, Madam." Robert had opened the door at her knock and ushered her in. She raced down the wide hall, past the Thomlinson clan portraits, and all but bumped into Collier, who was just coming out of the library. He pulled off his glasses.

"Maggie?" he questioned.

"Oh, Cole, I'm so glad you're here." Maggie rushed up and stopped in front of him, hands outstretched, then dropped them to her side when he didn't acknowledge her greeting. He just sat there staring at her with cold grey-blue eyes. An injured wolf in a trap.

Maggie asked, "Can we talk, please?" Collier nodded, and led the way into the drawing room. She started talking as soon as they got into the room.

"I know why you're leaving. I've come to explain a misunderstanding. You think my mother had an affair with your father. But you're wrong. My father is Liam Evans."

She saw Collier turn toward her. His face was drained of all color. The white of his skin, in contrast to the mat of fiery red hair, would have been a challenge for Titian to paint. He didn't say a word, just sat staring at her. Then, abruptly, he swung the wheelchair around, and rode past her to the terrace, where he sat looking out over the lake.

Maggie watched the pantomime. A performance of rejection as well executed as any she could imagine on the stage. She slowly turned and started out of the room.

"What's happened?" her mother asked, entering the room.

"He doesn't care. I thought he did, but he didn't say anything." Evelyn took Maggie's hand, and they both walked out to the verandah where Collier sat staring at the lake.

"Hello, Mr. Thomlinson." Evelyn Murphy walked up, and drew up a chair at the side of Collier's chair. Maggie did the same, and sat silently.

"Collier, you must listen to me." Her mother's English accent was quite evident. "George Thomlinson was not the father of Margaret Ann. I ought to know. I'm her mother." The words were blunt, but had the desired effect, for Collier looked over at her from under bushy brows, and appeared to be ready to listen to the woman.

"Bert and Clifford did have something in common, they both hated George Thomlinson. And both men believed that George had fathered the girls they were raising. George Thomlinson did father Jessie, but not my child. Liam Evans was the father of Margaret Ann." Evelyn looked at Maggie. Collier didn't say anything.

"Before we married I told Bert about my baby-on-the-way and that James Patrick Bonner, an Englishman that I'd met and married, but who had died before Margaret Ann's birth, was the father of Maggie. Bert never did believe me. He continued to be jealous, believing that I'd had an affair with Mr. Thomlinson. He would not be satisfied for it to be any other way. As I told Margaret Ann, your father was my employer. That was all.

"My Liam died before Margaret Ann was born. I married Bert because I thought that I couldn't raise a child without a man's help, but my heart has always been with Liam." Evelyn Murphy pulled a handkerchief from her purse, and wiped away tears from the corners of her eyes before she continued.

"I've kept the secret much too long. I'm relieved to tell the truth. I'm very sorry for the pain I've caused." The three sat silently.

The circle of fate, or God's master plan, had put the three together. It was much too mystical to understand how they'd been led to this moment. Perhaps it was best to realize they'd been blessed after a long time in the wilderness of their lives. Like Job's faith, not understood, but believed, they had been blessed in a way that would never be forgotten.

"Mrs. Murphy, thank you. Maggie, as you suggested, we aren't related." Collier eyes were alight with relief and a hidden fire.

"Suggested? I told you, and you sat there like an executioner as if it didn't matter. Why didn't you believe me?

Why didn't you share your fears?" Maggie's voice got steadily fainter until the last question was asked in a whisper.

"And another thing," Evelyn fussed with the buttons on her jacket. "I did some checking this morning. Clifford Wright was the person who drove the pickup that hit Collier's bicycle. He'd seen the boy coming along the street and turned his truck into the oncoming bicycle." Evelyn never took her eyes from Maggie's.

"Apparently Clifford's hate of the Thomlinsons fueled by the parenting of Jessie made him go over the edge when he saw an opportunity for horrible revenge. I just saw Thelma Wright. She told me that she'd known ever since it happened that Clifford was the driver of the pickup truck that had hit Collier. She said she'd kept Clifford's secret as Clifford had kept hers about Jessie." Evelyn's voice caught. She cleared her throat.

"It's painful and tragic to harbor jealousy and hate." The pleading look Evelyn sent to Maggie seemed to convey her mother's shame and contrition for the hate she'd harbored for Collier's mother. Maggie hoped her own smile showed that she understood and was glad that her mother was able to let go of the past.

Maggie's emotions seesawed from relief to shock. She was relieved that her stepfather hadn't hit Cole, and shocked that Clifford Wright could be so filled with hate and jealousy, even envy, and perhaps fear, that he'd had to take his warring feelings out on others. If nothing else, from her mother and Clifford Wright, Maggie had learned that evil feeds on inadequacies.

Collier had swung his chair around, and leaned over to take Mrs. Murphy's hand. "Long ago, I put the day of my accident out of my mind. I thought I'd never know for sure who hit me. Now, the question can be laid to rest forever. Thank you." He kissed Evelyn Murphy's hand.

Evelyn nodded. "I've one last thing to tell you, Maggie. I went to see Derrick Evans and told him about Liam, you and me. He said he was glad that his brother had loved before he died. His words gave me some peace."

Evelyn wiped away a tear, slowly stood, and looked at Maggie. "I must go." Maggie got up and walked to the front entrance with her mother.

Cole went beside the two as far as the entrance where he thanked Mrs. Murphy again, then looked at Maggie.

"I'll be in the library if you can stay."

Maggie nodded as if to say she would stay, then walked out with her mother to the car as Collier moved back down the hall to the library. Evelyn accepted Maggie's arm as they walked.

"Margaret Ann, I know it won't be easy to forgive me. It all seemed a dream when I told you everything. It was as if it all happened to another person."

"You're still my mother, and I love you. That will never change." The two hugged for a long time. Maggie helped her mother into the car, and watched her drive away.

Maggie went back to the library, where Collier sat looking out toward the lake. He heard Maggie come into the room, and without turning said, "Margaret Ann, please come here."

Maggie walked over to him, he turned and asked her to lean down. When she did, he placed a hand on each side of her face and kissed her lips. Not a kiss of passion, but one of finality. Maggie straightened and silently gazed at him as he whispered.

"Our kiss has closed all that has passed before, and holds all the potential for what may happen in the future. Sit by me, please." Maggie drew up a chair to sit close, and took his hand.

"Maggie, I thought I'd lost you. I had every intention of not seeing you again, for I couldn't abide being your stepbrother."

"And why was I not given the opportunity to say how I felt about it?"

He put a finger on her lips. "Maggie, I love you." He smiled a one-sided little boy smile that conveyed his uncertainty as much as his words.

"We're not related, but we could be by marriage. Will you marry me?" He pulled her over to sit on his lap.

She snuggled in and gently touched his cheek. "I've something to tell you about Jessie..." He interrupted.

"I didn't tell you, but yesterday I went to see Jessie in Royal at the home of your friend, Linda Jenson. I told Jessie the story of her birth, and who her real father was. She seemed neither interested nor indifferent. She said that if it were true it wouldn't make any difference. She said the past couldn't be changed, and that she was doing just fine with Mrs. Linda, Mr. Jenson and the baby. She said it was nice to keep the child, almost like having another chance to have one of her own. She didn't want anything from me. Maybe the best thing I can do for her is to set up a trust. What do you think?

"Oh, I forgot to tell you. I had a cup of tea with Linda and John. We visited, and Linda gave me a hug for you. They seem like a nice couple. I'd like to know them better."

Maggie pushed up from his lap and walked toward the terrace wall and the lake view. Arms folded tightly around her waist, she stood there stiffly erect.

"For god's sake, Maggie, what's the matter? Did I say something wrong?"

Maggie turned toward him. "There's something else you should know about Jessie—she was raped by her stepfather. Clifford Wright was the father of Denny Wright."

"Dear Jesus!" Collier pushed himself up straighter in his wheelchair. "I'll nail him to the wall with this."

"No!" Maggie's voice shook. "If you do, Jessie's life will be ruined."

"This isn't gossip, Maggie. It's the truth. Cliff Wright must be stopped, and this will stop him since Denny's death didn't. We can expose him for what he is. Get a new trial. The man is a child abuser, a menace, and possibly a murderer who got off. We'll get the others to come forward and give evidence of the man's physical abuse of his family. We can't get a new trial for murder, he's been acquitted for that, but we sure as hell can get a trial for criminal abuse. No, I believe the statute of limitations is just seven years. Possibly we can prosecute for abusing the grandson?" he questioned, then continued his train of thought aloud.

"Tim Edwards may be able to give some help on how to prosecute him again."

"Cole listen," Maggie pleaded. "If Clifford is confronted with this, the whole sordid story of Jessie's rape will surely come out. Hasn't she endured enough?"

"He should be made to pay, Maggie."

"Yes, but the horrible wrong has been done. The victim's son is dead."

"My father was a womanizer. He got away with it. Clifford Wright should?"

"No!" Maggie's voice was sharp. "But he's in the Woods People Church. He keeps going back. He doesn't have to do that. Something is moving in him. Let's let it happen."

"You truly believe it's possible? That a man can change?" he asked, and Maggie nodded.

"Well, prayers have been answered about other situations. I hope you're right. Perhaps, I can do a little threatening so Cliff Wright won't be repeating his slimy deeds." Collier rubbed a fist over his mouth and felt his anger subside as he recalled his own prayers.

"And Cole, I just learned the true identity of my real father, Liam Evans. It hurts, but that doesn't give me the right to hate my mother because of the deceit."

"Maggie-mine," Collier stared at her for a moment, then added, "I don't know if I can live with an angel, but I'm willing to try." A broad grin lit up his face. His eyes teased as he rode over and pulled her on to his lap.

"Speaking of living—you don't know how our night together has changed me. I'm no longer afraid of a future. We shall be what before we only dreamed of becoming. Maggie-mine, I don't want you to be away from me for a minute. Will you marry me?" he asked.

"Yes, I'll marry you." Maggie gave him a lingering kiss.

"Shall we dance?" he asked and pulled her close.

"I'd like that." She wrapped her arms around his neck.

Snuggling closer, face pressed against his shoulder, Maggie closed her eyes and the two glided around the drawing room as Collier hummed the tune, "Will You Dance the Rest of Your Life with Me?"

THE END